EVERY WOMAN FOR HERSELF

Trisha Ashley was born in St Helens, Lancashire, and gave up her fascinating but time-consuming hobbies of house-moving and divorce a few years ago in order to settle in North Wales. She is a *Sunday Times* bestselling author.

For more information about Trisha please visit www.trishaashley.com, her Facebook fan page (Trisha Ashley Books) or her Twitter account @trishaashley.

TRISHA ASHLEY

Every Woman For Herself

AVON

This novel is entirely a work of fiction.
The names, characters and incidents portrayed in it are
the work of the author's imagination. Any resemblance to
actual persons, living or dead, events or localities is
entirely coincidental.

AVON

A division of HarperCollins*Publishers*
1 London Bridge Street
London SE1 9GF

www.harpercollins.co.uk

First published in Great Britain by Judy Piatkus (Publishers) Ltd in 2002

This edition published in Great Britain by HarperCollins*Publishers* in 2014
10

A catalogue record for this book is
available from the British Library

ISBN-13: 978-1-84756-282-1

Set in Minion by Palimpsest Book Production Limited,
Falkirk, Stirlingshire

Printed and bound in Great Britain by
CPI Group (UK) Ltd, Croydon CR0 4YY

MIX
Paper from
responsible sources
FSC™ C007454

FSC™ is a non-profit international organisation established to promote
the responsible management of the world's forests. Products carrying the
FSC label are independently certified to assure consumers that they come
from forests that are managed to meet the social, economic and
ecological needs of present and future generations,
and other controlled sources.

Find out more about HarperCollins and the environment at
www.harpercollins.co.uk/green

For my father, Alfred Wilson Long, with love.

Foreword

I'm delighted that Avon are reprinting *Every Woman for Herself*, because I have to admit it's still my favourite literary child – and it's obviously a favourite with readers, too, since not long ago they voted it one of the top three best romantic novels of the last fifty years, a great honour.

I haven't rewritten it, merely tweaked a couple of errors into shape, brushed its hair and made sure it had a clean handkerchief, so since it was first published by Piatkus in 2002, it's obviously very much of its time. But then, think how relaxing it will be to visit a remote Yorkshire valley with no phone signal for miles and only a dodgy dial-up internet connection. The Brontë family managed quite well without them and I hope you will too.

Happy reading, everyone!

Trisha Ashley

Chapter 1: Alien Husbandry: 2001

Got up at the crack of dawn to kill the Fatted Breakfast before driving Matt to the airport, only to discover that aliens had stolen my husband during the night and substituted something incomprehensibly vile in his place.

I expect their replicator was having a bad day. I distinctly remembered marrying a gentle, long-haired, poetry-spouting Jason King lookalike with a social conscience, but what was facing me over the breakfast table was a truculent middle-aged businessman, paunchy, greying, and flaunting a Frank Zappa moustache seemingly edged with egg yolk: but I knew better. The alien snot was the clincher.

It was not a pretty sight, but fascinating for all that.

I went to peer into the kitchen mirror to see if *I'd* changed as well: but no, I still looked like a miniature Morticia Addams.

'Charlie,' the Matt creature said impatiently, 'did you hear what I said? About wanting a divorce?'

I certainly had; what did he think had ripped the veils of delusion from my eyes? But I was temporarily deprived of speech as almost a quarter of a century of married life flashed before my eyes in Hogarthian vignettes: *Flake's Progress*.

The inner film came to a jerky halt. 'Yes,' I said finally, nodding. I understood.

Unfortunately my memory was not of the selective kind, a cheery sundial remembering only the happy hours, so my recollections were freely punctuated with loss. Lost mother, lost virginity, lost babies, lost husband, Lost in Space.

Charlie Rhymer, this was your life.

For some reason, Matt seemed disconcerted by my reaction. 'We've grown apart since I've been taking these foreign contracts, and I've come to realise that this will be best for both of us. In fact, we can divorce right away, since we've been separated for more than two years.'

'How can we be separated when you're here?' I asked, trying to get my head around this concept.

'But I'm not *really* here, am I?' he said impatiently. 'I'm in Saudi.'

'But you're back for quite long holidays between contracts – and you said it would be better if *I* stayed here.'

'You would have hated it – you know you don't even like leaving the house, let alone the country.'

'But that's just York – it's got the wrong sort of outside. I'm fine at home.'

'*This* is your home.'

'I meant Upvale, and Blackdog Moors.'

'You seemed eager enough to run away from it with me.'

'That was love, and unplanned pregnancy, and Father.'

Matt said earnestly, 'Charlie, it isn't that I'm not still fond of you . . .'

'Oh, thanks,' I said. 'In fact, thank you for having me.'

He ignored that; I'm not sure he even heard it, like most of the things I say.

'It's just that I'm not getting anything out of this marriage,' he continued.

'You make me sound like a bank. What were you expecting to get out? More than you put in?'

'At least there are no children to complicate things,' he said, which was a very low blow. He was starting to make me feel quite sick.

'I'm sorry it's come to this, Charlie, but we really can't go on. I've been offered a long contract in Japan, and I can't afford to continue maintaining two households.'

'But the house . . . the mortgage?' I said, my brain starting to limp onwards a bit, now the first shockwave had broken over my head. 'What will happen?'

'The divorce will go through quickly if we're both in agreement – my solicitor will send you things to sign. Then I'll pay you maintenance every month, so you won't have anything to worry about. The solicitor will get in touch with you and explain everything.'

'Will he? Is that what you've been doing this week, organising our divorce? Why didn't you talk to me about it, instead of suddenly handing me a *fait accompli* on your last morning home? After all, I haven't done anything, have I?'

'No, you haven't done anything,' he agreed curtly. 'Perhaps that's just it. I've moved on, and you haven't. Other women have families and careers and interests. Perhaps now you've turned forty, it's time you got out there in the real world.'

I'd been cocooned for the twenty-three years of my married life, and now suddenly I was to be ripped from my chrysalis and told to make like a butterfly?

He rose from the table. 'I'll ring you from Saudi, once you've had time to think it over.'

3

Questions were already beginning to bubble scummily to the surface, like: when did he see this solicitor? How long had he been planning this? What does he mean, he'll give me maintenance? Was there some other woman behind this? Who on earth would want him?

'Hurry up and get the car out,' snapped Alien Nation in a reasonable impersonation of my husband, 'while I get my bags.'

'What?'

'I've got a plane to catch. It's time to go.'

It certainly was. I went into the conservatory, locking the door carefully behind me. Although it was so tiny, once I was in the middle where my easel and table were, you couldn't see me for jungle plants.

Palms, bamboo and bananas, and a fig tree in a big pot . . . Dense foliage and warm, slightly steamy, air.

Matt banged on the glass a few times like a deranged moth, shouting, but I disconnected, picking up a brush and carrying on painting the tiny, naked, cowering figure at the heart of the rampant forest. It looked like Steve, the handsome young gardener at the park, and something threatening was *definitely* lurking in the undergrowth.

Probably me: I often had lustful thoughts about him when I went there to sketch in the greenhouse, but in reality there was not enough cover to drag him behind, even were he willing – and it was one of those ironic facts that as you age you lust after fewer and fewer men, and those are the very ones who wouldn't look twice at you. When my last birthday date-stamped me forty, I knew the writing was on the wall.

I really should have sown my wild oats before I got married, because I feared it was now too late.

Sometimes, too, I wondered if my body wouldn't have rejected my pregnancies if they hadn't been fathered by Matt. Now I knew he was an alien, perhaps, I thought, our genes were incompatible.

Too late for that, as well.

Much later I resurfaced to the sound of a familiar loud thud and yelp as Flossie, my spaniel, attempted to walk through the glass door again. But at least if she'd come out of hiding it meant Matt had finally gone.

Flossie was not big on brains, but she *had* grasped that Matt hated her, and it was safest to keep out of his way. Of course she forgot sometimes, especially when overcome by greed, like the previous morning, when she was drooling over his feet at breakfast, and he kicked her when he thought I wasn't looking.

Afterwards I went up to the bathroom and gave *all* my big silver rings a vigorous cleaning with his toothbrush and a bit of powdered floor cleaner. The rings came up a treat and I expected his teeth would, too.

Flossie now sat in the dining room outside the conservatory door, looking dazed, though this is not unusual. She wagged her tail happily when she saw me coming.

The breakfast debris still littered the table, and Alien Nation had left a note pinned down by the teapot that said he'd had to call a taxi, and if he missed the connection it was my fault.

There was also the name and address of the solicitor who would explain everything to me.

I wished someone would.

Why did I never seem to grasp anything until a couple of

years after it had happened? I never knew where I was going, only where I'd been.

As Joni Mitchell says, you don't know what you've got till it's gone. I only knew what I had to start with.

Or did I only know what I *thought* I had to start with? Or did I have what I thought I had, but had somehow swapped it for an alien? Could living with me for so long have *turned* him into an alien?

He was right about one thing – he'd changed, but I didn't think I had very much.

Clearly, that was my mistake.

I took stock of my innermost feelings and discovered there weren't any: I was a blown egg, all shell and void.

You might have heard the sea if you'd put your ear to me, but that was about it.

Chapter 2: Wrong in the Attic

Lay awake all night with my mind doing hamster-in-wheel impersonations, then came groggily down the following morning to find a letter from Matt's solicitor.

Wasn't this indecently fast? The letter said that since Matt and I were in agreement (*were* we?) and there were no children of the marriage, I didn't need to have my own solicitor: just sign on the dotted line when asked to, and don't make a fuss.

The only good thing Matt's sudden bombshell did was to make me realise that he *had* turned into an alien, and an elderly one at that. Otherwise, who knew how long it would have taken for me to realise that I was beginning the slow trek through that long, rocky hinterland before fifty, hand in hand with a grumpy old man? (And as Sherpas go, he'd have been no Tensing.)

A day or two later Matt phoned, his usual bossy self, and basically instructed me just to do as I was told, and he would see me right financially.

That would be a novelty.

And there was definitely an underlying threat there . . .

I'd finished the painting: miniatures of looming menace, my speciality.

When I lived on the moors among all those vast spaces I painted long, narrow landscapes where tiny figures were set like random jewels. But once transposed to the claustrophobia of a city (even one as beautiful as York), I began painting ever-smaller canvases in which the minute figures cowered under threatening jungle foliage.

They sold quite well through Waugh-Paint, a local gallery. Vaddie Waugh, the owner, said it was because they were so small that they were easily portable. Or maybe people just liked having something small, dark and threatening hanging on their walls?

I hadn't told anyone about the divorce yet because it didn't seem real. And anyway, there was only really the family to tell, and frankly I didn't want to phone home and confess that not only had I failed in the motherhood stakes, I'd also failed as a wife.

The solicitor *had* explained everything to me, but it all slid away from my grasp immediately. All I understood was that financially we are up Shit Creek without a paddle, so there was no point in my fighting for half the house or a huge chunk of maintenance. The maintenance Matt did propose giving me was a pittance, though combined with my painting earnings I thought I would survive: Remittance Woman.

I knew I wouldn't be able to keep the house, but the only thing I'd regret leaving was my conservatory. I'd have to return home to the Parsonage at Upvale – but where could I put my jungle? I couldn't paint without it any more.

I'd have to find some kind of job, and a house of my own if I could afford it, because much though I loved going home, it would be difficult to do it permanently after having my own place for so many years. I *could* live on my painting, but it would not pay a mortgage.

Having looked around the house, I found it totally amazing what Matt had removed without my noticing before! Still, I didn't wish to keep ninety-nine per cent of the household contents anyway, since they were never my choice, and in fact were as alien to me as Matt now was.

Perhaps it could all go to one of those auction houses that take anything, though I supposed I'd better ask Alien Nation if he wanted to keep any of it first – that is, if he ever phoned again. He'd gone from checking up on me every other night (although after all these years he must have known I was either here or in Upvale), to one solitary, admonitory phone call.

A couple of weeks after the discovery that Matt was an alien, I opened the door to a most unwelcome visitor: Angie, raddled bride of Matt's best friend and colleague, the revolting Groping Greg.

'Angie! What are you doing here? I thought Greg's contract didn't end for another three weeks?'

Of course, had I known she was home, I wouldn't have opened the door without checking who it was first, from the upstairs window.

She pushed a bundle of magazines and a box of chocolates into my arms. 'These are for you,' she said in the hushed tones of one visiting the sick. Then she trailed past me into the house, exuding a toxic effluvium of sultry perfume and nicotine.

If you dipped Angie into a reservoir it would turn yellow and poison many cities.

I followed her into the living room, where she draped herself into one of Matt's minimalist white leather and birch chairs. She looked surprisingly comfortable, but then, she's all sinew and leather herself.

'I had to leave Greg out there and come home early, because the cleaning service said we had weird noises in the attic. But anyway, after Matt told us about the divorce, I just *knew* you'd fall apart! And since you've got no friends except us, I said to Greg, "I'd better get back and help poor Charlie."'

Angie was not, and never had been, my friend. Her presence was about as welcome to me as a tooth abscess.

'I'm not falling apart,' I assured her, which I wasn't, because nothing lately had seemed at all real. I wasn't sure if I'd been living in a dream world for years and just woken to reality, or vice versa. Sleeping Beauty in her jungle. 'Actually, I feel more as if I'm imploding – hurtling inwards on myself. There'll be a popping noise one day, and I'll have vanished, like a bubble.'

'You poor thing! There, I knew I was right to come back. But look on the bright side, darling – you and Matt are having a *friendly* divorce, so it will go through really fast. Then he's going to pay you maintenance, although I don't suppose you'll need much because you'll just go back to that insane-sounding family of yours. Did you see your sister Anne on the news last night? There were bullets flying around her head, and she just kept on talking.'

'Emily – my older sister – has second sight, so she knows Anne's invincible to bullets. And I don't know why you say

10

my family's insane. Matt was keen enough to marry me once he found out who Father was, even if he can't wait to get rid of me now.'

'Anne, Emily – and your brother's called Branwell, isn't he? What were your parents trying to do, breed their own Brontës?'

'Yes – well, Father was, anyway. He thought if he recreated the hothouse environment and we *didn't* become literary geniuses, or *Branwell* became the literary giant, it would prove his point. You know – like in his book: *Branwell: Source of Genius?*'

From her puzzled expression, clearly she didn't know.

'And Charlie's short for Charlotte, of course. When the experiment palled on Father he sent us all to the local school, and although Em didn't mind being known as Effing Emily, I got very tired of being Scarlet Charlotte the Harlot. My family always called me Charlie, anyway.'

'Weird!' she muttered again. 'I suppose you *will* go back there?'

'I'll have to, but I can't just return as if the last twenty-three years never existed.'

Though, when I did visit home it felt as if I'd never left. Everything was the same: Em running the place and striding the moors composing her lucrative greeting-card verses, Gloria and Walter Mundi haphazardly doing the housework and gardening, Father writing his infamous biographies and installing his latest mistress in the Summer Cottage, Bran and Anne turning up on visits.

And the moors. Nothing ever changed on Blackdog Moor except the seasons, that was what made me feel so safe there and so very *un*safe here in York.

11

'You can get a little job, can't you?' suggested Angie. 'You're not too old.'

'What as? Besides, I might make enough from my paintings if I exhibited more.'

'A London gallery, that's what you need.'

I shuddered. 'Oh, I couldn't go to London! I'm a country girl at heart and hate big cities.'

'Don't be such a wet lettuce,' Angie said impatiently. 'It's time to stop being a shy, mimsy little wimp once you're past forty.'

I gave her a look. I may be reserved, stubborn and quiet, but I plough my own furrow, as she should have known by then. I'm an introverted exhibitionist. Why should I like crowds? I'm simply not a herd animal.

No one could accuse Angie of being mimsy or shy. She's at least ten years older than I am, but her hair was dyed a relentless auburn, she wore eyelashes like tarantula legs, and her face had had every cosmetic art known to science applied to it at one time or another. Her body was lean, brown, and taut, except for the crepe-paper skin.

Flossie wandered in from her basket in the kitchen, wrinkling her nose at Angie and sneezing violently, before climbing onto my lap and regarding my unwelcome visitor with the blank expression only Cavalier Queen Charlotte Spaniels can assume. I'm convinced they are the result of an early failed cloning experiment.

'At least there are no children to dispute custody of,' Angie said, staring at Flossie.

I'd learned not to look upset when people said this sort of thing to me, as if I hadn't desperately wanted children. 'No, there is that, and Matt has always hated Flossie, so we won't be disputing over *her*.'

'So everything's all right? Matt says the first part of the divorce will go through in a couple of weeks, and six weeks after that, it's finalised. Isn't it quick?'

'That's because I didn't contest anything – I haven't even got my own solicitor – and we can't go for mediation because we're in different countries.'

'Matt says you don't *need* a solicitor, because the house is in his name, and remortgaged to the hilt anyway, and there are lots of debts, so there isn't much to share. But I'm sure he will be generous with maintenance. You'll be fine.'

'Yes, though I do suspect any mildly generous impulses he has now will dwindle away, like in *Sense and Sensibility*.'

She looked blank.

'You know, Angie, where the widow and her daughters were going to be looked after by the son who inherited everything, only the allowance sort of dwindled away to the present of the odd duck?'

Angie isn't much of a reader. She carried on staring at me with her mouth open for a full minute.

'The odd duck?'

'Not literally, in Matt's case. How could he send me a duck from Saudi? Or Japan, which he's supposed to be going to next. What an awful lot of students want to learn English.'

'Just as well – and Greg's been offered a Japanese contract too. I quite fancy it.' She looked around her vaguely. 'What are you doing with everything? You can't take it all back with you to Upvale, can you?'

'No, but I wouldn't want to anyway – I've never thought of most of the furnishings as mine. They're all Matt's choice, and most of them were already here when we married. There's very little we chose together. Unless Matt wants any of it, I expect I'll sell it. There are places that come and pack it all up and take it to an auction for you.'

'Yes, but I don't think you get much for it. Doesn't Matt want it stored?'

'Apparently not. He must have been plotting this long before he came home for his last holiday, because he'd already removed all his personal stuff into storage without me noticing.'

'You're not the most observant of women, are you? Head in the clouds. Or the plants.'

'I might want a few bits and pieces, because I don't think I could live at home again for very long, not after living in my own house for years. And I need somewhere to put my plants.'

'I don't think Upvale sounds very exciting. Matt said it was just one steep cobbled road like a Hovis advert, with three streetlights, half a dozen houses, your Parsonage, and a lot of dirt tracks leading to farms.'

'There are a lot more houses than that in Upvale, but they're spread out. And the only cobbled bit is about a hundred yards in front of the pub.'

'I didn't know there was a pub. Civilisation!'

'Yes, the Black Dog, after the local legend. There's Blackdog Moor, too, haunted by this huge, hideous fanged creature, with blood-red eyes and jaws dripping with—'

Angie shuddered. 'No more, please. What with noises in the attic and demon dogs I won't sleep a wink tonight all on my lonesome.'

'Oh, yes – the noises in the attic. Are you haunted, Angie?'

She should have been, by the ghosts of all the creatures who died in animal experiments on cosmetics.

'No, it's squirrels.'

'Squirrels? You've got squirrels in your attic? What colour? Those nice little reddish Squirrel Nutkin ones, or the big grey ones?'

'What does it matter? They're all vermin, and they've chewed to bits the furniture I've stored up there! Squirrels! They've eaten all the wooden parts of the chairs, and the grandfather clock, and a nice tallboy. I suppose I'm lucky it isn't rats, which is what I thought when I got back on Wednesday and heard all those funny thumping noises. Isn't that what you'd have thought, Charlie?'

'What?' I said, dragging my mind back from my own problems with some effort. '*I'm* the madwoman in the attic, I think, or will be. Perhaps I should join your squirrels.'

'Who mentioned madwomen?' she demanded crossly. 'Do concentrate, Charlie. The little tree rats have eaten all the lovely furniture Mother left me. I mean, what am I going to say to the insurance company? "Squirrels ate my furniture"?'

'"Weasels Ripped My Flesh"!' I exclaimed, perking up. 'I'd forgotten all about that song, but my eldest sister Em used to play it a lot years ago.. Wasn't it Frank Zappa and The Mothers of Invention? Or no – maybe it was Jethro Tull. Those were her two favourite bands so it must have been one of them.'

Angie sighed. 'Not weasels, *squirrels*,' she said in cold, clipped accents.

What a matron she would have made if she hadn't got off with Greg and left the nursing profession! Or a wardress.

'Sorry, it just reminded me of that song and . . . but do go on. Squirrels ate your furniture?'

'Yes. Grey ones.'

'How did they get in? There must have been a hole somewhere.'

'A tiny one, but they found it. Still, I expect the insurance will pay up in the end.'

'Unless squirrels are an act of God, Angie.'

'Don't be silly. How can squirrels be an act of God?'

'You never know. When our garden wall fell down that time, they said it had been undermined by moles, and *that* was an act of God, so—'

'You *are* joking, aren't you?' she asked warily.

I smiled encouragingly. 'I expect they'll pay up – and what a shame about that furniture. I really liked some of it, especially that knobbly triangular chair. Although bottoms aren't that shape, are they? And with all those bits sticking out it wouldn't have been very comfortable, and although it would fit right into a corner of a room, you don't usually want to sit right in the corner, do you? So I expect you can replace it with something more practical when you get the money.'

'You do go off at a tangent.'

'I'll have to go off altogether, Angie – I've got my hairdresser's appointment.' Which I absolutely *loathe*; but my roots were showing.

'That dead-black Goth look with the dark eye make-up and purplish lipstick is very out of fashion,' she said, scrutinising me severely.

'I know, but Matt insists, and—'

Suddenly I realised that it didn't matter any more what Matt liked or didn't like. He wouldn't be here to throw a major wobbler if I stopped dyeing my roots, wearing heavy black eye make-up and vampire-style black clothes . . .

16

It was a look that seemed less and less *me* as I got older. I mean, it was what I was into at seventeen, when I ran off with him, but I didn't think I'd be stuck in a timewarp forever afterwards.

But now I could do what I liked.

'I can do what I like,' I told Angie, brightly.

'You always did,' she said sourly. 'Wasn't that part of the problem?'

'Only in the major things, the ones that mattered, like the painting. In little things Matt had it entirely his own way. And I hadn't realised we *had* a problem.'

I was about to add that until the morning Matt asked for a divorce I hadn't realised how *old* he was either, but just managed to stop myself in time: like Angie and Greg, Matt was a good ten years older than I.

Greg was an awful, red-faced old roué who tried to jump on women the moment he was alone with them. He was Father's type, I suppose, but without the leonine good looks – and Father did go in for his mistresses one at a time, as a rule.

'Greg will be home in a couple of weeks, if you want any help,' Angie offered.

'Oh, no thanks, Angie,' I said hastily. 'I'm sure I can manage.'

Her eyes fell on the stack of magazines she'd brought, and she pounced on the top one. 'Now, what's that doing there? I didn't mean to bring that old copy of *Surprise!*. I only kept it because it had photos of that gorgeous Mace North in it.'

'Who?'

She exhibited the magazine, and I scanned the man on the cover with no recognition whatsoever, although his was a very distinctive face. His slightly oblique, hooded dark eyes seemed to be staring back at me assessingly (and probably finding me wanting).

'You must know him! He's a well-known actor, and he's got this deliciously plummy voice, a bit like Jeremy Irons.'

'You know I don't watch much TV. But it sounds an unlikely combination with that face,' I commented. 'He looks a bit – barbaric.'

'It's the Tartar blood.'

'Oh? I thought tartar was something you found on your teeth,' I said disagreeably.

'Not that sort of tartar – it's a place in Russia. Mongolia? The High Steppes, or Chaparral, or something? His great-grandmother was a Tartar and that's where those fabulous cheekbones come from, and the come-to-bed eyes . . .' She gazed at the magazine and sighed. 'He's sort of like a young Bryan Ferry crossed with Rudolf Nureyev.'

'Rudolf Nureyev's dead.'

'You must have seen photos.'

'Yes, but I don't find men in tights very appealing. I'd never have made Marian.'

After a minute she smiled weakly: Sunrise over Yellowstone Canyon.

'You will have your little joke,' she said, hoisting herself to her feet and tucking the copy of *Surprise!* firmly under her arm. 'I'd better go and sort out the roof rats. I'll soon have the little buggers out of there.'

Her car was parked opposite, outside Miss Grinch's, who would not be pleased, because she liked the front of her house kept clear so she had a better view of what her neighbours were doing. Had Angie been a man visiting me while my husband was away she would have been straight across with a milk jug or sugar bowl to try to catch me out in some imagined misdemeanour.

I don't think I'd ever done anything to surprise her – I must have been *such* a disappointment. You'd think she'd have lost interest. Apart from Angie and Greg, Matt's friends didn't bother me when Matt was away, and if Greg came to the door when I was on my own I'd pretend I was out.

I always checked from the landing window first, after one nasty experience soon after I married Matt, when Greg found me on my own and was horribly overfriendly in a near-rape kind of way.

He was even like that in front of Angie at parties, but she didn't seem to mind particularly. Maybe she thought he was all mouth and no action. Maybe he *was* all mouth and no action when it came to the crunch – I didn't intend finding out.

When she'd gone I finally phoned Em, the Ruler of Upvale Parsonage, told her about the impending divorce, and asked if I could come and live at home for a while.

'OK,' she said.

'Will you tell everyone? Father?'

'He's always thought Matt was a waste of space. Anyway, he won't be very interested – he's got a new mistress.'

I groaned. 'Is she in the Summer Cottage yet?'

'Not yet. She's renting a house down in the valley. But she's always round here, and they're all over each other. It's revolting. And she's got twin little girls who sit about giggling. She leaves them here when she goes out with Father.'

I supposed it was better than leaving them in an empty

house, but not much – Em didn't like children, so she wouldn't see their presence in the house as being anything to do with her.

'He's never had one with children before, has he?'

'No, unless you count Bran's mother, and that was unintentional. He'll probably get tired of her, if she won't move into the cottage. You know how he likes everything convenient.'

'Flossie says hello,' I told her.

Em's voice immediately softened to a medium baritone that was positively sugary. 'Give her a big kiss on her shiny black nose from me, and tell her Frost can't wait for her to come and live here.'

Flossie was petrified of Frost, a giant grey lurcher with questionable habits (a bit like Father, really), but I appreciated the sentiment.

'I will – and thanks, Em.'

'I haven't done anything.'

'You're just – there.'

'Where else would I be?' she asked, sounding puzzled.

Chapter 3: All Panned Out

I didn't turn up for my hairdresser's appointment in the end, which made me feel like I was bunking off school. I realised I need never sit in one of those foul-smelling torture chambers again.

Things were moving so quickly now that I'd decided to start packing my belongings. I'd put the stuff I didn't want in the small spare room: it was half-decorated as a nursery, a place of abandoned hopes, so entirely suitable. Anything going with me would be stacked at one end of the living room.

I'd been looking at the heap of magazines left by Angie, and I was feeling extremely irritated: none of them seemed to have *any* connection with reality as I knew it. They might as well all be called *Rich Young Brain-Dead Anorexic London-Based Fashion Victim Magazine*, and have done with it. Where were the magazines aimed at women like *me*? *Skint Old Northern Woman*, perhaps? I'll have to write my own:

Skint Old Northern Woman: Issue 1

Our motto is: Every Woman For Herself!

Welcome to our new magazine for the older, more frazzled reader. While written primarily for the Northern woman, it may also prove invaluable for those Southerners harnessing their huskies ready to brave the Frozen North, containing as it does many cultural hints.

To any peripheral Skint Old Southern Women, why not write your own issue, addressing the topics you find important?

We welcome readers' letters, except those sycophantic ones saying how wonderful our magazine is: we already know that, so for God's sake write about something. If you have an embarrassing personal problem write in to Sister Charlie's 'In Confidence' page: she will only share it with the entire readership . . .

I thought I'd discovered a fascinating new hobby.

The house was now on the market, and Matt, via his solicitor, had said he'd give me half of any profit, though I could see that it would all be eaten up by these mysterious debts and the overdraft. It had never felt like my house anyway, so I didn't care.

He'd also said he'd stored everything that he wanted from the house, and he didn't mind what I did with the rest.

What a busy boy he must have been during that week at home – and how unobservant of me not to notice.

He was going to carry on paying the mortgage and utilities until the house was sold, but for some reason he hadn't transferred any extra money across that month for food, etc. Was this a mistake, or had I already dwindled to the present of the odd duck?

Seeing that I would have to start selling the furniture *now* (however odd an appearance that would give to prospective house purchasers) I went out to the supermarket and removed as many cardboard boxes as I could fit into my ancient 2CV.

I also laid in a large supply of long-life consumables, like baked beans, jars of olives, red wine and dog food, before the money ran out altogether.

Em phoned: the mistress and her children had got into the house, and were laying waste like Angie's squirrels.

None of the others had managed to sidestep the Summer Cottage like this, and Em had begun an offensive against the invader. Em did offensive very well. She hoped to have them out before I moved back, but in the meantime the mistress was domiciled in *my* room! I was highly indignant, even though Em had removed all my personal belongings from it and stored them in one attic, and the two little girls in another.

She would have much preferred squirrels, and so would I.

Why did it have to be *my* room? Why not Bran or Anne's? Having foreign bodies in my only remaining sanctum was the last straw. Think the aliens were now taking over Yorkshire.

'Don't worry, I'll get them out,' Em said grimly. 'Father won't be able to stand them around all the time once the sexual novelty's worn off – you know what he's like. Then I'll put your room back as it was.'

'But it will never be the same again,' I said sadly, for now I really did feel like a dispossessed person. I was blowin' in the wind.

I told Em about *Skint Old Northern Woman*, and she said it was a wonderful idea, and she would write some inspiring verse for it, or maybe cookery hints, like: 'In Yorkshire We Eat Faggots'.

Em has a knack for writing doggerel verse, which is very saleable: practically every greeting card seems to contain one of hers. Now she reminded me that we all had old portable typewriters. Father bought them when it became clear that we weren't going to write Gondal-type stories in the minute notebooks he kept giving us. Perhaps he thought we needed a bit of twentieth-century apparatus?

When I found mine, the ribbon had dried to paper tape, and trying to buy a new one proved to be a vain quest, for the computer age had long overtaken me.

When I eventually did track one down it was the wrong sort and I had to hand-wind it onto the old spools. I feared I may have red and blue hands for the rest of my life. Still, it worked.

Skint Old Northern Woman

In this issue:
   Tart up that skirt
   Normal women bulge
   Superfluous hair
   Bulimia for beginners: what to do if your body doesn't want to part with the food

My roots were turning slowly silver as the divorce proceedings trundled tumbrel-like towards the final division. I'd always had long hair, but I didn't think all that dye would come out. It looked quite interesting, though – more badgerish than Cruella.

My clothes I couldn't do much about, since they were all black; mostly culled from charity shops and jumble sales. There were one or two floaty Ghost things, purchased at who-knows-what-price or with what credit card by Matt in London, but they were black, too.

Since I was not the same person who'd eloped with Matt, it didn't seem right that I should look the same, especially if I was moving back to Upvale. I was going full circle on my life, but surely it should be a different me that returned?

New To You.

It was melancholy packing up the house, and my dreams with it. And there was that moment when the auction van removed the marital bed . . . Very symbolic.

Not that I ever liked it.

Angie had been ringing continually, offering to help, but that was just nosiness. And Greg was back, but he hadn't got in, even though he phoned first to make sure I was here. That should have got the message through.

Soon he'd be flying off again – they both would – and I need never see them or any of Matt's other friends ever again, so there was at least *one* good side of divorce.

Skint Old Fashion Victim, No. 1

Criteria for buying second-hand clothes:
1. It fits you
2. It has no noticeable holes or stains
3. You can (just) afford it
4. It doesn't say 'Dry clean only' on the label

5. *The colour doesn't make you look like a dead Martian*
6. *It conceals/reveals all bulging bits in a socially accept-*
   able manner.

Phoned Anne's London flat, and for once found her home. Her normal manner of answering the phone was so indistinguishable from the answerphone that I'd started to leave a message when she broke in.

'Anne, this is Charlie—'

'And you think I can't recognise your voice after all these years?'

'Oh, you're there! Good. Is Red there, too?'

'No. Bosnia.'

'I didn't think anything much was happening there at the moment.'

'It isn't; he's coming back.'

'Has Em told you I'm getting divorced?'

'Yes. Bloody good idea.'

'It wasn't mine, but I'm getting quite used to it. I've discovered that although I'm deeply shocked and upset, I'm not heartbroken. Mostly I'm annoyed that I stayed faithful all these years when I needn't have bothered.'

'Em says you're selling the house and going home.'

'Yes – I won't have much money, so I'll have to live at home for a bit, until I can rent a place of my own. But to do that I'll need to either sell more paintings or get a job of some kind.'

'Father's mistress has got in the house.'

'She's not only in the house, she's in *my* room. If Em doesn't get rid of her soon I'll have to stay in the Summer Cottage.'

'You might like it. Home but sort of independent. Eat in, live out.'

'Yes . . . Oh, I saw you on the news a few days ago. Nice waistcoat – khaki suits you.'

'Just as well; never wear anything else. Like you, with your black.'

'I might have a change.'

'Em's thinking of having a change, too: turning to the Black Arts, or maybe greyish. The darker side of Wicca, anyway,' Anne said noncommittally.

'Yes, but is it a good idea?'

'Who knows? No one can stop Em doing anything she's made her mind up to do.'

'That's true. I expect she's got the measure of the mistress by now, too. Do you think you might be visiting Upvale soon?'

'Might do, in a few weeks. Depends.'

She rang off after a few bracing words about getting a solicitor and a better settlement, but I didn't think Matt had got very much to settle, so it would be pointless and tiring.

Came back from the supermarket with a whole lot more boxes, and had to kick the front door closed behind me.

Flossie was still snoring in the kitchen, lying just as she had been when I went out: on her back in her furry igloo, with her head hanging out of the opening and her ears on the floor. She didn't wake up even when I started clattering unwanted cooking-ware in the boxes.

It was as I was standing on tiptoe on the very top of the high kitchen steps, unhooking the cast-iron frying pan from the ceiling rack (so convenient for Matt, who never cooked,

27

so inconvenient for me, who did), that I was seized extremely familiarly from behind.

'All alone at last?' gloated a horribly familiar voice. 'You can't know how long I've wanted to get my hands on these!' And he squeezed painfully, like an over-enthusiastic fruit tester.

These were, I fear, the last words ever spoken by Angie's husband, Greg. Had he known, perhaps he'd have thought of something a little less trite: but then, everything he uttered was straight out of a Victorian melodrama, so perhaps not.

Startled and off-balance, I couldn't stop the weight and momentum of the pan I'd just grasped from swinging down and connecting with his head.

What an odd, strangely meaty, but hollow noise it made against his skull! A sort of watermelon-hit-by-a-cricket-bat sound that I don't think I'll ever forget as long as I live.

It *was* only the smaller frying pan, but unluckily he must have had a very thin skull. Mind you, even with a two-handed swing I would probably have dropped rather than swung the bigger pan. Bad luck all round.

As I stepped carefully down, Greg twitched like a dying insect at my feet, then lay still.

Not dead yet? Not dead?

Someone let out their breath in a long exhalation, and when I looked up, Miss Grinch was standing in the doorway, her choppy fingers to her skinny lips, as Shakespeare has it. An empty milk jug hung from the lax fingers of her other hand.

'I mustn't have locked the door,' I said inconsequentially. 'I'm always careful, especially when I know Greg's home – but it was awkward with all those boxes.'

Naturally Miss Grinch would have been so consumed with

curiosity she'd followed Greg in. Probably tiptoed up the hall right behind him.

'Is he dead?' she enquired, stepping into the room just as I dropped the pan from nerveless fingers. (It landed on Greg's foot with a crunch, but he was beyond caring by then.)

'Did he fall, or was he pushed?' I quavered.

'Not that he doesn't deserve it, behaving in such a disgusting way to a defenceless woman,' she said severely. 'Find a mirror and hold it to his lips.'

I began to giggle helplessly: 'A mirror? Why would he want to see himself at a time like this?'

'Pull yourself together, girl,' she snapped. 'A mirror will mist up if he's breathing. Here, I'll do it.'

She unhooked the small pine square from the wall under the clock. 'You phone 999.'

I managed that, even though my fingers felt even deader than Greg looked.

'Ambulance – accident – emergency!' I babbled. 'There's no mist on the mirror!'

'Where are you speaking from, please?'

'This is Miss Grinch,' that lady said, taking the receiver from my hand. 'I don't think there's any rush. He's dead.'

She gave my name and address to the operator, then added, 'We just need the ambulance, no police. This is such a nice neighbourhood, and none of the Grinches have ever been mixed up with police.'

'Except the one who stole Christmas,' I said helpfully.

Of course, we did get the police, much to Miss Grinch's indignation, but never did I think I would be so glad to have a nosy neighbour!

Were it not for Miss Grinch I was sure I'd have been facing a murder charge, but she described how she'd followed Greg right into the house and had seen the whole unfortunate accident.

If Greg hadn't suddenly assaulted me just as I was reaching down the pan, with no idea that I wasn't alone, it would not have occurred.

The frying pan was impounded, but I wasn't, although I felt so guilty at having taken a life I'd have gone without a struggle.

Flossie finally awoke at one point during the noisy and exhaustive débâcle, took a look out of her igloo and retired back in, until everyone was gone except Miss Grinch and me. Flossie was easily confused by loud voices and big feet.

Later, Miss Grinch gave me a small glass of colourless fluid and insisted that I drink it. I was positive she said it was gin and laudanum, but surely that couldn't be right?

Whatever it was, it put me out like a light.

Chapter 4: Sheared Off

Late that night Angie came to the door and beat on it, screaming hysterically, 'Bitch! Whore! Murderess!'

The last was the only one I felt truly applied.

Fortunately I was sitting in the upstairs bay window, sleep being something I'd lost the hang of, and my legs had gone too numb to go down, otherwise sheer guilt would probably have made me go and let her in.

After a while lights went on in several neighbouring houses, including Miss Grinch's, and shortly after that a police car coasted quietly up and removed Angie.

There was a faint, receding cry of, 'Pigs! Pigs! Arrest the murderess!' and then the street slowly sunk back into dark silence.

I'd been wondering how I could break the news of the accident to Matt, but in the end I didn't have to, because Angie did it for me.

He phoned to inform me tersely that henceforth all communication would be through the solicitor, and then put the phone down.

I suppose murdering his best friend *was* a pretty irreconcilable marital difference.

Miss Grinch continued to be my comfort and guide throughout this nightmare. I didn't know what I'd have done without her, which was a far cry from the way I felt about her before she became the star witness for the defence.

She was now my bestest friend. Not so much a mother figure, as an acidulated spinster figure – everyone should have one, but they are a dying breed.

Em would have come to stay for a few days, but Father's latest mistress was still infesting the house.

The housekeeping was, and always had been, Em's preserve, and she wouldn't stand interference, let alone a takeover bid. Outright war had been declared.

Normally this would all have interested me extremely, especially since one of the combatants was occupying the hallowed ground of my bedroom, but now I moved through the days like an automaton. I signed everything the solicitor sent me; Matt, true to his word, having ceased personal contact.

I'd be lucky if I even got the duck now.

Miss Grinch, like Anne, urged me to get my own solicitor and a better deal, but so far as I could see there wasn't anything but debts and an absent husband, and I didn't want half of either of those.

Anyway, I didn't feel I deserved anything any more.

All I could think of was that ghastly thud as the pan connected with Greg's head, and I was tortured with wondering whether I could have prevented it: I mean, when I hit him, I *wanted* to hit him – so was it really an accident?

Was there a moment when I could have diverted the fatal downward swing?

I didn't think so, but I wasn't sure. And I *felt* like a murderess – I *had* killed someone.

Miss Grinch didn't understand that. She said God would look into my heart and judge me, but I was afraid He already had. He just hadn't told me the outcome.

We had had several people round to view the house, though I didn't know how many were simply motivated by the thrill of blood. Miss Grinch had been conducting the sightseeing tours with a brisk efficiency reminiscent of Anne and Em. Perhaps that was why I liked her so much.

She had also helped me pack up most of the house contents, and soon everything except a few necessities had gone to auction. I didn't keep a lot – I felt a certain revulsion at the things that reminded me of Matt (and through him, Greg), which most things did. Anything unsaleable had gone to the nearest charity shop, or in the bin.

I sent a small van of things to Em to store for me: the driver was cheap, but he certainly wasn't willing, especially when it came to my plants. He said he had hay fever and wouldn't take *any* of them, so I would just have to fit as many of them as I could into my 2CV when I moved, with the roof open, even though it was pretty cold to be trans-porting tropical foliage. I gave a lot of the smaller ones to Miss Grinch, who was delighted, so at least they'd gone to a good home.

Eventually there was just me, Flossie, and a few vital odds and ends left. Like the survivors of a shipwreck, we were marooned until after the inquest.

Angie had made banshee late-night appearances twice more on my doorstep, but been removed much faster than the first time.

I had been buying head-sized melons.

Skint Old Gardening Tips, No. 1

Always keep margarine tubs of compost on your window-sills, and whenever you eat fruit, push the pips or stones in. Water daily, and eventually something *will come up. The novelty of this method is that you won't have the faintest idea what it is.*

Even in my numb state – which by then seemed part of me, like permafrost – I found the inquest appalling, although but for Miss Grinch it might have been a murder trial, which would have been very much worse.

The kindly coroner treated me like a frail little flower, and Miss Grinch with respect, but was firm about having Angie removed from the room when she became hysterical and demanded the death penalty.

She was still screaming, 'Murderess! Murderess!' as she was escorted out.

I knew in my heart of hearts she was right, even though the coroner assured me it wasn't my fault at all, and urged me to put it behind me. The verdict was brought in as accidental death.

The coroner added a little speech to the effect that people who succumbed to the current craze for heavy cast-iron pans would do better not to hang them from the ceiling, and I'd have to second that one.

By the time I got out of the hearing the reporters from the local paper were encouraging Angie to stage the scene of her life.

She spotted me. 'Murderess!' she screamed with a certain monotony, tossing her black veil over her shoulders and then lunging at me with blood-red talons like a deranged harpy. 'Murdering harlot!'

Well, that was different – but why harlot? Surely it was because I'd resisted her leching husband that he was dead? And she knew what he was like.

Fortunately, one or two people were holding her back, since I was transfixed by all the avid stares.

'I'll never let this rest until my poor Greg has justice!' Angie howled. 'Wherever you go I'll find you, and make sure people know the sort of woman you are!'

I wished *I* knew what sort of woman I was.

'You'll *never* be able to forget it.'

Well, that was certainly true.

'Wherever you go, I'll follow you,' she added, sounding suddenly exhausted, and dangling limply from the hands that a moment before had been restraining her. 'You'll never escape.'

Nowhere to run to, nowhere to hide . . .

'Why, Angie?' I asked. 'You must realise by now I didn't mean to kill him. Don't you think I feel badly enough about it already?'

'No, but I'll make sure you know what it's like to suffer – to be friendless and alone . . . like me.' She drew a dramatic hand across her eyes and gave a broken sob.

'But, Angie, Greg walked into my house uninvited and indecently assaulted me! And you must have known he was serially unfaithful?'

'Yes, but none of them ever *killed* him!'

Well, there was that. And the more I protested, the guiltier I felt. Could I really not have diverted that fatal downward swing?

'Besides, whatever his faults, he loved me,' declaimed Angie, looking tragic.

'Maybe he did, but he slept with anyone he could get,' I pointed out.

'They weren't important.'

The voices of the listeners now rose in a babble of questions, but Miss Grinch popped up suddenly at my side, seized her chance, and hurried me through a gap to the waiting taxi.

'How tall was Greg?' I whispered as we climbed in. 'Did you find out?'

'Five feet, ten inches exactly, dear,' she replied.

Looking back, I could see Angie still holding forth on the steps like Lady Macbeth.

'I wish I was dead,' I said dully. 'There doesn't seem any point to living any more.'

'Clearly God still has a use for you,' Miss Grinch said placidly.

'Compost?' I suggested.

'We are all God's compost, if you like,' she said. 'Interesting – I've never thought of it like that before. However, I am sure he has something in mind for you before that. He moves in mysterious ways.'

'Like the frying pan,' I agreed, and we were silent until we reached the house.

Miss Grinch bought the local papers, and thankfully I hadn't merited the front page. Even with Angie's theatrics I suppose they can only get so much story from a domestic accident without insinuating something libellous.

I was described throughout as Mrs Charlotte Fry (although I've always called myself by my maiden name), and there were several photographs of me looking very small and weird, like a glaze-eyed rabbit cowering under the menacing overhang of Angie's bust.

My hair was now a clear white for about an inch at the roots.

'I always wondered about that very dense blue-black shade,' Miss Grinch said, scrutinising a particularly hideous photo.

'It was my natural colour.'

'Believe me, it is a mistake, once a woman reaches forty, to dye her hair a dark colour. Your skin has lost the fresh bloom of youth and the contrast is too severe.'

'I know, but Matt wanted me to keep it black. He liked this sort of Goth look with the long hair and the dark eye make-up, because he thought it made me look young. He was so much older, so I was a sort of a Trophy Wife, you know?'

'Yes, but you can do what you like now, dear.'

'I don't think I care.'

'I'll have my hairdresser come round and do something with it – have it made as God intended.'

'God intended my hair to turn silver at thirty, like my mother's, but my eyebrows and eyelashes to stay dark.'

Mother is Lally Tooke and when I see her on the jacket of one of her radical feminist books, or on TV, she looks a bit like she's wearing a powdered wig, but she also looks good. We have the same big dark eyes, the purplish colour of black grapes.

Matt was always impressed by Father's fame (or notoriety), dragging his name into conversations like a dog with some malodorous and grisly find. 'My father-in-law, Ranulf Rhymer . . .'

He never felt the same way about my far-flying mother, but then, neither do I: *that* hand did not so much rock the cradle as break off shards and wage a bloody battle with them before leaving the field for ever.

'You could start wearing prettier colours than black,' suggested Miss Grinch, who had been pursuing thoughts of her own.

'I don't have anything else. Most of my clothes come from charity shops and jumble sales anyway.'

'Time for a change.'

'I can't afford a change.'

'My hairdresser's very cheap,' she assured me, and looking at her frizzed ginger-grey curls I could believe it.

She was right: her hairdresser *was* cheap. In a moment of madness induced by receiving the decree nisi in the post, I summoned her and had all my hair chopped off: very cathartic.

It was now clipped short and close to my head like a convict's, but at least it was all silver. I left off the heavy eye make-up, which made me look like a marmoset in combination with the cropped head, but the loose black clothes (I'd lost weight) and big boots now looked ridiculous.

I'd forgotten how to eat as well as sleep, which was why my clothes hung on me, but there was no more money so the escaped fugitive look would have to remain for the time being.

* * *

A rare phone call from Mother in America.

The last time she'd called me was after I married Matt, when she'd said that I was a pathetic, downtrodden negation of everything the women's movement had ever fought for.

Perhaps I was. And perhaps I might have turned out differently had she taken us children with her on her flight from Father; but then again, maybe not.

This time it was a congratulatory phone call, she having heard about Dead Greg.

'Well done!' she said. 'A blow struck right at the heart of male oppression.'

'More the head, Mother. And I'm not proud of it. I'm finding it very hard to live with the idea that I've killed someone.'

'The guilt was his: it was his own fault.'

'True, but somehow that doesn't seem to make it feel any better. Mother, did you know Matt and I are divorcing? We're waiting for the final bit to come through.'

There was a pause. 'I'd have loved to have had you to stay with me,' she said eventually, as though I'd asked. 'But I'm afraid I'm about to go on a lecture tour for my next book, and – wait, though! – you could come with me, and tell everyone about—'

'No, thanks,' I said hastily. 'I'm going home to Upvale.'

'You can open the cage door, but you can't force the animals out,' she said cryptically, sighing.

Chapter 5: The Prodigal Daughter

It was strange to be going home for good and yet not to be going back to my square, high-ceilinged bedroom, with the teenage-timewarp décor.

Of course, I'd escaped back from time to time over the years, usually alone. Among so many big, self-assured people Matt always felt very much the small Fry in the pond, I think. (Which he was.)

Father, Em and Anne petrified him, but I don't think he found Branwell threatening, just loopy. When I asked Bran soon after I was married if he liked Matt, he just replied vaguely, 'Who?'

Matt was always jealous of the stretched but uncut umbilical cord that connected me – and all of us Rhymers – to Upvale, though strangely enough I hadn't even realised it existed until I tested its limits by running away with Matt.

Even Anne, globetrotting TV correspondent that she was, returned from time to time to recharge her batteries on Blackdog Moor, before going back to foreign battlefields. Wherever in the world there was trouble, there also was Anne in her khaki fatigues and multi-pocketed waistcoat.

Wars didn't seem to last long once she'd arrived – I think they took one look and united against a greater peril.

Since the Ding of Death I'd tried to phone Anne a couple of times at her London flat (stark, minimalist, shared with her stark, minimalist, foreign-correspondent lover, Red), but there had been no reply other than the answering machine. Em said she'd managed to get hold of the lover once, but he'd just said Anne was away and put the phone down.

Anne, Em and Father are all big, handsome, strong-boned, grimly purposeful types, with masses of wavy light hair: leonine. Maybe that's why they made Matt nervous – he thought he may be the unlucky zebra at the waterhole.

I'm small and dark – now small and silver-haired – like Mother, but I'm not the fragile little flower I look. Bran is slight too, but wiry, with dark auburn hair like a newly peeled chestnut, and strangely light brown eyes. We think he must take after his Polish mother's side of the family, but we barely remembered her brief tenure as au pair, mistress, and oh-so-reluctant mother; even Em, who is the eldest.

Em had run the house as far back as I could remember, with the help of Gloria Mundi and her brother, Walter. Funnily enough, housewifery didn't sort of seep into me by osmosis – I had to go out and buy a book. But you can't say I didn't try; it's just that nature intended me to be an artist, not a housewife.

Upvale Parsonage has never seen a parson in its life – that was just Father being Brontëan. It stands foursquare in stone, with a small formal garden of mossy gravel and raddled roses dividing it from the road. Behind it the ground falls away steeply down to the stream, so the kitchen and sculleries are built into the hillside below the road level, facing across the valley.

And even below *that* is the undercroft, which we call the Summer Cottage, also partly built into the hillside, and linked to the house by a twisting and rather dank spiral staircase with oak doors top and bottom.

The Summer Cottage gives on to the narrow, rough track that leads down to another cottage, derelict last time I saw it, but recently renovated and sold to some kind of actor, according to Em. Then there's Owlets Farm, where Madge and her old father, Bob, live.

Em had always kept the hinges on the Parsonage door to the Summer Cottage unoiled, so she'd know by the squealing when an alien invader (i.e. one of Father's seemingly endless string of mistresses) was entering her territory.

But this time the invaders had sneaked in behind her back.

Kitchen Pests
1) Your Father's mistress
2) Your Father's mistress's children
3) Your Father . . .

'The van got here OK,' Em said when I phoned her from my strangely naked house. 'I had everything put into the cottage, including all the stuff from your bedroom that I'd stowed in the attic. Walter took it all down.'

'It seems odd coming back to the cottage. Still, I suppose I do still have a lot of things and I'm going to have a car full of plants, despite Miss Grinch having taken some. I don't know where I'm going to put them, but I'll need them if I ever paint again. I can't do it now without the jungle round me.'

But would I ever paint again? I'd had painter's block since the Great Pan Swing . . . and if I did paint, would I revert to the old style at Upvale, or perhaps evolve something between the two?

'You *will* paint again,' pronounced Em, like the word of God – or maybe the Word of Wicca – 'and Walter's making you a conservatory in front of the cottage, only of course he calls it a veranda.'

'Out of what?'

'Someone gave him some old doors and windows, and he's using clear corrugated plastic for the roof. I told him you needed somewhere like his friend George's pigeon loft, only much lighter, and he got the idea immediately. He's been at it a week – I can hear him hammering now.'

'That's wonderful,' I said, a lump coming to my throat at this extra kindness.

'Father's been complaining, but he isn't working – too busy banging away himself. That woman's so insatiable it's embarrassing. I caught him carrying her up the stairs the other night, which won't do his back much good.'

'He was always like that, though, Em.'

'This one's different. She's got into the house, for a start, with her brats.'

Like Angie's squirrels. I hoped Angie didn't follow me here and get in the house, too.

'Does he mind my coming home for good?'

'He doesn't care, just says you'll have to pay for your keep, so the mistress must be expensive.'

'He's right, though, Em – and I can't stay in the Summer

Cottage for ever. He's bound to want it for the next mistress. I'll have to find a job of some kind, and rent a place. Matt hasn't sent me any money since I dinged Greg. I *knew* it would be the odd duck, and that only if I was lucky, but I don't think I want his money any more anyway. I don't deserve it after killing his best friend.'

'It was an accident, and you're entitled to some maintenance – we all keep telling you. You've got to live on something until you paint again, so—'

'*If* I ever paint again,' I said pessimistically.

She ignored that. 'So I've got you a part-time job, starting Monday.'

Panic clutched me round the midriff with sharp talons. 'A job! What on earth as?'

'Helper in the Rainbow Nursery down the road. You don't know it – they started a sort of self-sufficient commune in Hoo Hall, and there's a progressive nursery attached.'

'Montessori or Steiner or something?'

'Something. They don't keep their staff long, probably because they don't pay much, so they're always desperate.'

'Do they know I'm a murderess?'

'You're not a murderess, and the accident didn't make the national headlines, so probably not.'

'Oh, Em, I don't think I can do it. I don't know anything about children and—'

'You can try. Then maybe something else will turn up, or you'll start painting again.'

'Vaddie at the gallery keeps asking me for more – but they've got everything I'd finished.'

'You need to get back here and let the moors cure you,

44

and Gloria will brew you up a tonic. You'll see – everything will be OK.'

Gloria is a wisewoman, and taught Em everything she knows, but she brews the most God-awful-tasting potions.

'It'll be odd living in the mistress's house.'

'Gloria Mundi's cleaned it till it squeaks, and I've oiled the kitchen door so you can come and go as you like without anyone knowing.'

'Thank you, Em,' I said gratefully. 'I've put you to a lot of trouble.'

'No you haven't – you know I like organising. It's that Jessica woman who's making trouble – you'll have to help me to get her out.'

'Father's mistresses never last long,' I assured her. 'Bran's mother was the longest, but that was only because she wanted to have Bran before she went back home. I don't think she and Father were communicating in any way once Bran was conceived.'

'Ah, yes – Bran. He phoned me the other day from outside the university. Apparently the High Priestess of Thoth manifested herself, and informed him that he shouldn't use mobile phones any more because evil spirits escaped from them into his head. I couldn't hear him very clearly because he was holding it away from his ear, and then there was a swooshing noise and a splash before it went dead, so I think he threw it into the river.'

'Ah.'

'Yes, so I've put Rob's taxi on stand-by to go and collect him. I don't suppose Bran's students will notice his absence if he has to come home for a break. He doesn't remember he's got any, half the time, and when he does he probably

45

lectures them in some ancient tongue they can't understand. But apparently the book's going to be brilliant.'

'There has to be a good reason the University is prepared to put up with his little ways, other than his having an IQ greater than the sum of all the other staff.'

'He also has a whanger bigger than any of the other staff,' Em said, which was true; even skinny-dipping in the icy beck as children we'd seen he'd been impressive in that department. But unless the High Priestess of Thoth manifested herself in a more solid form and drew him a diagram, I feared that asset would be entirely wasted.

'I don't think that would particularly impress academic circles,' I said.

'Perhaps not. I've asked them to phone me if he doesn't calm down in a day or two, and Rob can set off.'

Rob knew Bran's little ways and was always quite happy to drive down to Bran's ancient and hallowed university (which had proved surprisingly accepting of his eccentricity) and transport him back without mishap.

'Well, I suppose you couldn't put *Bran* in the Summer Cottage,' I said, though it still rankled that I'd been the one ejected for the mistress.

'I had one of my visions – about Anne,' Em said, reading *my* mind too. 'She's in difficulty, and she'll be coming home soon, for healing.'

'Spiritual or otherwise? She hasn't been shot, has she? I thought you said she couldn't be shot?'

'I don't think it's that sort of wound,' Em said doubtfully. 'But I can't tell clearly – my predictions are getting more and more fuzzy: I think the vertical hold's gone. Really, what's the point of hanging on to my virginity in order to

46

retain my powers, when all I ever see is the boring and mundane? I've never clearly seen *anything* wildly exciting. I really think I might as well explore the darker side of witchcraft.'

'Well, don't do anything hasty,' I begged her. 'Especially anything . . . Aleister Crowley.'

'That poseur! Certainly not. No, I'm thinking more of joining the local coven and fully embracing the Ancient Arts – and perhaps a suitable man. Lilith's running one.'

'What, a suitable man?'

'No, a coven.'

'And just what do you mean by a *suitable* man?'

'Big, strong, silent and malleable.'

She could add 'courageous' to that list of qualifications. I've seen strong men turn and run when they see Em coming.

'That actor's quite dishy, up at the cottage,' she mused. 'And Gloria said his reputation with women stinks, so he'd be terribly suitable.'

'Em! You wouldn't really.'

'What time are you arriving tomorrow?' she asked, changing the subject.

'Early afternoon, I hope, but snow's forecast, which will make negotiating Ramshaw Heights and Blackdog Moor tricky. I don't know why, but that's the only way I *can* come back.'

'It's because you left that way the first time with Matt, and so you must describe the full Circle of Return,' Em said.

'It'll be dicey if it snows heavily.'

'You'll make it – the 2CV will glide over the top. Wrap Flossie up well, though. These little spaniels are inbred; she catches cold too easily.'

'Yes, and the plants, too. They're all a bit tropical for a winter spin on the moors with the roof down.'

'You'll arrive safely. I'd at least know if that were otherwise,' Em said deeply, then added more prosaically, 'See you then. Drive straight down to the cottage. The key is in the frog, and Walter will unpack your stuff for you while we catch up with things.'

When I came over Ramshaw Heights I could see Blackdog Moor – transformed into Whitedog Moor – glittering like quartz below me. I felt inwardly cleansed by the bright light bouncing off the vast whiteness.

I was a bit of a dog at that moment: a complete mongrel. Cropped white head and black clothes hanging long and loose . . . more Uncle Fester than Morticia.

And speaking of dogs, bubbling snores were coming from the depths of Flossie's fake-fur-lined igloo, which was on the floor at the front passenger side. The passenger seat itself, and all the rest of the car, was jammed with all my favourite huge plants – figs and lemons, palms and bananas – wrapped in newspaper and layers of bubble wrap, and sticking up out of the open top of the car like so many extras from *Invasion of the Body Snatchers*. My driving visibility was almost nil.

We'd received some strange looks when we set out on our journey, but the closer to home we got the less notice anyone took. West Yorkshire folk can absorb every last detail without looking directly at you.

Externally I was freezing, my hands stuck to the wheel. Inside, too, was still the feeling that all my organs had turned to ice, which I'd had since the moment Greg died, only now there was just the faintest tinge of warm hope.

'You're nearly home, Charlie: everything will be all right now,' I encouraged myself as we slid down Edge Bank.

But the Snow Queen whispered in Angie's voice: 'Nothing will ever be right again.'

'Maybe it won't, Angie,' I said aloud. 'But at least it will be all wrong in the right place.'

Chapter 6: Pesto in the Kitchen

Skint Old Crafts: Stick It, Stitch It, and Stuff It

Hint One: for those of you living south of Luton, I suggest you shred this magazine and reassemble it in a different order with Sellotape, since it will give you hours of fun and make just as much sense afterwards.

I turned down the snowy track behind the Parsonage and slid to a halt, more by luck than judgement, next to the wall of the unseasonably named Summer Cottage.

It's more of a Hobbit hole in the hillside than anything, with the heavy bulk of the Parsonage threateningly poised above, ready to toboggan down the hill sweeping all before it.

The front of the cottage now sported a ramshackle, half-glazed appendage, painted a vivid shade of Mediterranean blue. The door was in need of a second coat, for the word 'Ladies' could still faintly be seen, although I thought the heart-shaped cut-out very tasteful.

Walter had excelled himself.

I was just sniffling a few sentimental tears away when a voice as mellow and melodious as a cello suddenly addressed me from behind, making me jump and whirl around like a Dervish.

'Are *you* responsible for that excrescence on the beautiful face of Upvale?'

Icy fingers of Arctic wind undulated my numerous layers of loose black drapery, and I had to claw a web-fine woollen scarf out of my eyes before I could see the man who'd spoken.

He was very tall, even taller than Em, and his dark, heavy-lidded eyes regarded me with a sort of weary wariness, as though I was a surprise gift he didn't want. He was also carrying a giant teddy bear.

'I don't think a man who walks about wearing a red duvet and a jester's hat has any right to criticise my cottage,' I informed him coldly, although his strange garments didn't actually look quite as ludicrous on him as they might sound, while my veranda, as Walter would call it, certainly did.

I didn't mention the teddy bear in case he was sensitive about it. Bran always takes his soft toy, Mr Froggy, everywhere in his pocket with him, but at least it's small.

'It's ski-wear,' he said, looking down his remarkably straight nose at me.

'Not in Upvale it isn't. You might as well have "Oft-Comed Un" stamped across your back; but I suppose you're the actor – Em said we'd got one in the cottage down the track,' I said, making him sound like a disease. 'I don't think she mentioned your name.'

And the bit of him I could see, between upturned collar and pulled-down hat – high sculptured cheekbones and slightly slanting, droopy-lidded eyes – did look vaguely familiar, even to someone who rarely watched TV or films.

'I'm incognito.'

'It's all right with me. I don't expect the urge will come upon me to boast about meeting you. Or your teddy bear,' I added, throwing caution to the winds.

'My teddy bear?' he echoed, looking at me strangely, but that might have been because my knitted coat was flying up behind me like black bat wings.

'Am I not supposed to mention the teddy bear? It's moving,' I added, fascinated.

Indeed, it was now not only moving, but muttering. The head turned and I saw a little face screwed up in sleep, framed by honey-brown fur and round ears. Then it snuggled back into the red duvet.

What with that and the Mediterranean veranda I was starting to feel quite freaked. Upvale had always previously stayed the same, my one fixed constant in a threatening world. It was a relief when the actor edged past me without another word (unless you count what sounded like a muttered 'Crackers!') and strode off up the lane with his little furry friend.

I prised *my* little furry friend out of her warm nest in the car, and she looked around her with a sort of vague surprise: the world had moved while she slept, *again*.

The door key was in the mouth of the stone frog as usual, together with some small wooden tablets inscribed with what looked like runes, and a bunch of dried herbs. I left those where they were.

We went through Walter's Folly, and I opened the door of the cottage to be met and embraced by a warm miasma of lavender, furniture polish and bleach. There was no leftover redolence of mistress here, for Gloria Mundi had clearly excised every last iota of their existence. It simply smelled like home.

Flossie pattered across the flagged floor behind me as I climbed the stairs up to the Parsonage kitchen and opened the strangely silent door.

There was a delicious aroma, easily identified as steak and kidney pie with suet crust, and Em was sitting coring baking apples at the kitchen table, and plopping them into a big earthenware bowl of water.

'You've come, then,' she stated, without looking up from her task. 'Put the kettle on – you must be frozen. Where's Flossie?'

With a wheeze like a small pair of bellows Flossie hauled herself up the last step, looking vaguely around, then made straight for the wood-burning stove in the corner like a shaggily upholstered heat-seeking missile.

'She must be cold,' said Em fondly. 'I'll warm her some milk.'

'She isn't cold – she's been fast asleep in her igloo all the way here. I'm the one who's absolutely brass-monkeyed, because I had to have the roof open for the plants. Where's Walter?'

As if on cue the door swung open and in hobbled a gnarled and cheery little goblin. The bridge of his over-large glasses had been bound with a great wodge of Sellotape, and his baggy corduroy trousers were held up by Father's old school tie.

'Hello, Walter,' I said, giving him a kiss.

'I've got no eyebrows.'

'I know. How are you?'

'No eyebrows. No bodily hair whatsoever!' he proclaimed happily. 'I've made you a veranda, and now I'm going to put your plants in it and make a jungle.'

'It's a wonderful veranda, Walter – it's the best one I've ever seen. Thank you!'

Beaming like a lighthouse he hobbled off towards the cottage stairs, muttering, 'No eyebrows . . . no bodily hair whatso . . .'

Em plopped the last apple into the bowl and got up. 'There we are, now we'll have a hot drink. Don't worry about your stuff,' she added, as ominous Burke-and-Hare dragging noises wafted up from the cottage. 'Walter will bring it all in, and you can arrange it as you like later. I've put a couple of greenhouse heaters in the veranda to take the chill off, because there's no electric in it yet, of course, and the floor's just the old paving stones. Do you like the colour?'

'Yes. It's very bright.'

'Walter's choice. Gloria wanted dark green, but I thought that was a bit municipal. You can do your own thing with the inside of the cottage.'

Gloria is Walter's sister, and they don't so much work at the Parsonage as inhabit the space at odd hours between dawn and dusk, as the fancy takes them.

'Where *is* Gloria? Where is everyone?'

'Gloria is turning out Bran's room, in case. Father's in his study composing another epic.'

'Oh God – who is it this time?'

'Browning. Apparently, he didn't produce much good work while he was married to Elizabeth Barrett Browning because he was actually busy writing all her poetry for her.'

'The same line as usual then?'

'He doesn't change. But at least it's lucrative; everyone loves to disagree with him. Otherwise, the mistress has gone out shopping, and then she'll probably be picking up the two sprogs from school. Do you know, she wanted them to have Anne's room because she didn't like them sleeping in the attic? I told her that Anne locked her room between visits and even Gloria only cleaned when she was there, and that shut her up.'

'Any word from Anne?'

'No, but her answering machine's changed: it just says, "This is Anne Rhymer, leave a message," and doesn't mention Red at all.'

'Perhaps they've parted? Not that they ever seemed to be in the same country simultaneously anyway.'

'Something's happening – I can feel it.'

'She will tell us if she wants to.'

'Yes, or simply turn up. I'm starting to get the idea she might be coming home soon,' said Emily, her eyes getting that strange, faraway expression. Then it was gone and she was saying briskly, 'Funnily enough, I've had much more interesting foretellings than ever before since I made up my mind to embrace the Dark Arts, but I think I'm going to go ahead anyway. I've got three friends coming round soon to tell me about their coven. You know one of them – Xanthe Skye.'

'I don't remember *anyone* called Xanthe Skye.'

'She was Doreen Higginbottom until The Change.'

'Oh, yes? That will be nice,' I said dubiously. 'Didn't she have a brief fling with Fa—'

I stopped dead, for the man himself, possibly attracted by the smell of freshly brewing coffee, had wandered in: big and broad-shouldered, in corduroys and a shirt rolled up to show muscular arms. He still had a full head of light, waving hair like Anne and Em's, and though his face was looking a bit pummelled by time, the general effect was large, virile and handsome.

'Hello, Father.'

'Oh God! Keep the pans locked up, Em,' he said resignedly.

Silently she poured out a mug of coffee and handed it to him, and he took two Jaffa Cakes out of the Rupert Bear tin and went back out without another word.

The study door closed behind him with a snap.

While I unburdened my soul to Em she baked a batch of sultana scones and made the biggest treacle tart you could fit in the oven, intricately latticed over the top.

She didn't say much, but it was comforting all the same, as were the two hot, buttered scones she insisted I eat.

It was quite a while later before the front door slammed and a woman's voice shrilled, 'Hello everybody!'

Silence answered her. Even the zooming noise of Gloria Mundi's Hoover stilled momentarily.

'That's her – Jessica. Can't hear the sprogs; perhaps they're out for tea or something.'

A woman staggered in and dumped a couple of bulging carrier bags on the table with a sigh of relief. 'There you are!'

She was fortyish, with a firmly repressed dark downiness and an aura of elegant sexuality – a sort of hungry look about the shadowed eyes. Her body was diet-victim skinny, and the rather bird-billed face perched on top made her look like a duck on a stick.

'Hello. You must be Charlie?' she said, smiling.

'Charlie, Father's tart – Father's tart, Charlie,' introduced Em.

'Fiancée,' Jessica said, her smile going a bit fixed. 'Is that your sweet little dog? Is she all right? She isn't moving, is she?'

'She isn't dead, if that's what you mean. She's a Cavalier Queen Charlotte. They go into suspended animation at regular intervals.'

'King Charles?'

'Not unless he was a bitch.'

'Take this stuff off my table, Jessie,' Em ordered. 'I'm trying to get dinner ready.'

'I thought we could have something a bit different tonight,' Jessica said, with a sort of determined jolliness. 'The girls don't really like all this meat and stodge, and I'm sure it's not healthy for a man of Ranulf's age. And there *are* vegetables other than mushy peas, you know! So I've got some pasta, and sun-dried tomatoes and pesto—'

With one sweep of her muscular arm Em cleared the table, and Flossie found herself under a sudden rain of Cellophane packages. She sat up, looking vaguely surprised.

'Sod off out of my kitchen,' Em said. I was relieved she was taking it so well.

Jessica laughed and began to retrieve her goodies. 'Now, Emily, I know your bark is worse than your bite, so—'

'No it isn't,' I assured her earnestly. One of Em's bites from a childhood disagreement we had still aches in cold weather, and I certainly don't come between her and anything she wants, any more than I'd come between a hungry dog and a big, juicy bone.

'Perhaps we could have pasta tomorrow?' persisted Jessica. 'I'll just put everything in the cupboard, shall I?'

'You can put it anywhere you like, as long as it isn't in my kitchen,' Em said.

'I – I think I'll go and see Ran,' Jessica said, backing towards the door.

'Do that,' Em said, and added, 'Frost's behind you.'

The great grey lurcher had indeed silently approached up the hall, and was now looming with his sad yellow eyes fixed on her.

Jessica gave a squeak of terror and shot off into the study, slamming the door.

They didn't emerge until dinner was ready, when Father looked excited and exhausted in equal measure, which I don't think was caused by writing the book.

The giggly little twins, Chloe and Phoebe, were decanted by someone's mother at seven. They looked about nine, and were attenuated versions of their mother, with legs like liquorice laces. The presence of Father and Em seemed to subdue them, but once they were sent off to bed they could be heard giggling for ages.

Gloria Mundi (whose only comment on seeing my shorn, silver locks had been: 'Well, I'll go to the foot of ower stairs!') stayed for dinner, but Walter had eaten a coddled egg and several scones in the kitchen and gone off to the pub.

Gloria would generally have gone too, by now, but had stayed in order to make sure I ate enough for ten people, and went to bed early. But then, I always was her favourite – probably because I was the runt of the litter.

She sat opposite, smiling at me, her pale bright eyes glowing in her crumpled face like stars in a net. She was about as close to a mother figure as we'd ever got, and it was comforting that night to have someone trying to molly-coddle me, even if, as predicted, she did make me drink a herbal brew that tasted as if it had been strained through an old sock.

Miss Grinch had been an absolute tower of strength, but Gloria was glorious.

Skint Old Cook, No. 1

How to Tell Your Mushy Peas from Your Pease Pudding

These two northern delicacies are easily distinguishable from each other. Mushy peas are simply, as the name suggests, dried marrowfat peas soaked overnight and then cooked until they go mushy and give off liquid. Much runnier than pease pudding, they are often served with chips or pies. The canned variety can be an interesting shade of green – try them with potatoes and gravy for an enticing mixture of colour combinations. Your dinner guests will never forget it!

Pease pudding is a solid, grey-greenish stodge, sometimes sold in little tubs. Made from split yellow peas boiled to a thick paste, it's cheap, filling and full of fibre. For the desperately hungry and/or hard up, use it as a sandwich filling.

It tastes better than it looks, as so many regional delicacies do: after all, weren't jellied eels once memorably described as looking like a bad cold in a bucket?

Chapter 7: Enlightenment

Chivvied by Em, I walked reluctantly down to Hoo House to meet Inga early next morning before all the children arrived at the nursery. I was worried that she wouldn't take me on, and worried that she would, but I needn't have bothered; I suppose if I had two heads or something she wouldn't employ me, but after seeing some of the other members of the commune with their feet in the trough at breakfast, I wouldn't bank on it.

They couldn't know I was a murderess yet – but they might well have regarded it as a sort of minor peccadillo when they did find out.

The nursery was called Rainbow of Enlightenment, which is as close as they can get to the Japanese original. I've never heard of it, so it obviously didn't take off like Steiner or Montessori.

Inga, a squat, damp, limp Scandinavian (no, they're not all tall, blonde ice maidens) gloomily took me around the two big, square front rooms of the house that formed the nursery, pointing out the arrangement of the equipment: apparently the children have to complete a series of tasks in their right order. 'Building the Rainbow of Endeavour to the Further Shores of Enlightenment . . .' or something.

Susie, the other helper, was setting out paint pots and brushes.

'We have sixteen childwen,' lisped Inga, 'including my own – Gunilla – who is in the gawden, being at one with Natuwe.'

'Natuwe?'

'Ja, Gunilla loves Mama Natuwe.'

'Oh, right. Does she also love the Rainbow of Enlightenment?'

'Gunilla is being bwought up by obsewving the behaviouw of The Gwoup. But it is also impowtant that she mixes with other childwen. She often chooses to join in with her fwiends as they complete thewe tasks.'

'I see,' I said, and so I did; no wonder staff didn't stay long, if Gunilla was doing her own thing while the other children were put through their very structured hoops. I mean, I knew nothing much about nursery education, but it sounded a recipe for disaster.

Still, maybe Gunilla was a sweet little thing, and it would all work beautifully. Yes, and I'm Pollyanna and everything comes up roses.

I left just as the first children were arriving in a series of mammoth people carriers driven by Mummy or the nanny. The Rainbow must be trendy.

Inga greeted the children by name in the same gloomy tones: China, Poppy, Zoë and Josh were just a sample. I expected I'd get them all hopelessly mixed up.

'Ah, Caitlin,' Inga said to one little girl, her voice warming up to blood heat. 'You awe eawly. Is Daddy hewe? I wanted to speak with him.'

'Gone,' Caitlin said succinctly. She was wearing a teddy-bear suit, the head, which I now saw was a hood with ears, pushed back. On her feet she wore flowered wellingtons, like a frivolous Paddington. 'Daddy wants to be left alone, because he's writing a play. And resting. And looking after me, while Mummy's in a film. Then she's going to marry Rod, and I've got a bridesmaid's dress. Daddy says it makes me look like a meringue.' She eyed me curiously, especially the limp black drapery and lace-up boots, then informed me: 'My daddy's a famous actor – he's Mace North.'

'Face North?' I echoed, puzzled.

'*Mace* North.'

'Of course,' I said, trying to sound impressed, which isn't easy if you don't watch films very often, although the name *was* ringing bells faintly somewhere. 'Then I think I met him behind my cottage yesterday. I'm Charlie Rhymer, and I live at the Parsonage.'

'I know Em. And Frost. Em gave me a gingerbread dragon with chocolate drop scales.'

'Em's my sister.' And she wasn't usually prone to like children. What *was* she up to?

Caitlin gave me a look of disbelief, for which I didn't blame her. I can hardly believe I'm related to three such enormous entities myself.

'Daddy's frightened of Em, but I'm not.'

'I'm suwe youw daddy isn't fwightened of anyone!' Inga said. 'Wun along in; we awe neawly weady to begin.'

I took the hint and left as yet more expensive dinosaurs trundled up the drive to decant their small passengers, and as I walked home through the mushy, melting snow I tried to remember if I'd ever seen Mace North in anything (other than a red duvet).

I didn't go to the cinema and although Matt was wont to

62

hire DVDs, they were of the violence, sex and nastiness kind, which were not images I wanted stored in my subconscious for ever.

However, that made me think of the actor's barbarian cheekbones, so at odds with his rather posh, mellow voice, and then I remembered where I'd seen him before: the cover of *Surprise!* magazine, the one Angie'd whipped away again.

Tartar blood, that was it.

When I got back to the Summer Cottage Flossie was just waking up, so I took her for the hundred-yard stroll she considered a strenuous trek, which got us as far up the track as the actor's cottage (no sign of life) but not quite as far as the farm, although Madge waved from the doorway. Then I set to work to try to turn the cottage into a home.

It was just two rooms, really, built into the hillside, and partitioned off to provide a bed-sitting room and the usual facilities. The décor was a bit flowery – the last mistress's taste, presumably – and if I was going to be here for any length of time I would have to paint it.

I set up my easel in the veranda, a gesture of hope, and arranged my plants around me, though there now weren't enough of them to give me quite that being-towered-over-threateningly feeling. I'd brought the tall ones, it was just the thick jungle effect that was missing.

I would have to take a big chunk of the auction money, go to the nearest garden centre – and hope they'd deliver.

It wasn't very warm, either. The two paraffin heaters were only there to stop the plants freezing, and they gave out a pleasant but strange smell all of their own (a bit like Walter).

I could do with some coconut matting over the stone flags, and electricity so that I could have lighting, and some heating . . .

Which sort of presupposed I was ever going to spend some time in there painting; but Em and Walter had done their best to encourage me.

I went up the stairs to the kitchen to see if Em fancied a trip out plant-hunting, and Flossie trailed wearily after me, wheezing. I felt sure all the exercise would do her good.

The kitchen was deserted except for Frost, who lifted his head and gave Flossie a leer.

Walter was in the small front room, watching TV and carving a walking stick. He grinned, but didn't say anything. His wig, never worn, occupied its usual place of honour on the mantelpiece, draped carefully over a polystyrene head.

Father's study door was shut with his 'Do Not Disturb' sign on it, though if anyone was already disturbed it was Father.

There was no sign of the Treacle Tart, and the children must be at school, but the sound of hoovering was still audible from above, where Gloria Mundi was singing Gilbert and Sullivan in a falsetto.

She was the very model of a modern major-general.

I found Em eventually in the sitting room, the curtains half drawn, which is why I was well into the room before I saw that she had company.

'Sorry,' I said, 'I didn't know you were entertaining, Em. I was just going to tell you I was off to the garden centre.'

'That's OK – you know Xanthe, don't you?'

Xanthe nodded graciously at me; she did look vaguely familiar from her days as Father's Flavour of the Month.

'And this is Lilith Tupman and Freya Frogget.'

Lilith looked like she'd been blanched under a pot. Freya was large and clad in billowing white, like over-exuberant ectoplasm.

'I'll leave you to it, but let me open the curtains first,' I offered, taking hold of the heavy velvet drapes.

There was a gasp from Lilith, who held her hands to her temples and exclaimed hysterically, 'No! No! The light must not touch my face!'

I hastily unloosed the curtains. 'Sorry.'

Maybe she was a vampire? But then, how had she got here?

'Would you like me to make you some coffee or something before I go?' I offered in atonement.

'Thanks, Charlie,' Em said. 'There's a tray ready in the kitchen – just fill the pot with boiling water and bring it in, will you?'

'You could join us,' said Lilith, recovering. 'If you wished?'

'No, no, her aura is *blue*!' Xanthe cried. 'I cannot have blue near me . . . it drains my psychic energy.'

If Father hadn't managed to drain her powers, I couldn't see how my blue aura would.

'Ice, I must have ice!' gasped Freya, in a parched voice.

'A bowl of ice from the freezer, too, please,' said Em. 'Do you want a hand?'

What, the Hand of Death? The Hand Of Glory? The Hand of the Baskerv—

'No, that's OK,' I assured her, backing out, and starting to puzzle over the ice. Still, Em's friends all appeared to be women of a certain age: Freya might be having a hot flush of mega proportions.

I brought the tray, which contained all sorts of home-baked goodies, plus a pot of some disgusting-smelling herbal brew reminiscent of Gloria's best, then left them to it.

Flossie was now snuggled up to Frost, the hussy, and showed no interest in accompanying me, to the garden centre or anywhere else.

Tips for Southern Visitors, No. 1

It is possible to have any variety of Northern accent in conjunction with an intellect.

At dinner it emerged that Father had also inadvertently crashed Em's tea party, barely escaping without being ravished by Freya, Lilith and Xanthe (well, that was *his* version, anyway).

'Congratulations, Em,' he said through a mouthful of home-made chicken pie. 'Not one of your friends is normal.'

'Speaking of normal,' Em said coolly, 'your son is coming home tomorrow for a rest.'

Jessica helped herself to a lettuce leaf, looked at it doubtfully, and put half back again in the bowl. 'I haven't met Branwell yet,' she said. 'Is he as dishy as you, darling?'

The two little girls, who were doing full justice to the despised stodge, giggled.

'He's nothing like me,' Father said tersely. 'Charlie's nothing like me, either.'

'I'm like Mother, though, and I expect Bran takes after his.'

'Your mother's very famous, isn't she?' Jessica asked. 'Big in America. But I do think all this writing books and talking about feminism does more harm than good, don't you?'

'Someone's got to speak out, especially when men are trying to claim great works of women's fiction as their own,' Em commented pointedly, but Father refused to rise to the bait.

'Yes, wasn't Elizabeth Barrett Browning lucky, having such a clever husband to write her work for her?' I said innocently. 'I wonder how on earth she managed before he came along? Perhaps one of her brothers?'

'You mustn't tease,' Jessica said earnestly. 'Ran researches very thoroughly. He works very hard.'

'He has to research thoroughly to find scraps of evidence that can be twisted into proving what he wants,' Em said.

'And you, of course, are a great writer and know all about it?' he said sarcastically. 'My dear Em, I don't think writing doggerel for greeting-card manufacturers quite qualifies you as a literary critic.'

'No, but I don't just write for greeting cards – I'm also Serafina Shane.'

While this was a bit of a damp squib as far as Father and myself were concerned, Jessica laid down her fork and stared.

'What, Serafina Shane out of *Women Live!* magazine? *Womanly Wicca Words of Spiritual Comfort*? I've ordered the book!'

'Advance orders *have* been very brisk,' Em said complacently, and bestowed a slightly warmer gaze on Jessica than I had ever seen before. She might just live, after all.

'Well done, Em,' I said. 'If I'd known I'd have read them, but I never buy women's mags – they're all *New Woman*, and *Never Admit You're Forty Woman*, and *Rich Bored Bitchy Woman*, when all I ever wanted was something like *Skint Old Northern Woman*.'

'You're right,' Em said. 'Weren't you going to start one?'

'Yes, in fact my hobby during the last few weeks has been writing articles for the sort of magazine I'd really like to find. I've got quite a lot.'

'Do I understand, Emily,' Father broke in, 'that you've been writing your ghastly doggerel for a women's magazine, and it's now coming out as a book?'

'Yes – inspirational verse and prose. I'm very popular.'

'Serafina what?' I asked.

'Shane.'

'At least it isn't Rhymer!' Father said.

'Well done, Em!' I enthused.

'So what were you plotting with your abnormal friends when I came in this morning?' enquired Father.

'We were trying various means to discover where Anne is. There's something the matter with her, and I can't get any reply from her flat. Xanthe tried the crystal pendulum.'

'And Xanthe knows everything?' He frowned. 'And why does she look so familiar?'

Em ignored this. 'The crystal showed us where she was – somewhere near her flat. Then Freya did a reading, and discovered that Anne's had an operation, but she'll be here soon to recuperate.'

'I suppose you know this because Anne's phoned,' he said sceptically.

'No. You know Anne, she'll phone when she's nearly here. Gloria Mundi's turning out her room, now she's finished Bran's.'

'What makes you think the Three Witches got it right?'

'They always get it right. That's why I'm joining their coven. I've been pussyfooting round the mealy-mouthed

68

edges for long enough, and now I'm going to wholeheartedly embrace the Ancient Arts.'

'Prostitution?' suggested Ran. 'I hear it's very well paid.'

Em gave him a look. 'The Ancient *Black* Arts,' she said.

Jessica gasped, her eyes widening in alarm. 'You mean – black magic? Oh, my God! The children!'

But the little girls, bored with the conversation, had crept away unnoticed. One of the dishes of meringues from the sideboard had gone too.

'Oh, Emily – promise you won't say anything about it in front of the girls! Don't they sacrifice little children, and sell their souls to the Devil?'

'Hands up all those present who've read the entire oeuvre of Dennis Wheatley and believe every word?' I said. 'Really, Jessica, grow up!'

'Charlie's quite right. I wouldn't harm *any* animal, even your children,' Em assured her.

'Thank you!' Jessica said, slightly hysterically. 'Ran, are you going to sit there and—'

Father stood up abruptly. 'No, I'm off to the pub. Coming?'

'How can I leave the girls?' she shuddered.

'I'll listen out for them,' I offered.

'But *you* killed someone . . .' she began.

'And I'm Spawn of the Devil,' Emily finished for her.

Father sighed. 'Lock up the pans, Em, and don't sacrifice the children. Satisfied, Jess? Come along!'

There was a brief internal struggle as Jessica's maternal feelings fought a losing battle, and then she hurried out after him.

'Tell me more about this *Skint Old Northern Woman* magazine,' Em said, passing the port.

In the woods the wild violets bloom.
From a distance,
the crumpled cigarette packet
is no less beautiful.
              From 'Words from the Spirit'
                      by Serafina Shane

Serafina Shane's first book, Womanly Wicca Words of Spiritual Comfort, *is available, price £5.99, from the Fishwife Press.*

Chapter 8: Dangerous to Melons

Skint Old Northern Woman: The Love Quiz

Would you exchange your husband/boyfriend/significant other for:

1. A box of chocolates?
A) Yes
B) No
C) A big box

2. A bag of pork scratchings?
A) Yes
B) Snatch your hand off
C) No, I'm Jewish, but try me with pistachio nuts

3. A night with Robert Plant?
A) Yes
B) Never heard of him, but yes anyway
C) No, never liked blonds/heavy metal/men even older
   than my father, but try me with Johnny Depp

I'm afraid our resident thespian caught me taking a swipe at a large yellow melon with a frying pan the following morning, so now probably thought I was demented, which I wasn't: merely obsessed.

It was not the *fatal* frying pan, of course, because Miss Grinch cleaned that up once the police had finished with it, and sent it off to a jumble sale.

I hoped it wasn't haunted by the red, bloodhound face of an elderly roué. I mean, imagine *that* materialising by the cooker, just as you were getting your omelette all puffy.

The melon was balanced on the gatepost, and I was standing on a large crate. It wasn't ideal – the relative heights were wrong, and the melon kept trying to roll off the perfectly flat surface as though possessed.

I'd just started the downward swing on a ripe yellow honeydew when I caught the glint of weak sunlight on raven's-wing hair above the stone wall that separated my strip of garden from the track, but by then the momentum was unstoppable: the pan connected with a meaty *thunk!* and the melon bounded past me and ricocheted off the veranda.

Mace North stopped by the gate, and surveyed me briefly with unsurprised, world-weary dark blue eyes. (Funny, I sort of expected them to be brown.) His black hair looked as if it had been casually hacked off with a sword – something fancy in gold, with a jewel in the end – and covered his head with feathery artlessness.

Then there was just the clatter of loose pebbles as he headed for home.

Good morning to you, too.

From my vantage point on the box I'd seen becoming

strands of purest silver among those black locks, so he was no spring chicken, though I didn't think the weary look was an age thing – he'd probably always looked like that.

Isn't it odd how much you can notice about someone in the briefest moment, even when you're not particularly interested in them?

He certainly made off quickly enough, probably afraid I'd fling myself on him pleading for his autograph, or something. But he could be permanently incognito, as far as I was concerned, and I didn't expect he would be bothered by crowds of admiring followers up here unless he was in a popular soap.

Still, I didn't suppose that, as an actor, he found my behaviour in any way unusual.

The previous night Father, who has got acquainted with Mace up at the Black Dog, warned me that he liked to be treated just like everyone else (although not, perhaps, to the point of being struck by a frying pan). That was fine by me – I wasn't about to follow him around with an autograph book clutched in one sweaty hand and my tongue hanging out, and he'd probably keep a healthy distance from me, too, now he knew I was armed and dangerous, if only to fruit.

But the most interesting thing about our encounter was that I'd noticed him just as I'd lifted the pan above my head ready for the swing, and I still hadn't managed to stop it or even divert it. If I could try that again with the heights properly measured . . .

It would be a bonus if the sound was right, too. If I could hear it once more outside my head instead of in. It was all pretty cathartic, but I felt that if I could find one that made the right sound, I'd be exorcised to the point where I could at least paint again, especially if I could convince myself without doubt that it really had been an accident.

I'd never be able to forget I'd killed someone, but at least I'd know I hadn't intended to do it.

I tried melon number three, a smallish watermelon, but it still didn't make quite the right hollow, meaty noise. Then I took the battered fruit upstairs to the Parsonage kitchen and put them on the table.

'Canst tha not bash something more useful than a melon?' demanded Gloria Mundi. 'A turnip, maybe? There's none here will eat melon.'

Em, who was removing perfect loaves from the oven, said over her shoulder: 'I've got a recipe for melon and ginger jam. I'll make it later. We all like ginger – and you're forgetting, Gloria, that Bran likes melon.'

'Yon Branwell's one on his own.'

'Rob's set off to fetch Branwell from the university. I told him to make sure Mr Froggy doesn't get left behind this time.'

'How is he?'

She shrugged. 'Talking a bit fast. Then yesterday he told one of his students that a spirit ordered him to speak in only ancient Amharic from now on.'

'Not too bad then – he'll be right as rain after a little rest at home.'

Jessica stuck a cautious head through the doorway. 'I'm just off to school with the girls and . . .' She stopped, and looked from the battered melons on the table to me. 'You know, when I looked out of my bedroom window just now, I could have sworn I saw you hitting one of those with a pan.' She laughed uncertainly.

We stared at her. Gloria gave an audible sniff and went out past her with her mop and bucket.

'Well,' said Jessica into the silence, 'I'd better be off and – oh, that's what I came to say: Ran says he'd *love* to try a pasta dish tonight – perhaps with a big salad, and some garlic bread and—'

'He'll get what he's given,' Em said shortly.

'If you don't know how to cook it, I've got a recipe book you could borrow.'

'Hark at Lady Muck!' said Gloria, briskly and sloppily swabbing down the flagged passage round Jessica's feet so that she jumped back. 'She'll be giving out the household orders next!'

'Mummy!' shrilled the girls. 'We'll be late!'

With another uncertain look Jessica went, skidding on the damp floor with a certain coltish grace. I bet she can ice-skate.

'I wonder if we could put something in her food?' mused Em.

'Not unless you can coat a lettuce leaf in it – she doesn't seem to eat anything else.'

'Well, I'll have to take some action – our Ms Tickington-Tingay's getting on my wick.'

'Is that her real name? Jessica Tickington-Tingay?'

'Oh, aye,' said Gloria. 'Double-barrelled names are breeding up here.'

'Look at the time!' Em exclaimed. 'You should be on your way to the nursery. You're supposed to be there well before the children, to set things up, aren't you?'

I shifted uncomfortably. 'Em, I don't really think I can do this. I mean, they can't know about the Greg thing, and I've had no experience with children.'

'Forget about the accident with Greg, and as to the experience with children, you'll pick that up as you go. You need the money they'll pay, until you start painting again.'

I glared at her a bit resentfully. She's never had to go out and earn her living, although she does run the house like clockwork, cooks wonderfully, and makes what money she needs writing her verses . . . and now the book.

OK, that's all working, I admit.

She also does a little magic and fortune-telling, too, when asked, but she doesn't take money for that, just trade goods.

'Off you go; Inga's expecting you,' she said firmly.

'That Inga's a miserable bugger,' said Gloria, now giving the kitchen floor a sort of third-degree water torture. Frost, sighing deeply, got up from his rug and jumped onto the safety of the settle, where he sat looking resigned.

'She's Scandinavian,' said Em excusingly. 'They all sound like that, even when they're telling jokes. It's to do with having only two hours of daylight a year, or something.'

'Couldn't you come with me, Em?' I whined cravenly.

She sighed. 'I suppose I could walk down there with you. We'll take the dogs, and I'll bring Flossie back for you.'

'Flossie's still asleep. She doesn't usually get up until lunchtime.'

'She's not a dog, she's a cushion on legs. Go and get her, it will do her good.'

Flossie was disgusted, but consented to accompany us down the long, winding road to Hoo House, though whether she would walk back up it again was a moot point. Perhaps Frost would pick her up in his long jaws and carry her home like a puppy?

We were the only walkers; a series of immaculate four-wheel-drive vehicles passed us, all converging on the nursery, each giant petrol-eater containing one adult and one mutinous infant.

Em strode through the decanted parents and offspring, grunting at anyone who dared to wish her a good morning, and dragging my reluctant self and the dogs with her.

Our resident luvvie, exiting too hastily from the doorway, fell over the entwined dog leads, gave me a look of surprise and then, collecting himself, strode off with a nod and a grunt as brusque as anything Em could produce.

'Morning,' said Em affably. I stared at her in amazement.

A small, bun-faced woman in riding breeches and Hunter wellies cantered out in hot pursuit, crying shrilly, 'Oh, Mr North! Hef you got a minute?'

'He's incognito,' I said to her helpfully.

He was certainly fit – he was halfway down the drive already. And he hadn't come in a car, though I wouldn't put a four-wheel-drive past him.

'Incognito? He's gorgeous!' muttered bun-face, drooling after the retreating actor (tall, broad-shouldered, expensively hacked hair – no jester's hat today).

'You can't call someone wearing a bright red duvet gorgeous,' I objected.

'It's vintage Kenzo,' she said absently.

'Is that sort of like judo kit?'

'Judo? No,' she said, getting a grip on herself and really looking at us for the first time. 'Ah, Emily, is this your sister?' she said graciously. 'Inga said she was going to be the new helper.'

'Charlie,' Em said shortly, 'this is Elfreda Whippington-Smythe. Bought that half-ruined farmhouse up by the Donkers. Husband looks like Monet on a bad day. One sprog.'

'Er . . . yes, Satchel,' agreed Mrs Whippington-Smythe nervously, but then, Em often has that effect.

'Satchmo? Good name!'

I'd have expected something more stolid, like John or Charles, or even Ethelred or Wolfbane.

'No, not Satchmo,' she corrected me. '*Satchel* – like Woody Allen's son.'

'I thought Woody Allen's aura was a bit tarnished round the edges these days?'

'Oh, no – he's such a genius! You simply can't believe all those fairy tales Mia was putting about; she's the jealous, unbalanced one.'

Genius? Enough people seemed to think so, although I'd never been a fan. Maybe I just didn't have an ear for that sort of thing, like understanding classical music, or opera.

'Satchel . . .' I mused. 'It's pretty odd as a name when you think about it, isn't it? I mean, I wonder what made him think of *Satchel*? Why not Handbag? Or Portmanteau, if he wanted to be posh: "Come on, our Portmanteau." Or even Bumbag.'

There were limitless possibilities to luggage names.

'Tea Bag?' suggested Emily, interested.

Then I noticed Elfreda's fixed stare of offended incomprehension and got the giggles, which offended her even more.

'What's the matter with *her*?' asked Em, as the small figure strode away in her green wellies like an outraged plum duff.

'I expect the thought of Tea Bag Whippington-Smythe was too much for her.'

It had made *me* feel better, though.

It was a bright, cold day, the kind I like best, the children were all milling about in a non-threatening sort of way, and anyway they were all even smaller than I was. So when Em said a brief, 'See you,' and loped off, I didn't feel too bereft.

Flossie gave me a look of entreaty as she was towed along behind. Bet Em ended up carrying her.

Resolutely I passed through the portals to the sound of small voices raggedly singing.

Chapter 9: Nature in the Raw

How good it was to see Bran again, even if at that moment he was more one *with* us rather than *of* us. Were any of us able to speak in Amharic, I was sure we could have had many interesting conversations, but I expected he would descend to our level soon, even if only through the translation skills of Mr Froggy.

He had brought his manuscript and reference books, which took up most of the car, and refused to come down to breakfast until he had rebuilt them into a wall of Frantic Semantics across the floor of his bedroom, in exactly the same order as they were in his college room.

Tips for Southern Visitors, No. 2: Lancashire

Contrary to popular belief, a Coronation Street-style conurbation does not cover the entire county.

After breakfast I went down to the nursery alone, trying to convince myself that it hadn't been *too* awful the previous day. I could survive it.

Resolution – that's what I needed – and money. I'd put

melons on Em's shopping list again, although they were dear just then, but I was sure I'd hit on the right one soon – literally.

Walter was kindly making me a pole on a stand, exactly five feet ten inches high, to impale them on. If I could just get the sound right, as well as the relative heights . . .

'Good morning, Inga! Isn't it a lovely day?' I said, coming into the light, sunny classroom.

Inga was kneeling, trying to coax a pencil from between the floorboards with the pin of her edelweiss brooch.

The sun seemed to have leached the colour out of her so that her sad, beige hair dripped down her shoulders like a frozen waterfall, and her pale eyes reflected dully back like a dead fish.

'Ja,' she agreed mournfully, with a voice that held the long, dark despair of centuries of Scandinavian winters. 'It is a beautiful day. The sun is shining, but you can nevew be suwe. Later it may wain, and the stowms come, and the big, black clouds, heavy, heavy! And the lightning and the big wolls of thunder – and then I must get into the cup-bowd.'

'In the cupboard?'

'Ja. Always, since I am a little giwl, I must go in the cup-bowd.'

'Any particular cupboard, Inga? Just so I know where to find you if necessary.'

'Is the cup-bowd under the stairs – dawk and safe. When the lightning stwikes and the house falls down, the staiwes will stop the big stones fwom falling on my head.'

'Right. And Gunilla? Does she go in the cupboard, too?'

It was only my second day, and already I was wishing that Gunilla would go in the cup-bowd on a permanent basis.

81

'No-o,' sighed Inga heavily. 'She will not go in, though I plead with hew and say it is the only safe place. But she is excited when the thunder sounds and the lightning cwackles, so she likes to wun about, scweaming.'

'Sounds like fun.'

'Ja. It is her natuwal way of expwession. And when the wain is heavy she must take off hew clothes and wun outside.'

'Must?'

'Must.'

Since Gunilla was supposed to be modelling her behaviour on that of the adults – The Group – around her, it posed the question: which members of the community ran about in the rain, naked? And surely not in the winter?

'Is that a good idea, Inga?'

'Ja. If you twy to stop hew she bites. Sometimes she does not put hew clothes on again for the west of the day, because she must be as one with Natuw. In the summew,' she added heavily, 'we awe all at one with Natuw, but only when school is finished. Some of the pawents, they do not feel the need to be at one with natuw.'

'No, I can imagine.'

Mrs Whippington-Smythe, for instance, is only at one with large, hairy, four-legged creatures that neigh.

'The childwen come now,' Inga murmured unnecessarily, as a tide of shrieking banshees raced towards us.

'Stop!' bellowed a male voice from the hall. 'Sing!'

Sudden silence was followed by the ragged, reluctant voices of fifteen children droning something unintelligible.

'What *is* that song?'

'It is the Wainbow song – to inspwire them for the wowk.'

'Funny, it sounds a bit like Japanese.'

'Ja, that is so. They awe singing: "Build the wainbow, bwidge the world with coluw, and walk acwoss into the clouds of happiness. Go fwom flowuw to flowuw, and sip the knowledge of life thwough Natuw."'

The roar began again and the door bounced back on its hinges with a crash.

'Here they come for a taste of that, then, Inga.'

Gunilla, predictably, was first in. Snot streamed from her nostrils like twin green pennants as she made for the easel and paints. Or rather, paint: only pots of liquid black were supplied, and big bamboo brushes.

'Aren't they supposed to start at one side of the room and then move around in a big arc, from task to task?' I said, baffled by the milling tots. Yesterday I'd observed rather than joined in, but hadn't managed to make a lot of sense of it.

'Ja – see, Susie has them beginning with the thwee discs of logic now.'

Indeed, some of the children were slapping multicoloured discs onto a pole, with the fierce concentration of those desiring to progress quickly to something more interesting.

'But Gunilla is—'

'Gunilla is mowe at one with Natuw than the othews; she is beyond this stage and must be allowed her fwee expwession. Besides, she is being bwought up puwely thwough Natuw.'

'I think she has a cold.'

'Ja, it is because she wuns awound naked in the wain in winter, as in Natuw,' agreed Inga.

Nature in the raw. 'Right. Er . . . what do you want me to do?'

'I think today you can help them to build the Wainbow

83

of Happiness. That they always find hawd – always it falls down befowe the Key of Enlightenment is insewted into the Hole of Stability.'

'My whole life's been like that,' I said, and she nodded a sad agreement.

That morning was the first time that I felt almost glad that I hadn't got any children, although one or two were quite appealing in an untrammelled sort of way.

En masse, of course, they were all monsters; but none more so than poor, natural Gunilla (or Godzilla, as I kept accidentally saying).

Gunilla was everywhere, pinching the other children, screaming with rage if she couldn't get her own way, and shoving in anywhere she wanted.

'I want to put the Stone of Enlightenment in!' she declared, using her elbows to break into my group, who were laboriously constructing the rainbow, eyes crossing with concentration.

I smiled at her: 'Sorry, Godz— I mean Gunilla, this is Josie's turn. But then you can help to build the rainbow back up and put the stone in.'

Gunilla stared at me incredulously. 'I'm putting the sodding stone in *this* time!' she declared, stamping her foot.

'No, Gunilla,' I said patiently. 'It's Josie's turn this time, but you can do it next – we will build a very special rainbow just for you.'

'Do it fucking *now*!' she screamed, trying to shove the large, stolid Josie aside.

'No, Gunilla. Why don't you go and find a hankie and blow your nose, and then it will be time to build your rainbow?'

Josie inserted the central stone of the arch while Gunilla stared at me with a sort of malevolent incredulity.

Goblins were alive and well, and living in Upvale.

Then, turning, she bit Josie, who overbalanced, screaming, onto the rainbow arch, which collapsed.

Gunilla threw herself to the floor and went into a paroxysm of rage, and Inga hurried over to snatch her infant to her bosom, which instantly became smeared with viscous green.

She rocked, crooning in lightly fractured English, 'What is the matter with my baby? Tell Mama, and she will make it all wight again.'

Gunilla darted a glance at me, as I tried to comfort poor Josie, who now sported a crooked circle of bite marks on one hand.

'Horrible cow wouldn't let me put the stone in the rainbow!' Gunilla whimpered.

I looked up. 'No, because it was Josie's turn – she'd built the rainbow. Gunilla could have had her turn next.' I turned back to Josie worriedly. 'Inga, Gunilla's teeth have pierced the skin – I think I'd better put some antiseptic on the bite, if you'll tell me where the first-aid stuff is.'

Inga rose to her feet, cradling her four-year-old to her chest like a baby. 'Nevew, nevew must you cwoss Gunilla! How could you? She is lewning thwough fweedom to be one with Natuw.'

'But surely during the Rainbow Nursery sessions she must fit in to some extent with what we are doing with the other children? With the Rainbow ethos? Is it fair to teach them a rigid structure, and then let Gunilla come in and disrupt everything by doing just what she wants?'

'I want my mummy!' sobbed poor little Josie. 'I want to go home.'

'I want the nasty lady to go away!' screeched Gunilla.

'Mama will build the wainbow for you, and you can put the stone in now,' soothed Inga, pushing her jumper up to reveal a breast like an elephant's ear. She proceeded to breast-feed her hysterical child, ignoring both the wounded infant and the small circle of watchers, one with a thumb in her mouth and a couple noticeably damp round the edges.

'Big baby!' Caitlin commented critically, standing stolidly on the sidelines, watching play, with her hands thrust into her dungaree pockets, rather like a miniature Em.

'Quite right,' I agreed, picking Josie up and going to look for the antiseptic.

Gunilla's little yellow teeth gave promise of tetanus, if not rabies, and I only hoped the little girl's inoculations were up to date.

When I returned her to the class later (much happier, due to the fortunate discovery of a rather strange tin of biscuits and a story book, which I'd read to her three times) Gunilla ran up and kicked me hard on the shin.

With a gasp of pain I picked her up so that she was nose to nose with me and said furiously, 'Don't ever, *ever*, do that to me again!'

Her eyes were two startled discs – Discs of Enlightenment, I hoped. 'Mama!' she screamed.

But Mama had already flown to the rescue like a virago. Not to *my* rescue, though: frothing at the lips she seized Godzilla and pointed at the door.

'Go!'

'Go?' I bent down, hitched up my skirts and peered at a

promising bruise. It was unfortunate that my assailant had been wearing clogs with wooden soles when she'd committed her onslaught. 'Yes, you're right. I'd better put some antiseptic on this, too. I'll be in the kitchen when Gunilla is ready to apologise, Inga.'

Susie popped her head into the kitchen a few minutes later and winked. 'Good for you! But they won't let you come again, you know, if Gunilla's taken against you. Keith will be in soon to tell you, in a deeply understanding voice, that it's all your fault. Make sure they pay you for the two days before you go.'

'Right. Thanks, Susie,' I said.

Keith, a tall, skinny man with a head like a light bulb, duly informed me in hushed tones of reproach that Gunilla's behaviour that morning was entirely due to my own aura of hidden aggression, which the poor sensitive creature had sensed, and therefore he unfortunately did not feel that I should work with the children any more.

'I'm not aggres—' I began indignantly, and then stopped. Maybe I was? Maybe I was wearing a permanent aura of Frying Pan Murderess? But aggressive . . . I didn't think so. And certainly not towards children, even poor little Gunilla. Firmness isn't aggression, and the other children seemed to like me.

'I don't agree with you,' I said politely. 'I think Gunilla is simply confused by being allowed total freedom, while attending a nursery with a very rigid structure that the other children have to stick to. It isn't fair to her or the others.'

'The lesson that life isn't fair will benefit them all,' Keith said deeply.

Little twerp.

'It's a pity Gunilla hasn't learned that one yet, isn't it? Still, if you'd like to pay me for the two mornings I've worked, I'll be off.'

He looked taken aback. 'But surely after what's happened you don't expect—'

'The labourer is worthy of her hire. And look on the bright side: I won't claim any money from you for this top, which Gunilla ruined by wiping her paint-covered hands up the back. It's got poor little Josie's blood over the sleeves, now, too.'

He stared at me, chewing his moustache, then grudgingly dipped into his pocket and counted out my measly wages in small change. 'There. Now, perhaps you could go to Gunilla before you leave and make peace with her? Her sensitive nature has been troubled by your aggression, and—'

'No,' I interrupted firmly, 'but if Gunilla would like to come to me and apologise before I go, you could fetch her now.'

'Apologise? Gunilla?'

Seeing we had reached an impasse in understanding I left the house, jingling my money and limping, and Inga and Gunilla glowered at me silently from the schoolroom door.

For a moment as I turned away I felt like a horrible, evil, child-eating witch, but really, I didn't want to hurt anyone, and would never have struck Gunilla however hard she kicked me.

But Natuw had a lot to answer for.

Then a small figure in an unzipped teddy-bear suit wriggled out between Inga and the door frame, ran up and hugged my legs fiercely – and painfully. Caitlin stared up into my face with her usual pugnacious expression and then ran off ahead of me to where the parents were gathering.

The actor swung Caitlin up into his arms as I walked past down the drive, and he did it with such infinite grace that I half-expected someone to roll out of the bushes on one of those trolley things with a camera shouting: 'Take two, scene one!' or something of that kind.

But nothing happened except for my very nearly being flattened by Mrs Whippington-Smythe's big red off-roader hurtling up the path.

Skint Old Cook, No. 2

Savoury Ducks aren't.

Chapter 10: Small Change

When I looked at the paltry coins Keith paid me, three were French and one German, which were of no earthly use to anyone, but perhaps my feng shui money frog would like them. I could sort of heap them round him like a dragon's hoard.

One by one the little gremlins passed me, homeward bound in their monster carriers. The only ones walking up the hill were the actor and Caitlin, and they didn't catch me up until I was nearly home.

I heard the thump of small feet behind me, and then Caitlin was embracing my legs again. I nearly fell over. When she held her arms out to be picked up I did, and hugged her, though I didn't know what I'd done to deserve it. Still, it did make me feel a bit less of a witch, and also suffer a sharp pang of regret for my lost chances of motherhood. A sort of strange, low pain inside.

Maybe my heart was in the wrong place.

'Are you crying?' asked Caitlin anxiously.

I smiled. 'No, it's the cold making my eyes water.'

She peered into them alternately from two inches away. 'They're a very funny colour.'

'Em says they're the colour of black grapes.'

'Trodden-on black grapes,' amended Caitlin. 'The insides are sort of purply.'

'Caitlin seems to like you,' her father said, catching us up.

She looked at him severely. 'She's OK, Daddy. Gunilla bit Josie, and then she kicked Charlie, and Charlie sorted her out. She calls her Godzilla, and I'm going to call her Godzilla too, because she's a monster.'

'She's just a confused little girl,' I said to the actor, who was raising one eyebrow.

(How did he do that? I could never do it, even though I'd spent hours in front of a mirror trying. It was both, or nothing. I could twitch the end of my nose without moving my lips at the same time, though, and I bet he couldn't.)

Mace had to be older than me, but he'd worn in a sophisticated, lounge-lizard sort of way. Nature, as well as artily silvering the odd strand of hair, had given him interesting lines around his dark eyes to map out what he'd been up to for the last forty-odd years. He also looked fit (as far as you could tell from someone wearing a duvet) without giving the impression his personal fitness trainer flew in by helicopter every day to put him through his paces.

Caitlin slid down again and took his hand.

'So we meet again,' he said, with more resignation than enthusiasm. 'Em says you're her sister?'

I didn't blame him for sounding surprised. (And just when did Em get on chatting terms with him?)

'Yes – Charlie Rhymer. I'm living in the Summer Cottage because my husband's divorcing me and Father's mistress has taken over my bedroom.'

'Now why doesn't that surprise me?' he mused.

'Which bit?'

'The divorce.'

'Like you and Mummy,' commented Caitlin, swinging on her father's arm like it was an exercise bar.

'Mummy's marrying Rod,' she told me. 'He's very nice but *thick*, and he can't be my daddy, because I've already got one. He says I can just call him Rod.'

'That's nice,' I said weakly.

A faint spasm of something that might have been either pain or annoyance passed across the actor's face, and he abruptly changed the subject.

'I still think that lean-to is an excrescence on the beautiful face of Upvale,' he said, his lovely posh and mellow voice at odds with his exotic face.

'Like that duvet you're wearing,' I said shortly.

'It's Kenzo.'

'So I've heard from Elfreda Whippington-Smythe.'

'Which one's she?'

'Small, bun-faced, always wears jodhpurs, talks from up her nose.'

He shuddered. 'Oh God, that one. She rides past every day, and lingers. And if I go for a walk, she always just happens to be crossing my path.'

'I expect she keeps her binoculars trained on you from the other side of the vale. You should wear something more inconspicuous. My sister Anne's an expert in camouflage, and she's coming home soon – you could ask her.'

He looked down critically at himself. 'Perhaps you're right – this does look worryingly at one with your lean-to. Garish.'

'Veranda. But don't worry, I expect good taste is optional for the acting profession.'

'Speaking of good taste, that's the biggest garden gnome *I've* ever seen,' he said blandly, pointing behind me.

I turned. Walter was standing just inside the veranda, wearing a red woolly hat and his usual voluminous corduroy trousers. He was beaming and pointing at where his eyebrows would have been had he got any. I blew him a kiss.

'Walter made the veranda as a welcome-home present,' I said, 'and I think it's perfect!'

Mace North and I stared at each other, then a most disconcerting smile appeared on his even more disconcertingly beautiful pinky-brown lips.

Wow.

I could probably have prevented my own plebeian mouth smiling back had I coated my face in concrete.

Caitlin, tired of jumping up and down waving at Walter, tugged his arm. 'Come on, Daddy – I'm hungry.'

She turned to wave as they carried on up the path, but Mace didn't.

Walter's presence in the Summer Cottage was easily explained: an electrician was just putting the finishing touches to the socket and lighting he'd installed, probably illegally, in the veranda. Walter doesn't trust any tradesmen not to make off with the family stainless steel.

'Anne's come,' he informed me over his shoulder before escorting the electrician up the stairs to the Parsonage.

I changed and tidied up. There was no sign of Flossie, so she was probably up with Frost in the kitchen.

Anne was striding up and down the kitchen in her usual fashion, in khaki cotton trousers and a camouflage waistcoat that would have blended the actor into the woods quite nicely.

'They entered from the left and circled—' She broke off briefly to thump me on the shoulder and say: 'Hi, Chaz. —circled the enemy before attacking.'

'Where have you been? Which battle is this?' I demanded.

'Hospital,' Em informed me. 'Anne's fighting the Big C.' She carried on shearing chickens into pieces and tossing them into a big pot.

I recognised nourishing chicken soup in the making, and looked at Anne more closely. She did look fine-drawn and tired.

'You don't mean . . .?'

'Cancer,' Anne said. 'Lump – left breast. I was just telling Em – they circled the little bugger, and whipped it out before it could invade.'

'Oh, Anne! Why didn't you tell us? We could have been with you.'

'Enough on your plates already. Fight my own battles,' she said.

'Did Red go with you?'

'Spineless git. Couldn't face any of it – cleared off.'

'Is – is that it, now? Do they think the cancer's gone?' I asked, worriedly.

'So they say. Took a lymph node, too, and it wasn't in that. Got more puckers than Bride of Frankenstein. Just as well I've got no boobs to speak of anyway.'

I sat down at the table next to Em, feeling limp.

Em tossed the last chicken piece into the pot with the vegetables. 'They took the gland from under her arm to check if it had spread, but there was no sign of it,' she interpreted. 'So she's clear.'

'Left arm's a bit sore,' Anne admitted. 'Got to go over to

the hospital every day for six weeks for treatment – back-up stuff. Then back to work.'

'Have you told them?'

'Told them it was a small op on my dodgy knee – rest up, back right after Christmas.'

'What about Red?'

'Break *his* knees if he says any different.'

'Why don't you go and lie down for a bit?' suggested Em daringly.

'Fall back, regroup, and fight another day,' she agreed, to my astonishment. 'You'd better not have put that tart Jessica with the see-through blouse in my room: where does she think she is, the bloody Cannes Film Festival?'

'No, she's in Charlie's room.'

'Bad luck, Chaz.'

'Never mind – I quite like it in the Summer Cottage,' I said. 'Did Em tell you Bran's home too?'

'Seen him – didn't know he spoke Croatian.'

'I've put your stuff upstairs, our Anne,' Walter said, hobbling in. 'Outside the door.'

'Good man. See you've got no eyebrows yet.'

'No bodily hair whatsoever,' he agreed, beaming.

Tips for Southern Visitors, No. 3: Fashion

1) *It is socially acceptable now, and always has been, to wear white stilettos with jeans.*
2) *If going out for the evening in a big city, remember, even in winter, that* one *layer of clothing is enough. Coats and tights are for wimps.*
3) *If you are wearing a bra you do not need a handbag.*

'Well,' said Father sarcastically, gazing at the complete family circle around the breakfast table next morning. 'All my little chickens come home to roost?'

'Cluck,' said Anne, who was eating French toast lovingly prepared by Em, who was inclined to hover over her – but then, we'd never seen Anne looking ill before. She moved stiffly, and there were dark circles under her eyes.

Bran stared across at her and smiled. 'There's no reason why we can't *all* use the click language,' he said in perfectly intelligible English, before resuming the creation of a strange triple-decker sandwich that involved a lot of marmalade and bacon, watched with fascination by the two little girls.

Frost came in with a mouthful of letters and spat them onto the carpet.

'Must all my post be covered in dog saliva?' demanded Father distastefully.

'Beats me why folks bother writing to you at all, you great lump of nowt,' Gloria said, coming in just then with more toast and the teapot.

'Thank you for that vote of appreciation,' he said. 'Do you think you could ask Walter if he'd take a look at my desk? One of the legs is a bit wonky.'

He and Jessica exchanged fleeting but meaningful glances.

'I'm not surprised,' Gloria commented cryptically, and patted me on the head like an infant in passing as she went out again.

Jessica was rather daringly eating a boiled egg, but I didn't think she would make it through the whole gargantuan repast; she'd already had one spoonful and a bite of dry toast.

'Well, it's nice to meet all Ran's family at last,' she said, 'even if Anne and Em do rather dwarf poor little me!'

'Bran and I aren't much taller than you,' I pointed out.

'No – you two certainly don't take after Ran, do you? In fact, it's hard to believe you are related!'

'Charlie looks exactly like her mother – Lally Tooke,' Ran said, looking up from his paper.

'And does Bran look like *his* mother?' asked Jessica, slightly waspishly.

'I don't know. I can't remember,' he replied calmly. 'It was all a long time ago. Aren't those girls going to be late for school?'

Jessica looked up at the clock, squawked, and dragged her protesting children away. I peeled the rest of her boiled egg and tossed it to Frost, who ate it in one gulp.

Not having to go to the nursery ever again made me feel inordinately happy – until I discovered the hate mail from Angie, dewed with dog drool, under the table.

. . . better start looking over your shoulder, Charlie, because I'm coming to Upvale. Soon everyone will know you're a murdering whore, leading men on and then turning on them . . .

Life was just a rollercoaster of pleasure lately.

Chapter 11: Parting

Health Check, No. 1

There are few minor ailments that cannot be alleviated by the application of two large gin and tonics.

'Get your coat,' Em said, appearing on the stairs after dinner.

'Why, where are we going?'

'Freya's house – it's her turn.'

'What for?' I asked, obediently pulling on my coat and hurrying after her. Flossie's snores reverberated up the stairs behind me.

'The discussion group. It was a reading group, but now we just meet and discuss – stuff. And anyway, Freya's husband's coming back tonight to collect his things, and he has a violent temper.'

'I didn't know she had a husband.'

'Had's the operative word. She's thrown him out and got an injunction against him, but a fat lot of use that is. Still, she's being fair – she's letting him come round tonight to remove his half of their belongings.'

'But I thought she had magic powers. Can't she just do something nasty to him?'

'You've never seen so many boils on one man's neck,' Em said. 'But that was Xanthe Skye – Freya's powers lie in other directions.'

I didn't ask what. Already it sounded like a fun evening.

'Who else will be there? I'm not feeling very sociable.'

'Madge comes, and she isn't terribly sociable either – and Susie from the nursery, and Xanthe Skye and Lilith, of course. Madge's old father is driving her mad – and ours is driving *me* mad. And *you* can have a good moan about Matt. We could get Freya to do something nasty to Matt, if you still have any of his belongings.'

'I think I already did, killing his best friend, and I've cleared out everything to do with him.'

'Purged,' she agreed.

'In every way.'

We trudged up the hill in icy darkness, lit at irregular intervals by the small yellow circles grudgingly cast by three old streetlamps. The Black Dog looked terribly warm and inviting; Father and Jess were probably in there already. The last bus up from town stopped just ahead of us and decanted Inga and Godzilla before chugging slowly onwards.

Inga gave me a sad, pitying smile as she passed us, but Godzilla lingered, pulling faces at me and capering, until she looked at Em instead, and suddenly ran off crying: 'Mama! Wait!'

Freya lived at the end of a terrace of old stone weavers' cottages right at the top of Upvale. The bus passed us again on its way down, a brightly lit and empty *Marie Celeste*.

The tiny sitting room, already full, became crammed to bursting point with our arrival.

Freya pushed past us, gasping: 'Ice, ice – I must have ice!' in a parched voice, but she came back fairly soon with coffee, gin, and crackers smeared with something that probably only *looked* like road-kill hedgehog.

All the time we were drinking and chatting heavy footsteps thumped about overhead, with muffled cursing. From time to time something bumped down the stairs and was dragged out.

Then the footsteps and creakings from above were replaced by the sound of frenzied sawing, and flakes of plaster drifted down into my cup.

'What's he doing?' enquired Madge.

'Sawing the wardrobe in two,' replied Freya calmly.

'Isn't that taking the "his half" business a little too seriously?' I said.

'He's taking it to the letter, but I don't know what he thinks he's going to do with half a wardrobe. I'll use mine for firewood. Mind you, if he'd asked I'd have given him the whole thing. I don't want it. I was never big on white melamine.'

'I know what you mean,' I agreed. 'My ex-husband liked angular modern furniture, all cream and white, with no colour or pattern.'

'No wonder your aura is still faintly blue,' Xanthe said, edging a little further away.

'Sorry. Is there some way I can clean it off? Sort of Magic Flash?'

'Are you joking?' Xanthe asked, looking at me severely.

'No, she's serious,' Em explained. 'She just doesn't know

100

much about that sort of thing. I'm the only one who ever listened to Gloria Mundi.'

'You have a natural talent for the Ancient Arts,' agreed Lilith. 'Far beyond Gloria, who is a mere wisewoman.'

'Oh, nothing's beyond Gloria,' I assured her. 'Em's just gone in a different direction.'

There was more frenzied sawing from upstairs.

'The dressing table?' suggested Lilith, and Freya nodded.

'Yes – he's taken it very hard; but then, so did I when he tried to slap me around.'

'Your having already found a much younger lover seems to rankle particularly,' said Xanthe.

'Have you?' I said with respect. 'Who is it?'

'He's new – a teacher from the valley – but I'm teaching *him* one or two things. He lives on that new Mango Homes estate – Raspberry Road, just off Strawberry Street. You've just bought a house there too, haven't you, Susie?'

'Yes, but mine's Galia Gardens, up Honeydew Hill.'

'Fruity,' I commented.

'Well, I drew the line at Passionfruit Place, but otherwise I don't mind,' Susie said. 'They renamed my old road Mandela Street, and every time someone forgot to put the town on my mail it went on a round-Britain tour. There's a Mandela something in every town in the country.'

The halved furniture descended the stairs in a series of crashes, and a few minutes of dragging and swearing later the van drove away.

'I'll just pop out and perform a protection spell for you,' Lilith said. 'In case he tries to come back.'

'And I'll go round with the Bowls of Cleansing,' offered Xanthe. 'Mix us a large G&T, dear, for afterwards.'

Rituals accomplished, things got quite merry, and after some urging from Em I told them all about *Skint Old Northern Woman* magazine.

Everyone came up with suggestions for more articles, some so rude I'd probably be prosecuted if they came to anything.

'You should publish it,' suggested Madge. 'Everyone would love it. It would go down a treat at the WI.'

'Publish it? I couldn't possibly do that – it would take a fortune to start up a magazine.'

'Yes, but you could try it as a one-off issue, and see how it went.'

'It would be great!' Susie said. 'My sister Jen works for a small publishing company. I'll ask her how much it would cost.'

I shook my head regretfully: 'I can't afford anything at all.'

'It should be published!' Em said, as if she'd just received Divine Revelation. 'Anne thought so too, when I told her about it. Perhaps we could pay for the first print run?'

I shook my head. 'No, you'd just lose your money – but it's fun writing the articles. Anyone got any more ideas?'

'How about an 'Are You a Victim' quiz?' suggested Freya.

Are You a Natural Victim? Try our quiz and find out!

Your partner slaps you around, and then goes out. Would you:
A) *Put up with it, because it was your fault after all, and he won't ever do it again, will he?*
B) *Balance a large heavy item on top of the half-open kitchen door and await events*
C) *Leave (May be combined with answer B)*

*D) Fell the bastard with a large heavy object as he turns
to go, thus giving you plenty of time to pack.*

On the way home Em and I stopped in at the Black Dog, where we found the new vicar playing darts with Walter, Bran and Father, with Jessica sitting in the corner looking bored over a Martini.

Bran, surprisingly, can throw a mean dart. You just have to remember not to stand between him and the board when he's got the darts in his hand, because he throws them fast.

I was introduced to the vicar, whose name was, entirely suitably, Christian, although he likes to be called Chris. He was a different species from our last one, being very tall, rangy, fortyish, and with a long, iron-grey ponytail and drooping moustaches, like a handsome but slightly melancholy Wyatt Earp. He wore small gold rings in his ears with dangling crosses, and a T-shirt with a dog collar and waistcoat printed on it.

The moment he set eyes on Em he dropped his darts and assumed the unmistakably sheepish expression of the seriously smitten male, but I don't think she noticed.

She looked especially nice that evening, I thought. The red T-shirt under her dungarees had washed out to a flattering faded rose, and her light blue eyes with their blacker-than-black pupils looked like a very intelligent goat's.

Em joined in the game while I took my drink and sat with Jessica, who seemed pitifully grateful for any company, even mine.

'God, this is boring!' she confided. 'I thought Mace North might come in – he does sometimes when Madge babysits for him – but not tonight.'

'Madge was at Freya's house for the discussion group.'

She yawned. 'Then Mace won't be coming. The vicar's quite dishy, but he won't flirt – that's the trouble with vicars. I think I'll go home.'

'I'll walk back with you,' I said, draining my pint of bitter and blackcurrant. 'I'm pretty tired – it's been a long day.'

'I'm going home, Ran,' she called, and pouted when Father just smiled and waved a hand at her before taking careful aim with his next dart.

I thought lust's first bloom had rubbed off already. But it would be a bit worrying if Jessica left, because the next mistress would probably need the Summer Cottage, which was just starting to feel like home.

Chapter 12: Jumbled

'Chris – the vicar – gave me a message for you, Emily,' Jessica said a couple of days later. 'Did you ask him to find you a plumber, or something? God knows, the bathrooms are still in the last century, and none of the locks work. I walked in on Bran the other day while he was showering. He's a big boy,' she added thoughtfully, a faint smile crossing her face.

Oh, well, I don't suppose she really registered on him. If he's got a sex drive he hasn't found the on switch yet.

'What was the message?' Em demanded curtly.

'The message?' she echoed blankly. 'Oh, yes, the message – silly me! Chris said to tell you that Barkis is willing. Willing to do what?'

'Barkis is willing?' I repeated, staring at Em in astonishment, and she went a faint but becoming shade of pink.

'Chris is quite dishy,' Jessica said, 'for a vicar. He's invited me round tonight.'

'He can't have done,' Em said shortly. 'It's the jumble sale.'

'Yes, he invited me to that.'

'You don't invite people to a jumble sale, you just tell them about it,' I informed her. 'Are you going?'

'Oh, no – I get all the girls' stuff from Gap, and *I'm* so petite . . .'

'Skinny,' interpreted Em, but Jessica was impervious.

'. . . that I have to buy most of *my* clothes from children's departments too!'

So *that's* why the shops are so strangely full of sexy clothes for little girls – they're really meant for all the tiny stick-women like Jessica. I'm glad to have that explained to me.

'I wouldn't say it like it was an asset, being a bag of bones – "bag" being the operative word,' Em said disagreeably, but Jessica just laughed.

Her bones must be rubber, because she always bounced back. Or maybe she didn't take in everything Em said. She certainly seemed immune to her little whitish spells – I hoped Em didn't call in the Black Dogs of War in the shape of Freya, Lilith and Xanthe.

I was getting to sort of like her a bit, but trying not to, because of loyalty to Em.

'I'll go to the jumble sale,' I said. 'I'm tired of black, and nothing fitting. I might find a pair of jeans or something.'

'If you lost another stone, you'd probably fit into my clothes,' Jessica offered.

'If she lost another stone she'd be even more skeletal than you,' Em said. 'We're trying to build her back up again. Anyway, she doesn't wear tart clothes.'

'Thanks, though, Jessica,' I said hastily. 'Fashion's a funny thing, isn't it? Remember all those transparent dresses women wore with just knickers under? I mean, people went *out* wearing those and no one much said anything. It was just like the Emperor's new clothes.'

'Which emperor?' Jessica said, puzzled.

'In the fairy tale,' Em said. 'You're right, Charlie – no one dared to tell the Emperor he was totally nude and the family jewels were on public display, because he'd been brainwashed into thinking he was wearing a magic suit.'

'Except for a little boy, who didn't understand, and shouted out that the Emperor was in his birthday suit – and then the crowd all got the sniggers,' I finished.

Anne came in, looking exhausted. Even the multi-pockets on her battle fatigues were limp, although her light hair still stood out round her face like a dandelion clock.

'Clear off,' she said to Jessica, although not with her usual energy.

'You Rhymers!' Jessica said, laughing, but getting up all the same. 'I told Ran he'd made a bad job of bringing you up. All that isolation has warped your social skills.'

'Go to bed, Anne,' Em said tersely. 'Charlie will bring your tea up in five minutes.'

'It's no wonder you're tired, if you keep going out when you're supposed to be convalescing after an operation,' Jessica babbled. 'I suppose it was a hysterectomy or something, and that's why you're not telling us what it was?'

'Telling *you* what it was,' Anne said pointedly, and Jessica gave up probing and went off to pick up the girls from school.

'Was it OK?' I asked when I took Em's lovingly prepared tray upstairs to Anne. It was odd seeing her in bed during daylight hours, but she did look exhausted.

'Quite bearable. Only for a few weeks.'

'Your hair's not going to fall out, is it?'

'No, different sort of treatment.'

'Will you have to have anything else done?' I ventured, since this was talkative for Anne.

'No. This is a back-up – they got the bugger. Gave up before the battle began. Like Red – one mention, and he cleared off. No guts.'

Even cancer's got more sense than to tangle with Anne twice.

'Doctors wanted me to take some drug for ten years "just in case". Told them to stuff it up their jacksies.'

'Should you do that?'

'What, stuff it up their jacksies?' she sniggered.

It was all that hanging around with soldiers. Anne's language sometimes had to be heard to be believed. I was always afraid she was going to slip up when she was broadcasting live, but she hadn't yet.

There was a familiar wheezing noise as Flossie appeared in the doorway, wagging her tail in a mildly pleased way. Then she scrabbled up onto the bed next to Anne.

I stared at her in surprise. She didn't usually take a liking to people; I wasn't even sure she could distinguish *me* from everyone else half the time.

'Do you want me to take her away? She'll cover the bed with hair.'

'No, leave her,' Anne said, leaning back and closing her eyes. 'She's company.'

That's another thing Anne's never sought much before. I backed out, feeling a bit ruffled, but leaving the door slightly open for Flossie when she remembered food and attempted to find the kitchen.

Anne's hand was on Flossie's head, in a touchingly dying-Brontë way, but Flossie's tongue was just starting to explore the perimeter of the tea tray.

I put my head into Bran's room on the way down. He was

standing by the window, saying something calmly, but in an obscure-sounding tongue, to Mr Froggy.

'Tea, Bran? Hot cheese scones?'

His light brown eyes regarded me amiably. 'Buttered angel cake?'

'Yes,' I agreed. Em always has to make angel cake for Bran. He interpreted this for Mr Froggy, and then stuffed the toy unceremoniously into his pocket before picking his way through a drift of books and papers. Someone, either Em or Gloria, had put new leather patches on the elbows of his corduroy jacket.

I led the way down. 'There's a jumble sale tonight at the church hall, Bran. Do you want to come? Books?'

'Books,' he agreed.

Jumble Sale Etiquette

Step one: queue in an orderly fashion in front of the door, peering in to see where the best-looking tables are, if you get the opportunity.

Step two: as soon as the doors open, stampede in, jostling for position at your chosen table with your elbows. (As Mae West once so memorably put it: 'He who hesitates is last.')

Step three: grab anything that looks remotely interesting without stopping to examine it until you have an armful and can't grip any more. Then retire to a corner of the room and sort through them, returning to put the rejects back on the table and pay for your chosen items.

Stow paid-for items in a bag and repeat step three.

Em, Gloria and I formed a cordon around Branwell to prevent him wandering into the hall and rifling the books before the doors officially opened. Walter had somehow managed to insert himself at the head of the queue, and could be heard informing Madge that he had no eyebrows, and, probably, that he had no hair anywhere else either.

It was a good jumble sale, and well attended, since word had got out that Lady Hake-Hackett had been having a major clear out. Word had also got out that the vicar was including some of the obscure volumes left behind by the previous incumbent, but no one except Bran was showing much interest in those: I had to go back and get the car at the end and load them in.

The vicar helped. He seems drawn to Em like an unwary moth to the flame.

'Barkis is willing to what?' I asked her later while we examined our booty in the kitchen, Bran having retired to his room with his books.

Jessica and Ran had gone to the pub in our absence, leaving the girls in the nominal care of Anne, but they'd gone to bed when we got home. Anne said she'd told them a few stories first, which seemed unlikely, because the only stories I'd heard her tell usually ended something like: '. . . and bugger me if the next second he didn't tread on a landmine and get himself blown to smithereens!'

Em shrugged, pulling a voluminous mass of tawny crushed velvet out of her bag. 'Marry me, presumably,' she said off-handedly, holding the dress against her dungarees and squinting critically downwards. 'Do you think this will fit me? It looks big enough – must have been a Hake-Hackett. They're all built like barn doors, except Felicity. She's the runt of the litter.'

'I've never seen you in a dress!' I said, amazed. Come to think of it, I'd never seen her in anything other than dungarees over a T-shirt or jumper, and big boots.

'I need to make an impression, or I'll die a bloody virgin.'

'But Barkis is willing.'

'I can't seduce a vicar when I'm about to embrace the Dark Powers. You can't seduce vicars anyway. It isn't done. You have to marry them, which is impossible.'

'It's not impossible, and he's rather attractive.'

'I don't want to marry, I'm quite happy with my life the way it is, or I will be, once we've got rid of Jessica. No, I just want casual sex, preferably in a place of power, like the standing stones on the moor. Besides, I couldn't have any sort of relationship with a man who thinks Dickens is the greatest British novelist!'

'No, I suppose not. Er . . . you do *know* all about safe sex, don't you, Em?'

'Wasn't born yesterday,' she said indistinctly as she pulled the dress over her head. It fell in loose folds about her and would have been flattering had it not been for the layers of bulky fabric underneath, and the boots. 'I'll wear this next Friday, for Father's birthday feast.'

'It will have to be cleaned first.'

'It's clean already – still got the cleaner's tag pinned in the neck.'

'Is anyone else coming on Friday?' I asked. There had to be some reason for the dress.

'Mace North – Father's invited him. Jessie's delirious with pleasure.'

'Big deal.'

'He hasn't accepted any other invitations, though that

111

Whippington-Smythe woman's been shameless. Maybe he only *looks* nervous when I talk to him – you watch him on Friday and tell me if you think he fancies me.'

'I will, but you're flogging a dead horse on that one, Em. Even ugly middle-aged men can pull pretty young girls if they're rich or famous enough, so he's probably got a queue waiting to jump into his bed.'

'I'll put something in his drink. And he's not ugly.'

'I didn't say he was – it was just a generalisation. He's . . . interesting-looking, and he has a very attractive smile.'

'Hmm,' Em said, staring at me. 'Why's he smiling at you? You don't want him, do you?'

'No, I've gone off men permanently, except family, of course. And I don't mind the vicar, he's rather sweet. Otherwise, even casual sex seems pointless now I can't get pregnant any more.'

'What have you got in your jumble bags?' she asked, changing the subject, to my relief. I was not a rival for anyone's affections; I'd been through the sex/marriage/dwindling sex/divorce cycle already; I didn't want to repeat the whole damned thing with anyone else, even on a temporary basis.

'Jeans, and a lot of sea-green stuff. Dresses, T-shirts . . . a dark green suede jacket . . . matching desert boots, sandals . . .'

'Now that definitely *was* Felicity. She had a green phase last year; thought she was a bloody naiad, but it didn't suit her. Too yellow. That's a nice dress.'

'I think it's a nightie really,' I said doubtfully, holding up a wispy green chiffon number. 'But it has got an interestingly Peter Pan touch about it – frondy.'

'Well, call it a dress and wear it next Friday. When do we ever dress up?'

'Never?'

'We *shall* go to the ball,' Em said.

Chapter 13: Jam Tomorrow

I spent a couple of days washing, altering and mending my new wardrobe; Felicity was a little larger than me, even though I was starting to fill out a bit. I'd had to filch one of Bran's belts to keep my jeans up, but I didn't suppose he'd notice.

The two little girls (who, under Anne's practical influence, had started calling themselves Clo and Feeb) helped me to paint a jungle on the inside of the veranda's glass walls in poster paints. It would come off eventually, but gave me the right dense green atmosphere to work in until I got enough plants.

I was glad the paints were non-toxic, because Flossie tried licking the glass and smeared several leaves before she decided she didn't like the flavour.

Clo painted a sort of monkey in her bit, and Feeb did lots of butterflies and a lizardy thing like a salamander.

I did a snake. The serpent in the Garden of Eden.

Skint Old Gardening Tips, No. 2

Spider plants have no reason for existence – they are simply a sort of green chain letter.

1) *Place in a cardboard box and abandon them somewhere they will be found quickly: e.g., outside a charity shop just before opening time.*
2) *Include the macramé potholders.*
3) *Walk away: just feel that relief!*

One afternoon Em appeared at the Summer Cottage in her loomingly silent way, followed by Frost, who tried to poke his head into Flossie's igloo, and got short shrift.

Since a blast of dank, icy air had fingered its way in with them I deduced that they had come in through the veranda. They'd taken to using the place as a short cut up to the Parsonage after their walks, which was fine, except for the surprise; I wasn't big on surprises after the Dead Greg episode.

With my meagre wages from the nursery I'd purchased an economy-sized can of pale yellow one-coat emulsion and was obliterating the flowered wallpaper in my kitchen/diner/bedroom.

'I've got you another job,' Em said casually.

'What do you mean? What sort of job?'

'Caitlin's nanny. Mace took her away from the Rainbow Nursery because she didn't like it, and now he's finding it hard to concentrate on writing his play, so he needs someone to look after her in the mornings while he works.'

'But he doesn't like me!'

'I don't know why you think that – and anyway, Caitlin likes you; she said she wanted you. It'll be fine. You can bring her to the Parsonage, and take her for walks and things. You're starting at nine thirty tomorrow, and he's going to pay you London wages.'

'But, Em, he saw me bashing melons the other day – he can't want someone he thinks is loopy. And he can't know about Greg either! You must have forced him to offer me the job.'

'Of course I didn't force him. I just suggested it when I popped in with some melon and ginger jam,' she said, slightly self-consciously. 'He probably thinks you have to bash the melons as part of the process or something. He didn't mention it, anyway. And I don't think anyone round here other than the family know about Dead Greg. It only made your local paper, after all, thanks to that earthquake and the lurid sex-murder trial.'

'Jessica knows.'

'Yes, but I told her if word got out we'd know it was her, and we'd kill her and drop the body down the old well, so that's OK.'

The image of a tiny Jessica looking up from the bottom of a well sort of twitched my painting nerve.

'Did you take the vicar any jam?' I asked curiously.

'Not yet . . . but I might,' she said, smiling in an unusually Mona Lisa way. 'And one of my advance copies of *Womanly Wicca Words of Spiritual Comfort*.'

When Em and Frost had gone up the Parsonage stairs I assembled my melon-bashing equipment in the garden. (Ripe ones are *so* messy.)

First, the stand Walter made, Greg-height and spiked to hold the melon still. Then I positioned the fatal kitchen steps and climbed up holding the pan . . .

This time I checked there was no one on the track before I took the first swing.

The blow connected solidly, but the sound was too soggy.

The second landed fair and square too, and it almost sounded right . . .

I set the last one up, climbed back up on the steps, and lifted the pan high, as if it was hanging on the hook. Then I shifted to a two-handed tennis racquet grip to swing it down and—

'What are you doing?' enquired the vicar curiously, his head bobbing up right next to me.

The pan had begun its inexorable swing, missing Chris by a hair's breadth and connecting with that oh-so-familiar-from-my-nightmares meaty 'thunk!'

The melon bounced off its spike rather gruesomely and rolled away.

'That was the sound!' I said, amazed. 'That was it! And I *couldn't* stop the pan, even though I was afraid I was going to hit you.'

'No, I'm sure you couldn't, not from that height and holding it like that,' he agreed. 'Once it started to swing down, that would be it. Did you mean to hit the melon?'

He sounded interested rather than surprised, so after he'd helped me take everything into the cottage I made some coffee and prepared to Confess All, which I suppose vicars are quite used to.

'I expect people tell you this sort of thing all the time,' I finished.

'Not really,' he answered thoughtfully. 'Still, I hope you are now truly satisfied that you didn't mean to kill this Greg?'

'I am *now* . . . and even the noise was right. It felt – cathartic.'

'Good. Accept that what happened really wasn't your fault,

117

and although it will be hard to live with the memory of it, it was just an accident brought on by his own actions.'

'I only hope his wife, Angie, accepts that too. She was feeling very bitter and vindictive towards me after the inquest, and she's sent me poison-pen-type letters threatening to come here and tell everyone about me. I expect she's left a million nasty messages on my mobile too, only of course you can't get a signal within five miles of Upvale, so I've left it switched off since I came home.'

'Poor woman,' he said charitably. 'If she does, I'll speak to her and offer her comfort.'

She might have been interested, at that, but I didn't think they'd both define 'comfort' in the same way.

I sat back in the old wooden rocking chair and everything suddenly looked subtly different, as if it had all shifted in space slightly and become brighter. I felt reborn: a slightly dazed new phoenix Charlie arising from the ashes of her old nest.

'Do you know, Chris, I think I could paint again? I'm going to paint Jessica down the old well.'

'Oh? I understood from Em you only painted the jungle.'

'I do, but Jessica's going to be at the heart of the next one, far, far down a well, looking up.'

He looked thoughtful. 'I expect there's something deeply Freudian about that, but we won't pursue it. I'm glad you're feeling better.'

'Yes, and once I'm painting I won't need another job. Em's got me a temporary one, looking after Mace North's little girl in the mornings while he writes, but I expect the cottage is just a whim. A famous star won't want to hang about in Yorkshire for very long, will he?'

'I rather selfishly hope not,' he confessed, looking glum. 'She – Em – likes him, doesn't she?'

'She does find him interesting,' I admitted, 'but he's frightened of her. I expect that's how she got me the job.'

'Frightened of her? How can anyone be frightened of her?'

I looked at him with dawning respect. 'Yes, but she's a *witch*.'

'She certainly is,' he agreed enthusiastically. 'She's put a spell on me. Do you happen to know if Jessica gave her my message?'

'What, the Barkis one? Yes, and it's taken her by surprise.'

So long as she didn't take the actor by surprise . . . although I supposed he would be more suitable for Em's purposes than a vicar, even if I didn't particularly like him.

Poor Chris! He was obviously seeing her through the eyes of love – and he was really rather attractive. And I never had been keen on the idea of Em embracing the Black Arts – she was so *very* thorough.

But could an alliance between Wicca and Church work? I decided to speak to Gloria and see what she thought.

And I'd made up my mind that I was going to tell Mace about Dead Greg before he found out from someone else. If he didn't want me to take care of Caitlin after that, it was fine by me.

Tips for Southern Visitors, No. 4

In some parts of North-east England, a man would rather kill himself overtaking on a blind bend at seventy miles an hour than drive a hundred yards behind a woman.

When I went up to his cottage next morning there was a sleek, sporty red car pulled up outside, which hadn't been there before. The actor's car is some low, dark thing.

Caitlin opened the door, her fingers to her lips: 'Ssh! Come into the kitchen – Mummy's here, and she and Daddy are having a talk in the living room.'

Indeed, even as she drew me into the kitchen I heard a husky voice drawl: '. . . buried out here in the cultural desert!'

But there she was quite wrong, for there are lots of blue-blooded Russian émigrés in Huddersfield, all enjoying soirées, the dance, theatre, ballet. A stray Tartar would be quite at home.

'Perhaps I should go away and come back la—'

'*There* you are,' snapped Mace North from the doorway, as if I was hours late. 'Caitlin, go and put your things on and Charlie can take you for a nice walk.'

'It's brass-monkey cold out there,' I objected. 'I'll take her up to the Parsonage.'

'Wherever,' he said abstractedly.

'Is that the nanny you mentioned?' said the low, slightly husky voice, and Mace's ex-wife, the actress Kathleen Lovell, peered around him. She looked me up and down critically with huge brown eyes in a gauntly pretty face.

Up to that moment I'd felt quite good in my jumble-sale jeans and dark green suede jacket, but now I felt like the hired help. Come to that, I *was* the hired help.

'You're tiny, aren't you? And not so very young – I expect you're glad of the job. Would you like to come to America with us after the wedding?'

As job interviews go, it was a bit sketchy.

'No,' I said. 'I'm staying here.'

120

'And so is Caitlin,' said Mace with a steely note in his voice.

'Of course – for now,' she agreed. 'I'm just back from Morocco,' she said to me. 'I've been filming *The Return of the Sheik* – you must see it, it's too scary for words! The Sheik is a ghost, drawn back by my golden-haired, voluptuous beauty, but ours is a love that can never be.'

'No, I can imagine,' I agreed.

'That's the last *fat* part I'm going to play,' she added firmly. 'I'm going to lose a stone for the wedding, and then I'll be thin enough for roles in America – you have to be skinny to get *anywhere* over there. My fiancé, Rod – Rod Steigland, you know, the actor? – is going to insist I'm the female lead in his next film.'

'I don't think you've got a stone to lose,' I said, amazed, for she looked even more of a collection of bird bones than Jessica. 'Or even an ounce!'

'Sweet of you,' she drawled. 'But thin is the new fat – it simply isn't good enough. Are you *sure* you don't want to be our nanny and come to America?'

'I wonder if you'd excuse us, Charlie?' Mace interrupted. 'Kathleen and I have got a lot to discuss before she has to leave. Caitlin will be down in a minute.'

'But—' I began, because surely Kathleen would want to see something of her little girl before she went off again? But the door to the living room closed firmly behind them. And then, as is the way with old doors, quietly clicked open again, just a hairline.

A better person might have gone to round up Caitlin, or waited outside. I edged a little nearer to the door, and listened, fascinated. It was like hearing a play on radio with an exceptional cast: the enunciation was *superb*.

'I'd like to have Caitlin make her main home here in England with me, Kathy,' Mace said quietly. 'If you remember, I didn't go for custody because we agreed that we'd share time with her and do whatever was best for Caitlin.'

'Well, we have, haven't we? And you can still see her. I mean, Rod's got a flat in London, you've got a house there, and you come over to the USA sometimes to make films.'

'Not so often – my ambitions have changed in the two years we've been apart, Kathleen. I see my future now mainly playwriting and maybe the odd cameo role.'

'Well, I suppose that's right for you. Go while you've still got what it takes.'

'Yes, but it means I'm the one with the stable home, while you're jetting about from one place to the next leaving Caitlin with a series of nannies. It would make more sense if she lived with me and came to you for holidays.'

'You're just jealous of Rod, because Caitlin likes him! You can't bear the idea of another man being her daddy!' said Kathleen, her voice rising. 'You only married me because I was pregnant!'

'I'm *glad* she likes Rod – I like Rod too, the poor harmless mutt. But I'm still her father, and I don't want her living on the other side of the world.'

'Well, I'm her mother, and you will just have to put up with it!' she exclaimed triumphantly.

'Not if I apply for custody. I know one or two things about you, Kathleen, that a judge might be interested in!' he said, his voice hard.

'Well, here's something you didn't know,' Kathleen said with deadly venom. 'Caitlin isn't yours!'

At this interesting moment Caitlin galloped back into the

kitchen, wearing her teddy suit and with her wellies on the wrong feet, so I quickly ushered her out of the cottage.

Behind me it had gone ominously silent, until I heard Mace say, in a quiet but carrying voice that brought goose bumps up on the back of my neck: 'What do you mean?'

Then I regretfully had to close the front door.

I began to feel sorry I'd never seen him act in anything.

Em was in the kitchen, and so, to my surprise, were the twins, perched on chairs with their arms up to the elbows in mixing bowls.

Frost and Flossie were in hopeful attendance, lightly dusted with flour.

'What are you making?' demanded Caitlin excitedly, bouncing up and down in her little flowered wellies.

'I'm making rock cakes, and Feeb is making gingerbread,' Clo said importantly. 'Do you want to join in?'

I divested Caitlin of her teddy suit and wellies, wrapped her in a pinafore and stood her on a chair.

'You can make chocolate slab,' Em said, tossing digestive biscuits into another bowl. 'Here, take this rolling pin and bash these biscuits to pieces.'

'Where's everyone?' I asked Em as the girls beat the ingredients to death, squealing.

'Father's working. His agent's taken to calling him on an hourly basis, so he's finally shaken off the tart and got on with it. The said tart's gone off in a huff, shopping, but the girls didn't want to go.'

'I thought they liked shopping?'

'Seem to have gone off it – and they wouldn't put dresses on this morning, only jeans. She didn't like that, either.'

123

'Well, they're only children. You can't have much fun if you're trying to keep expensive clothes clean.'

'Anne's gone for her treatment, but she says she'll tell them some more stories later – and she's bringing them an effing *present*.'

We exchanged slightly incredulous stares.

'Bran's in his room, working – he's nearly fit to go back, I think. It's not long before he'll be home again for Christmas, anyway. Walter's watching the TV, and Gloria's in there too, with the ironing.'

How cosy it all sounded ... and soon it would be Christmas – at home – without Matt!

'Mace was having an argument with his ex-wife when I came out,' I told her. 'She's beautiful, but even skinnier than Jess.'

'Gloria says Mace's reputation with women is terrible,' Em said.

'Does she? How does she know?'

'*Surprise!* magazine. She gets it every week. She doesn't like you going down there to look after Caitlin so she's going to read your tea leaves, to see if you're safe.'

'Of course I'm safe! I hardly think he's even registered that I'm a woman – just a useful version of the village idiot,' I assured her.

When I took Caitlin home, tired, grubby and with a cake tin of edible goodies for Daddy, there was no sign of the sports car or its glamorous occupant.

In its place was a battered motorbike, and the vicar and Mace were in earnest discussion in the kitchen.

It seemed a bit early for whisky.

124

It was certainly no time to explain about Dead Greg either, which was a pity, for in my brief absence someone had scrawled 'Murderess!' on the veranda windows in harpy-red lipstick.

Looked like Angie'd arrived.

Chapter 14: In Combat

Tips for Southern Visitors, No. 5

People will be quite kind to you when they realise you are from the South, because you can't help it.

My painting, *Jessica Down the Well*, was coming along nicely, and I had a little row of tiny primed white canvases awaiting my attention.

Jessie was not at her best the following morning: first she kicked up a fuss because the washing she left in the machine the night before had been decanted onto the floor, although she should have known from past experience that getting up early to take it out herself was her best option.

Then she made a bit of a scene at breakfast, when the twins showed her the presents Anne had brought them back from town, although they were only new outfits for their Barbies.

The girls' dolls were now fetchingly attired in army fatigues *à la* Action Man.

'They don't do Action Woman yet,' explained Feeb earnestly, 'or Anne would have got those, but these fit OK.

Anne usually buys men's clothes anyway, especially waist-coats, because you need loose, practical clothes in a war zone. See – my Barbie's wearing a flak jacket.'

'And mine's got army boots on, and when we get home from school, Anne's going to help us to camouflage their helmets with grass and twigs!' said Clo eagerly.

'But Barbies aren't soldiers,' Jessica said earnestly. 'And Action Man is for little boys!'

'But I've just explained – these are Action *Women*,' said Feeb impatiently. 'Really, Mummy!'

'But Mummy's always taught you that war is wrong!'

'Yes, but if it happens, someone's got to report it, haven't they?' Feeb said sensibly. 'Anne goes on the TV. When she's better she's going back, and then we can see her on the news!'

'Mummy,' wheedled Clo, 'could I have a movie director Barbie?'

Thrown off balance, Jessica said, with relief: 'Of course, darling! That will be much more fun, won't it?'

'Oh, yes – then *my* Barbie can be the camerawoman recording Feeb's Barbie for TV,' Clo agreed.

'Call your sister Phoebe, Chloe. I don't like these abbreviations.'

'Clo, Mummy. And Phoebe's always going to be Feeb now: we've decided.'

That was the final straw and Jessica forbade them to have anything more to do with Anne, a condition impossible to impose in the circumstances.

Father had had enough by then, and said he was glad to discover the twins were not just the brainless, giggling little imbeciles he'd thought them, and then Jessica turned on him and tried to have a row.

Father doesn't like rows, so he scowled and went off into his study, locking the door; so at least he could get some work done.

'Em, can we have treacle tart and cream tonight?' wheedled Clo. 'It's my favouritest pudding in all the world.'

'And mine,' agreed Feeb. 'Mummy, Em calls you the Treacle Tart – is that because *you're* scrumptious, too?'

'No, it's because she's dark and sticky,' Em said, smiling.

Bran, who'd been sitting silently stirring sugar into his porridge in slow motion, looked up and answered the smile. 'Sticky pudding?'

'After dinner,' Em said.

'I don't know what your problem is, Jess,' Anne said, from behind the newspaper. 'You don't want them to grow up thinking being a giraffe-necked blonde bimbo is the height of ambition, do you?'

Jessica was sulking again. Em looked about to win the battle after all.

I had packed up my black clothes and Gloria was going to take them to a charity shop. I wore only my jumble-sale finds now, and a crocheted cardigan in multicoloured yarn that Gloria had made for me, in a pattern of daisies in squares.

Other than my cardigan I seemed to be moving towards the sea-green and silver spectrum, which I supposed was more suitable to a cool and fishy Pisces than black.

Horrorscopes: what your star sign says about you!

PISCES are cool: watch them slither off on their own business just when you thought you'd caught them in a

128

net of the mundane. But don't worry, there's nothing scaly about them and they always return home to spawn.

Mace was definitely taciturn next morning, but that was all right because Caitlin talked enough for all of us. I didn't think he was brooding over what his ex-wife had said, though, because it was probably something she'd thought up in the heat of the moment.

He did seem to be a devoted daddy, whatever Gloria said about his reputation, while I couldn't say I was impressed by Kathleen's maternal instincts. But clearly she'd got some, or she wouldn't want to take Caitlin to America with her.

Mace sort of loomed in the kitchen doorway and glowered while I helped Caitlin into her teddy suit and made sure her wellies were on the right feet.

'Take her out for a walk,' he ordered, like she was a dog.

'That's what I intend doing,' I snapped. After all, *I* hadn't done anything to make him mad – yet. Not perhaps the most opportune time to confess about Dead Greg?

We left him stewing in his own juice (Tartar sauce?) and I took Caitlin up to Ramshaw Heights in the car, feeling in need of the air and exercise and a space in which to compose my explanation to Mace about Greg, before Angie broadcast it to all. It had to be done sometime.

Em was going to try to find out where Angie was staying, by one means or another: better not to ask.

She did take the vicar some jam, and he said he'd treasure it for ever, though I hope he doesn't because it would go mouldy. She didn't tell me what he said about *Womanly Wicca Words of Spiritual Comfort*, but she looked thoughtful when she came home.

129

I left Flossie behind, snoozing noisily, but with the Parsonage door open at the top of the stairs in case she woke and fancied company. She likes a touch of Frost, in small doses.

At first Caitlin walked quietly by my side through the lightly iced woodland, pulling me to a halt from time to time in order to point out some marvel.

'This,' she announced importantly, 'is rabbit poop, and this is sheep poop, and this is dog poop.'

Feeling some answer was expected of me I said vaguely: 'Oh?'

'But I don't know what squirrel poop looks like,' she went on, satisfied that she had my full attention. 'And there are lots of squirrels here, so there should be some. I wonder where it is.'

'Under the trees?' I suggested. 'Though I suppose they're swinging from tree to tree, or whatever they do, and let fly at the same time, so it will be scattered everywhere.'

Caitlin giggled. 'We could be showered in squirrel poop at any minute! I'll tell you a joke,' she added.

'Go on.'

'What's got a hazelnut in every bite?'

'I don't know. What *has* got a hazelnut in every bite?'

'Squirrel shit!' she said, laughing like a hyena.

I recalled that Sylvia Plath used to walk in the woods at Hardcastle Crags, not so very far away, and write poetry. Either she didn't have her children with her at the time, or she was much better at blanking out small, piercing voices.

We wound our way up along the valley and came out high up where you could look way, way down from the jutting rocks.

'I like you,' Caitlin announced unexpectedly. 'You don't say things like: "Get away from the edge of that rock this minute, Caitlin!"'

Startled and guilty I realised that her wind-whipped slight form was precariously balanced near the edge of a slab of rock.

'Of course, that's the sort of thing I should be saying, isn't it? Only I'm not used to children, so I forget.'

'I'll remind you – after I've done it. I don't go right to the edge anyway, because Daddy let me once, while he was holding my hand, and I felt like I wanted to jump off and whirl round and round like a sycamore helicopter. Only Daddy said I'd plummet straight down like a conker, and when I got to the bottom I'd be spread out like raspberry jam, so it wouldn't be worth it.'

'Er – no,' I agreed.

'And he'd be very angry with me,' she added, as a clincher.

'Does he often get angry?' I asked tentatively.

She giggled: 'Yes, but not with me. Mostly with people on the telephone, and magazines when they tell fibs about him. And Mummy,' she added. 'He's a big grumpy bear.'

'This is a long walk, isn't it? What have you got in your pockets?' I asked, hoping for sweets, even old fluffy ones.

'What's it got in its pocketses?' she screeched. 'I've got *The Lord of the Rings* on CD and Gollum hisses and says that, and when I first heard it I had nightmares every night for a week!'

'I'm not surprised – it's too old for you.'

'No it's not. I could read it now. I can read *anything*. I can read the newspapers.'

'I wouldn't bother. The only interesting women they ever tell you about are in the obituaries.'

Still, that explained her wide vocabulary. Not having much experience with small children I'd assumed all the others at the nursery were a bit dim, but maybe that was just in contrast to Caitlin?

'My brother, Bran, could read when he was two, and he learned French from a set of old Linguaphone records when he was four,' I told her, but she didn't seem noticeably impressed.

'Those people over there are snogging.'

'Kissing. Snogging's not really a nice word.'

'I snogged Joel last week, but I didn't like it, so I'm not going to do it again.'

'It's a pity *I* didn't think of that earlier.'

'Not snogging, because you don't like it?'

'Not doing anything twice that I didn't like the first time.'

'But sometimes you have to do things you don't like,' she pointed out like a miniature philosopher. 'Daddy usually manages not to do the things he doesn't like, but then sometimes it makes other people cross.'

'Yes, that's the price you have to pay.' I held my hand out. 'Come on, let's get back to the car – we've got time to stop for a hot chocolate with whipped cream on the way back if we run!'

Mace greeted us at the cottage door, and he didn't look any more cheerful than when we left.

He silently handed me a note on horribly familiar blue paper, and stood there, arms crossed over his broad chest, watching me read it.

Light blue touchpaper and retire.

'You are trusting your innocent child to a murdering whore!' it said, rather predictably.

'Is it true?' he asked, (quite mildly, considering) as Caitlin ran off past him into the house, her teddy-bear ears flapping.

'Which bit?' I said brightly, wishing I'd got in first with the explanation.

'The murdering bit. I can see the possibilities of the other myself, now you aren't dressed like a small perambulating Bedouin bag-wash any more.'

I scowled at him. 'I meant to tell you, but you didn't seem in the mood for conversation this morning.'

'You were going to tell me you were a murderer?'

'Of course not. I didn't murder him, it was an accident – ask the vicar!'

'*Chris* knows about this?'

'Yes, I told him when he caught me hitting melons the other day, although actually I've given it up now.'

'Murder?'

'Hitting melons. You see, I accidentally hit Angie's husband, Greg, with a frying pan, and he died, and Angie – that's who sent you the letter – is a bit upset about it, and she's followed me here. I don't know why she keeps calling me a whore, though, because I didn't lead him on – I haven't led anyone on, except my ex-husband, and look where that got me.'

He stared at me. 'I find your conversation curiously oblique, but I think I've got the gist – and,' he added thoughtfully, 'I'm not altogether sure I still fancy that ginger and melon jam your sister Em presented me with.'

'We had to do *something* with the melons. They're very dear just now.'

'Yes, I can see that.'

I sighed. 'Well, I don't suppose you will be wanting me to come and fetch Caitlin tomorrow?'

'Why, you aren't likely to hit her with a frying pan, too, are you?'

'Certainly not! I like Caitlin – even *Em* likes Caitlin. I wouldn't hurt a hair on her head.'

'No, that's what I thought. We will carry on as before, then, and I'll keep my melons hidden when you're around,' he said, with one of his sudden, absolutely demoralising smiles.

I wished he wouldn't do that.

'I told you I'd given melon-bashing up.'

'So you did,' he said, still smiling: a ravaging horde in his own right.

On the way back to the cottage I tried to remember exactly what he'd said about whores and Bedouin washing to see whether I'd been insulted or not.

I would have immediately asked Em's opinion, but Xanthe Skye was sitting in the kitchen with her, eating rich fruitcake and drinking something green out of a Russian tea glass.

I stopped in the doorway. 'Is my aura all right today?'

Xanthe examined the air around me with an expert gaze. 'A bit sultry, dear, but not blue.'

'Oh, good,' I said, coming further in. 'The sultry bit's probably because Mace's found out about Dead Greg, Em. He's had a poison-pen letter from Angie.'

Dead Greg was clearly no surprise to Xanthe, but of course all the people who *matter* in Upvale would know, they just wouldn't drag it into the conversation.

'How did he take it?' Em asked, cutting me a slice of cake.

I considered. 'Quite well, really, I suppose.' And I recounted what he'd said as well as I could remember it.

Had I known Gloria was within earshot I'd have left the whore bit out. She bounced out of the nearby scullery.

'Cheeky bugger!' she said. 'You don't want to go near that one, he's *wicked*!'

Xanthe sighed. 'He certainly is!' she agreed dreamily.

Gloria gave her a look.

'At least you won't be going to look after his little girl now.'

'Yes, I will. I told him Dead Greg was an accident.'

'I hope you told him you're not a whore as well!' she said tartly. 'Or that your sister would be, if he gave her half a chance.'

'That's enough, Gloria,' Em said firmly. 'There aren't any whores these days, everyone's at it, apparently – except me. And I only want to utilise him on a temporary basis, while Charlie is only interested in his money.'

'He's not for either of you,' Gloria said, glowering. 'I know what I've seen in the tea leaves.'

'Earl Grey?' enquired Xanthe interestedly.

Chapter 15: Taken Out

Anne gave me an article she'd written for *Skint Old Northern Woman*, to be published anonymously, which read more like one of her war correspondent reports than anything. But I was deeply touched by it, and felt I understood Anne more than I'd ever done before.

Health Check, No. 2: The Body as Battlefield: One Woman's Fight Against the Big C

As a war correspondent I'm fit and healthy, but battle-scarred. Any threat to my health I always expected to come from outside, but this time I carry a war wound caused by a traitor within myself: cancer.

The enemy sneaked in and set up an advance position in the form of a small lump in my left breast, hoping to go unnoticed until reinforcements were well entrenched.

However, fortune favours the flat-chested: when you have boobs like two fried eggs even a tiny bump stands out like a beacon.

Even then, I just assumed it was a troublesome cyst – there was nothing impressive about something the size and shape of a petit pois *under the skin. But within two days I found myself diagnosed with malignant cancer, and offered a range of exciting clinical procedures.*

I opted for a lumpectomy, and with amazing speed was summoned to hospital where the surgeon circled the little bugger and whipped it out, also taking a gland or two from under the arm to check for any spread to the lymph glands.

The arm was sorer than the boob, but the glands showed negative for cancer spread, so it was worth it.

The outlook was good, but six weeks of radiotherapy was advised as back-up, which I accepted. It's no big deal.

Then they offered me the drug Tamoxifen, 'just in case'. You take it for ten years, and when I asked if it had any side effects they gave me a leaflet to read.

The possible *side effects included hot flushes, skin rashes, genital itching, menstrual disorders, breast pain, hair loss, weakness, muscle and joint pain, and sickness.*

This didn't sound like a whole lot of fun, but then I turned the leaflet over and found the possible serious *side effects: liver problems, yellowing of the skin and eyes, visual disturbances, feverishness and unusual bruising and bleeding of the skin.*

After a brief exchange of views on the matter (I told them to stuff it where the sun don't shine, they told me I was very lucky to be offered the drug at all), I elected to decline it.

Lessons I learned from this experience are: 1) Watch your back (and your boobs). 2) Don't rush into anything, but study your position carefully and weigh up the options. 3) Don't panic – you need a clear head to fight and survive. 4) If you've got all the facts, you are as expert as anyone else and can make your own decisions. 5) Your operation scar's just as much a battle scar as any other, and you don't need to be ashamed of it.

Finally, 6): Live each day like it's all you've got. I've always done that anyway – today is the only day we can be sure of. Don't waste it.

'Anne,' I said, 'the magazine isn't going to be published at all – I'm just doing this for fun.'

'Yes it is, Chaz, and I will see to that. It's the sort of thing that should be published, if only once.'

'That's right,' Em agreed from the other end of the kitchen table. 'I've got the advance from my book, and Anne's got some savings, so we're putting it into the first and possibly only edition of *Skint Old Northern Woman* magazine – or comic. Susie says it might turn out looking a bit more like *Viz* than *Woman's Own*. I've got lots of pieces written for it already.'

She bent her head back over her cookery books. 'Do you think duck pâté would be good as the starter tomorrow?'

'Do your vichyssoise soup. Everyone likes it, and it's cold, so it doesn't matter what time you eat it,' Anne said.

'Yes, but listen you two,' I interrupted. 'I can't possibly let you pay for the magazine to be published. It won't sell enough to pay for itself, and you might need the money!'

'We think *Skint Old Northern Woman* should exist,' Em said. 'If only briefly. And that's that. The rest of the discussion group are coming round here tonight to help sort out which articles go where, and Susie's bringing her sister, Jen, to help us – the one who works for the small publisher.'

'He's a little man?' Anne asked, interested.

'No, he's small as in not a huge publishing house. But efficient. We can have it out before Christmas.'

'Bloody fast, Em!'

'That's modern technology for you – stuff it in one end, out comes the finished product at the other.'

'I think there might be a bit more to it than that,' I said feebly. 'Besides, you can't have a magazine without pictures.'

'We'll have that painting you've just finished – *Jessie Down the Well* – on the front cover,' Em said.

'Yes, and Susie's done some good cartoons. That should do it,' added Anne. 'There you are. All sorted, Chaz.'

'You don't think Mace or the vicar is vegetarian, do you?' asked Em, getting back to business.

'Mace looks like a meat eater to me, Em,' Anne said.

'When did *you* meet him, Anne?' I asked curiously.

'Out and about – don't spend all my time in bloody bed. And the vicar came to see me – don't know why. I quite fancied him, but he's got the hots for old Em.'

'Chris isn't vegetarian,' murmured Em, absently thumbing through Mrs Beeton. 'Can I do roast beef and Yorkshire pudding?'

'You certainly can, better than anyone,' I said enthusiastically.

'No, I meant, because of the Mad Cow – that Jessie won't touch it, for a start.'

'She won't touch anything with calories in anyway; she's even started saying the bubbles in fizzy mineral water make you fat,' I said.

'And everyone probably thinks we're the Mad Cows already,' sniggered Anne. 'Go for it, Em.'

'Right. And sticky toffee pudding with custard afterwards – men like their stodgy puds.' She closed the book. 'There.

That's that. I'm off to the shops. Shouldn't you be off to get Caitlin, Charlie?'

I jumped. 'Oh, yes, of course. I thought we could both paint in the veranda today so I've set the small easel up next to mine for her.'

'There are iced rabbit biscuits in the Beatrix Potter tin – take them down with you. But not the frog ones, they're for Bran.'

'OK. Thanks, Em.'

'And I'm off to the hospital,' Anne said, pulling herself up.

'The meeting's tonight at eight, after dinner,' Em reminded me. 'In here.'

I didn't try to protest any more: if Anne and Em were determined *Skint Old Northern Woman* would live, then live it would, and I started to feel quite excited.

> *We see the tip of history's iceberg.*
> *Entombed in the deep belly*
> *the women's mouths move*
> *silently.*
> From 'Words from the Spirit'
> by Serafina Shane

I don't know why Gloria felt that I should beware of Mace, because he has never shown the slightest inclination to drag me into his lair and ravish me, which would be slightly difficult with Caitlin in tow anyway.

I think he's more in danger of Em dragging him into *her* lair: if she makes her mind up, she is likely to pounce should she get an opportunity. Still, I think she also finds Chris attractive too, if she can only get over his double handicap of Christianity and the love of Dickens.

Mace did not even emerge from his study when I got there this morning. Caitlin was ready and waiting for me.

I painted *Caitlin in the Rainforest*, and Caitlin painted *Charlie with Blue Hair*. Time flew past on hummingbird wings, and before we knew it Mace had come knock, knock, knocking on heaven's door, and entered our paradise like a particularly beautiful, but potentially dangerous, snake.

Smooth and fatal, sums him up pretty well, really.

Caitlin proudly showed him her picture.

'It's a speaking likeness,' he said solemnly. 'Especially the hair.'

'Yes it is,' Caitlin said severely. 'You aren't looking properly, but Charlie showed me: look at Charlie's hair.'

He turned his oblique, midnight-velvet stare on me, and I shifted a bit under the searching scrutiny.

'It's very pretty – and unusual. Silvery hair combined with dark eyes, eyebrows and eyelashes – different.'

'It's natural,' I said coldly.

Caitlin tugged impatiently at his arm: 'You're not looking properly, is he, Charlie? The blue paintwork is reflecting onto it so she's got *blue* hair.'

'You're right,' he said, after another minute inspection. 'And there *is* a blue-green light up one side of her face, from the plants. If she weren't wearing jeans, she'd look like a wood nymph.'

'It's not good enough to look, you have to *see*,' Caitlin said importantly.

I hope *I* didn't sound that bossy.

Mace walked around me and stood close enough to radiate body heat, gazing down at my canvas. 'It's amazing how like

Caitlin that is, even though she is so tiny in the middle of it. Clearly Caitlin . . .' he added quietly. 'Herself – there's nothing of me in there.'

'No, she doesn't look like you or her mother,' I agreed. 'Though she has got your eyes.'

Then I suddenly remembered what his ex-wife had said about Caitlin not being his . . . though surely he hadn't believed that?

'Anyone could have dark blue eyes,' he said.

Surprised, I twisted and looked up into his brooding face: 'Well, no, they couldn't – didn't you do genetics at school? Besides, yours are a real dark navy blue, and you don't often see that.'

He smiled like the sun coming out over the High Atlas and said unexpectedly: 'I think I'll take you out for lunch.'

'Oh, yes!' Caitlin agreed. 'Let's take Charlie!'

'Thanks,' I said, somewhat taken aback. 'But I—'

I stopped and swallowed. Well, *you* try being invited to lunch by Mace North and finding an excuse on the spur of the moment.

And *part* of me wanted to go. I suspect it's the same bit that always wanted to drag the young gardener Steve behind the shrubbery.

'Were you doing something else?' he enquired, employing the ultimate weapon: the 'I'm going to abduct you on horseback, and carry you off to my tent – you don't mind, do you?' smile.

'No,' I conceded weakly.

Barbarian hordes, sweep me away.

'Get your coat,' Barbarian Horde said practically.

I was *so* glad to see that he wasn't wearing the red duvet today.

'So my little chicken's been going out with that actor,' Gloria Mundi said, parting the silver fronds of my fringe and peering searchingly into my eyes.

'What? Did you?' Anne said, surprised. 'Well, bugger me! Does Em know?'

'I didn't go *out* sort of out. I just had a pub lunch with him and Caitlin. I think he asked me on impulse.'

'Drink this tea,' Gloria said, thrusting a cup into my hands. 'I need to see what's coming to pass.'

'I don't feel like a cup of tea, thanks, Gloria. The discussion group will be here any minute, and I've got to fetch the magazine stuff up from the Summer Cottage.'

She stood over me, though, until I drained the cup, and then spent long minutes staring down into the tea leaves and muttering.

The coven might dismiss her as a mere wisewoman, but I was sure she knew a lot more than any of them. She just didn't share it, even with Em.

'Dead Greg's widow's staying at Hoo House with the other loonies,' Em said, coming in. 'Inga's up in arms – said I'd made her employ a "muwdwess".'

'Charlie's nicked your actor,' Anne said helpfully.

'Someone dark and strange is entering her life ... bringing change and trouble,' agreed Gloria, taking another doubtful look into the teacup. 'Storm clouds are gathering.'

'That might be Angie. She's naturally dark, she just dyes her hair, and she's certainly strange.'

'I've got *no* hair,' chipped in Walter, who was quietly rocking away by the stove, carving another walking-stick head. 'No bodily hair whatsoever.'

'And there's the Treacle Tart, too. She and Father have made it up, and they're even more all over each other than before.'

'It's a man,' Gloria said with certainty. She tilted the cup as though some trick of the light might show her something better. 'And I see a child . . . but—' she broke off, frowning.

'What?' I demanded.

'Never you mind.'

'They do a good lunch over at the Stone Cross,' Em said.

'How did you . . .?'

'Freya. In the back room with her lover.'

'You don't mind, do you, Em? It didn't mean anything, they were going anyway, and just sort of took me along. I don't want another man, even if Mace were interested in me that way, which he isn't. Anyway, he's a bit scary.'

'He does have a deliciously dark edge to him,' Em agreed. 'That's why he seems so much more suited to my purpose than Chris. I need the love of a Bad Man. We'll see tomorrow night. The way to a man's heart is through his stomach, so I'm going to mix a potion up that will make him appreciate me. Gloria, you're in charge of seeing it gets in the right glass of sherry before dinner, and I don't want any more of that "he's not for you" business, right?'

'Right,' conceded Gloria, with unusual meekness. 'I'll see

to that for you, don't you worry. And if you don't want that vicar, I could see that he falls for Anne instead?'

'No,' Em said quickly. 'No, I'm enjoying the novelty of having a Barkis, even if he's the wrong one, and Anne doesn't really want anyone just now. Do you, Anne?'

'No, just want to get fit and back to work. Besides, Red's phoned me up.'

'Red? But you wouldn't have him back, would you?'

'Might. Never trusted him in the first place, but damn good in the sack. I'll think about it.'

'There's that Freya at the door,' Gloria said absently, and I didn't ask how she knew. 'I'll be fetching the ice in.'

I noticed she took my teacup out with her.

We were there until nearly midnight putting the magazine more or less in order, with Jen to tell us what was and wasn't possible.

It was hard work, but I thought we'd got it right, and Jen had taken my painting of *Jessie Down the Well* for the cover.

Susie's cartoons were great.

Gloria hung around most of the evening, giving me strange, furtive, sideways looks, so goodness knows what she saw in the tea leaves.

But whatever it was, it certainly wasn't anything romantic, since that part of me had atrophied away to nothing. I would confess to faint lustful pangs sometimes when I thought of Mace North, but that was more just the last stirring of dying embers, and was balanced out by the slight *frisson* of terror he also somehow managed to inspire in me.

Probably half the female population of the English-speaking world felt the same way, since without being in any

way a hunk, he was still the sort of man women look at and
wonder about the body beneath the clothes.

Mmm . . .

When we were tossing filler article suggestions about,
Gloria suddenly said she had a winter tip for southern visitors: 'Never eat yellow snow.'

Well, thank you for that one, Gloria.

Chapter 16: Going Hairless

On the Friday of Father's birthday, everyone was preoccupied at breakfast, and immediately afterwards went their separate ways. (Rhymers don't do cards and presents, they have Feasts instead.)

Branwell was pretty much recovered, but he had received dispensation from his university to stay at home until after Christmas and put the finishing touches to his Great Work. There wasn't much term left anyway; universities seem to spend more time off than on.

Father abandoned *his* nearly finished book and went out somewhere with Jessica, dropping the girls at school en route. Jessica was upset at breakfast because she'd put two pounds on, and wouldn't eat anything at all, just drank black coffee, which Em said she'd probably sick straight back up again if she got the chance (but I think she was joking).

I couldn't see any sign of the two pounds either, but I suppose that's sort of like three extra layers of skin all over her little bird bones.

Anne vanished for her mysterious treatment, Emily readied herself for a mammoth cooking session, Walter went off into the dining room to polish all the glasses, and Gloria disappeared into the back scullery to brew mysterious potions.

I saw she still had my teacup from the previous night in there with her, when I looked, with a sticker saying, 'Do not wash this cup' on the side. I couldn't make anything of the contents, except that they were drying out like dark dandruff.

While I was getting ready to fetch Caitlin, Flossie emerged from her igloo and intimated that she wouldn't mind coming too, which was a surprise: extra exercise seems to be paying off.

We set off happily enough, but then some primal instinct made me look over my shoulder just in time to spot Angie, turning the Parsonage corner and starting down the track.

Call me a coward, but I did not in the least feel like a screaming match at forty paces, so I scooped Flossie right up off her flat, furry little feet and ran, bursting into Mace's house unheralded and panting.

Flossie may be a bit thinner and fitter, but she's still heavy.

Mace, elegantly disposed on the window seat with a cup in one hand like a *soigné* coffee advert, raised a surprised eyebrow.

'Come in, why don't you?'

'Sorry,' I panted, dumping Flossie on the rug. 'Angie – Dead Greg's widow – chasing me.'

Flossie, wagging her tail, ambled over and stuck her wet nose up his trouser leg.

'Brazen hussy,' he said, reaching down to fondle her domed and silky skull, inside which precious little went on. 'I don't let girls do that until the second date, and we hardly know each other.'

'That's not what Gloria says,' I commented unthinkingly.

He stared at me: 'I don't remember any Gloria.'

'Perhaps you haven't met her? She's . . . she helps . . .' I stopped. There *is* no way of describing Gloria and Walter's roles. 'She's Walter's sister.'

'*Two* old retainers? Well, well! And what does Gloria base her estimate of my character on?'

'Tea leaves. Oh – and *Surprise!* magazine.'

His face darkened alarmingly: 'Never mention that evil, slime-spreading rag again in my presence!'

'Why? What's the matter with it?'

We were interrupted by a sudden hammering on the door. 'Come out, you murdering witch – I know you're in there!' screeched Angie.

I thought of those long, blood-red talons reaching out for me, shuddered and backed away, but Mace got up.

'What are you doing?'

'Opening the door,' he said calmly.

I darted in front of him clutching at him with both hands. He simply swept me behind him like I weighed nothing, and turned the handle.

I peered around him; Angie, poised for another onslaught at the knocker, overbalanced and fell forward onto the path, where she stared up at him between witch-locks of violently auburn hair.

'Can I help you?' Mace asked politely.

The transformation from raging, unbalanced harpy to normal-if-drooling fan was astonishing in a science-fiction, shape-changing sort of way. Maybe the aliens were at it again. Probably recruited her at the same time as Matt.

'You're Mace North, aren't you? I loved you in *One Midsummer Night*, and – aargh!'

She flung herself frantically back as a clatter of hoofs heralded Elfreda Whippington-Smythe's sudden advent. Her large and expensive-looking horse slid to a stone-rattling halt and stood steaming, reeking and rolling its eyes, vast hoofs inches away from Angie.

'Oh, Mace,' Elfreda gasped, wrestling with the reins as her mount jerked its head up and down. Her little round boiled-gooseberry eyes under the pulled-down hat zoomed in on her quarry and I don't think she noticed anyone else was there.

'Hef you heard? That Charlie Rhymer's an actual murderess! Inga at the nursery—' She stopped as some elements of the tableau before her finally registered. 'Oh . . . you're there, Charlie?'

I stood on tiptoe and peeped around Mace, who was still holding me behind his back like a secret present. 'Yes, the murderess in person – and this is Inga's guest.' I indicated Angie, momentarily silenced. 'The murderee's widow.'

In the face of a new, expanded audience, Angie gave it her all: 'She killed my husband! She led him on, and then killed him when he made a pass at her!'

'I killed him, but I certainly didn't lead him on!' I said indignantly. 'He sneaked into my house and assaulted me, and his death was an accident.'

'An accident? You hit him with a cast-iron pan!'

'It dropped on his head, and I've got an unimpeachable witness to prove it.'

'If you mean that batty old cow who lived opposite you, she'd say anything.'

'Don't speak like that about one of my best friends!' I said furiously, trying to duck under Mace's arm, but he held me back with muscles like iron.

'I just thought you ought to be warned about the woman looking after your child,' Elfreda said to him stuffily. 'Especially after what she did to Gunilla at the nursery.'

'She didn't do anything to Gunilla. It was the other way around, and I have an eyewitness to that one – Caitlin,' Mace said pleasantly. 'But thank you for the warning, Mrs Whippington-Smythe. How nice of you to rally to a helpless man's defence.'

She stared at him, went faintly pink, and kick-started her nag into movement. 'I wouldn't have bothered if I'd known you were under her spell already,' she said nastily, and jolted away like a sack of potatoes. King Edwards.

'What spell? I haven't *done* any spell!' I yelled indignantly; trying again to release myself and get around Mace.

'*Will* you be still?' he said exasperatedly over his shoulder, then turned back to Angie. 'I'm so sorry about your husband, but I'm sure Charlie didn't mean to kill him – it was clearly an accident – and if you persist in trying to blacken her name like this there is a law in this country she can use to stop you. Haven't you got a life of your own to lead, instead of running a hate campaign?'

'Life? No – I *had* a good life, and we were going to Japan after Christmas! And there isn't even a proper pension, and the insurance are hanging back on paying out, and to top it all, the squirrels are an act of God! And it's all because of that innocent-looking bitch behind you.'

'I don't think you can blame the squirrels on me, Angie,' I protested. She ignored me, her voice rising.

'She hasn't always looked like that, you know. When she killed my husband she looked like the vamp she is!'

'Goth,' I corrected. 'Different thing. I'm sorry about . . .

151

well, about everything, Angie. Can't you just let it rest and get on with life?'

'Never,' she said, turning away. 'You just wait, Charlie Rhymer. I'm going to make sure your name is like mud, stinking mud, around here.'

'You could get her stopped,' Mace said, pushing me back in and closing the door.

'Anyone who matters around here knows already. The incomers are the only ones who won't have heard yet.'

'Like me? Don't *I* matter?'

'Well, yes, but I *was* going to tell you, Angie just got to you first. You can let go of me now,' I added pointedly.

'I'm not sure I dare – you've got quite a temper.'

'I don't think I even register as a blip on the Mace North scale of temper, and anyway, I'm not angry with *you*.'

He gazed down at me, his grip tightening rather than letting go . . .

'People were shouting, Daddy,' Caitlin said, pushing the door open with a large bag from which spilled clothes, teddy bears and hair ribbons in artless profusion. 'Why are you holding Charlie?'

'To stop her flying off.'

Caitlin giggled. 'Like a fairy?'

'Something like that. Don't you think it's a bit early to pack?' Mace said mildly.

Caitlin was to have tea with the twins and stay the night, while the grown-ups had dinner in a civilised manner – though actually no Rhymer Birthday Feast had ever quite managed that yet.

'Perhaps Charlie wouldn't mind going upstairs and helping you to repack it a bit?' he suggested.

'If we're not disturbing you?'

'I find you constantly disturbing, especially since you've given up the widow's weeds: but if you mean will it stop me writing, then no. I've come to one of those patches in the play where nothing goes right, and I need a break.'

I stared at him uncertainly, but he was looking so Mr Rochester that I suppressed the impulse to bleat out: 'What do you mean, disturbing?' and just followed Caitlin up to her room, where I repacked her case, and calmed her down a bit as she was wildly excited about spending the night with two big girls like Feeb and Clo.

'What sort of clothes should my Barbie take?'

'Practical ones. Clo and Feeb's Barbies are not really party animals these days.'

'Ski wear?' she pondered.

'As long as it's not a red duvet, like your daddy's.'

She giggled. 'Daddy calls it his duvet now, too!'

Daddy, six-four of soft, downy vermilion, went out for a walk with us later, thus entirely defeating the reason for employing me to entertain Caitlin in the first place. But he said he needed to stretch his legs and think.

We climbed right up to the beacon, and although I'm not sure how the conversation took such a turn, I ended up telling him all about *Skint Old Northern Woman*; only I called it a comic, since he seemed to have an acute aversion to the word 'magazine'. He said he'd order a dozen copies and send them to all his friends for Christmas.

I don't have a dozen friends. Come to that, apart from family (in which I include Walter and Gloria), Miss Grinch, and possibly Vaddie at the gallery, I'm not sure I've got any at all.

'You need an arts page,' he suggested. 'A sort of "What's on in the North".'

'"What's on in the North That's Worth Parting with Brass to See",' I corrected.

'Did you know there's a sort of natural amphitheatre in the rocks above the stream in the woods?' he asked. 'It reminded me of the Minack outdoor theatre at Porthcurno in Cornwall. You could start a campaign to have summer theatre there.'

'Yes, I know where you mean. It's on Madge's land, too, so her old dad could charge everyone going in – and out, knowing him.'

'Local people could be the actors, like the Passion Play at Oberammergau.'

'Or a Shakespeare a year . . . in the vernacular!' I enthused. 'I can see it now: "Enter Hamlet – he were a short, stiff man with no hair or eyebrows." Or "Romeo, Romeo, thou art got a right poncy name, flower."'

'That kind of thing,' he agreed, grinning. 'I could direct it.'

'I don't suppose you'll be spending that much time here.'

'I intend spending as much time in Upvale as I can, though I'll have to keep my London house on, as well. Upvale and the moors have got to me, in a way Haworth never did.'

'Don't mention Haworth – or the Brontës,' I shuddered. 'My brother and sisters and I are the result of a failed Brontë experiment.'

Then I described Father's attempt to replicate the conditions that had turned the sisters – or, in Father's opinion, the brother – into literary geniuses.

'So he chose a similar area, not too far away, as the crow flies, and settled there with my mother. She's Lally Tooke

– have you heard of her? She went to America, and she's *very* big on the radical feminist literature circuit – and they had Em and Anne and me. And by then their opinions of the Brontës had turned in opposing directions, Mother discovered that she hated childbirth, and wasn't that mad about children, and she bolted. Father carried on, since it made the situation more authentic, after all, especially after our first au pair had Branwell, and made the numbers up. But none of us was brilliant except Bran, and he's a genius of an entirely different kind.'

'I met Bran in the pub with your father,' Mace said. 'Well, I say met, but we didn't seem to be speaking the same language.'

'Not many people do.'

'Probably not. I've also had a close encounter with your other sister, Anne. She said she thought I would strip well.'

I choked: 'I think she just meant you look like you'd be a good man in a fight.'

'Let's hope it won't come to that – I think she'd win.'

By the time we got back it had been a longer walk than I'd intended, and Caitlin was ready for a snooze before being brought to the Parsonage.

There was no sign of Angie, except for something very rude scrawled across my door in spray paint, which Walter had already half-obliterated with Mediterranean Blue.

'I seen 'un off,' he said. 'I were up the back chopping firewood, and come to see what she were up to. She screamed and run off.'

'Were you still holding the axe, Walter?'

He nodded. 'Aye, that'll be it. Still, t'door wanted another coat.'

'Yes – it'll look lovely, Walter. You're very kind to me.'

155

He beamed. 'Don't you worry about the mad lady – Em's going to set them three witches on her.'

That would be interesting.

Father wandered into the kitchen, removed several candles from the top of his birthday cake, tossed them into the bin, and wandered out again, muttering darkly.

'I told you, Em, he wouldn't like the right number on it,' I said. 'Has anyone told Jessica how many it *really* is? He's wearing well for his age, but he's still getting on a bit.'

'Dining room's ready,' Anne said, appearing. 'Girls are in bed listening to that story tape I got them.'

'I thought Jessica confiscated *Rambo: Tocsin of Terror*'? I said.

'Ho bleeding ho,' said Anne. '*The Lion, the Witch and the effing Wardrobe.* They've got a load of biscuits, pop, and stuff. Said they were going to have a midnight feast.'

'I don't think any of them will last as long as midnight, and let's hope they aren't sick.'

'Em,' I added cautiously, looking at the hem of the magnificent amber velvet gown in which she strode about like a queen, 'I don't think gorilla slippers go with that dress.'

'It's that or boots.'

'No it isn't – bare feet would be better. And you look amazing – it could have been made for you.'

'You've all scrubbed up nice,' Gloria agreed, coming in with a furtive air and secreting something away in the pocket of her pinafore. 'I thought you were going to wear that lovely green dress, Charlie?'

'I think it's a bit much – I couldn't decide. It's very *wispy* for the middle of winter.'

'You go and put it on this minute,' Gloria ordered as the Parsonage doorbell sounded. 'That's your father's guests now.'

'Oh, all right, Gloria.'

Em said, 'You know what you're to do, Gloria, don't you?'

'Don't you worry, Gloria knows what she's doing.' She looked severely at me as I hovered on the stairs. 'Scat!'

I ran down and quickly changed into Felicity Hake-Hackett's rejected Tinkerbell costume and strappy sandals.

There is one thing Felicity and I have in common besides being the runts of our respective families: we may be skinny, but we both have busts. This dress showed more of mine than I thought I'd got.

And thank God I'd already lawn-mowered my legs and armpits even though it *was* winter when you're usually glad of the extra warmth in Upvale. Otherwise, I'd have been much, much later.

Skint Old Beauty, No. 1: Going Hairless

One of Nature's most cruel pranks is the way that, after forty, she starts to thin the hair on your head, while over-compensating by causing a sort of angora body stocking to gradually envelop the rest of you like mould.

And, to add insult to injury, there is no cheap, fast, efficient and painless way of removing it. (Or even cheap, fast, efficient and painful.)

One day, we hope, they will perfect the art of a total immersion in body wax from nose to toes, but until then we must suffer.

Now you know why Victorian bathing costumes covered you up like that – and it wasn't for modesty.

One of the Great Mysteries of the Universe is: just where did that three-foot spike of nose hair hide before it sprang from your nostril, fully formed, at an embarrassing moment?

Chapter 17: Surprised

Leopardskin prints and gold accessories complement each other perfectly.

The girls were hanging over the banisters in their pyjamas when I went up to the drawing-room floor.

'You look like a flower fairy,' Feeb said. 'If there *are* green ones?' she added doubtfully.

'You're *very* pretty,' Clo agreed. 'Mummy said you looked like a little ghoul in those baggy black things you used to wear.'

'*My* daddy says she looks like an abandoned nymph,' Caitlin said. 'Is that good?'

I thought it was . . . so long as she didn't get it wrong, and what he really said was 'abandoned nympho'.

'Em's got a pretty dress too,' Feeb said. 'The vicar walked into the door-post when he saw her. Even Anne's got her best denim shirt and trousers on!'

'We like to push the boat out at Rhymer Birthday Feasts.'

'Bran had his tea with us – he ate all the biscuits, but he

let me hold Mr Froggy,' Caitlin said importantly. 'He says he hasn't time for birthday dinners, he has to finish his book before anyone else gets in his head and interrupts.'

'And Walter was there, too,' Feeb said. 'We had our own party!'

'Why has Walter got no eyebrows?' asked Caitlin.

'It was the war – Gloria says he was a very sensitive young man and he found it so traumatic that his hair just fell out and never came back,' I explained. My neck began to ache from tilting back to look up at them, so I was quite relieved when Gloria popped her head out of the drawing room and beckoned.

She was holding a tray of sherry glasses. (That's how the Birthday Feast *always* begins – sherry and birthday cake *first*, then dinner.) 'Take that glass nearest you,' she instructed, 'and go and give it to Em while she's talking to the vicar.'

'Right. Will it . . .?'

'Just open her eyes to his good qualities.'

'I can see most of those myself, even from here. And wasn't it his goodness that was the stumbling block?'

'Love will find a way,' she said. 'Better him than that actor – for either of my little chickens.'

'I don't know what you've got against Mace. What *did* you see in the tea leaves, Gloria?'

'Trouble,' she said heavily. 'And that Mace – his first wife drove into a tree and killed herself.'

'*Did* she? How awful! But you can't blame him for that, can you? Poor Mace!' No wonder the poor man was bad-tempered.

'*Surprise!* magazine said she lost control of the car after a row with him,' Gloria said. 'After she found out about the other woman.'

I looked at her. 'But how did she find out about the other woman?'

'From the *Surprise!* "Stolen Secrets" column – though they can't name names.'

'I wondered what Mace had against women's magazines, and now I know. Was it true, about this other woman?'

'There's no smoke without fire, and that one's still burning,' Gloria said cryptically. 'Look at him!'

I turned; Jessica had cornered him, and he was standing, arms folded, glowering down at her. Tyger, tyger . . .

Then he caught sight of me, raised one eyebrow and smiled. It was the Ravaging Horde bit all over again.

'Here,' Gloria ordered brusquely, giving me a dig in the ribs with her sharp elbow. 'Take that glass to your sister this minute! Bloody tea leaves – I'll show 'em!'

Em and Chris seemed to be getting on fine without any herbal help, so it was easy to give Em the glass while she was looking at him.

They were in the corner, and Chris was leaning over her with one hand on the wall next to her head, in a very masterful way. I was sure Em was enjoying the novelty, because otherwise she would have released herself in a painful manner: painful to Chris, that is.

None of us except Father actually liked sherry, but Em was too engrossed to notice what she was drinking.

I'd evidently missed Father blowing out the candles on the cake, because Anne was now slicing it . . . and Gloria was purposefully forging down the room in the direction of Mace and the Treacle Tart, one solitary, twinkling amber glass left on her tray.

Something wicked this way comes.

She *wouldn't* – would she?

She would.

Mace had just lifted the glass to his lips when I said urgently: 'Don't!' and reached out for it – but too late.

He stared at me in mild astonishment.

'Excuse *me*!' Jessica said tightly, having been unceremoniously elbowed out of the way. 'Mace and I were having a conversation.'

'Sorry, was that your glass?' Mace said, relinquishing it to me.

'Yes. Gloria gave you mine by mistake,' I said feebly. 'Shall I get you another?'

'No. I don't really like sherry, though I don't mind sharing this one – with you,' he offered, with that irresistible smile – *and* smouldering dark eyes, so Gloria was right about the fire. 'You look like a creature from another world tonight. Beautiful, fragile, insubstantial . . .'

Disconcerted, I found I'd taken a sip of the potentially doctored sherry myself – then Mace took the glass, turned it around, and drank from the very place my lips had touched, his eyes holding mine.

Do not ask me why this was the sexiest thing that ever happened to me, because I don't know. Take it from me, it *was*.

I was dissolving faster than a love philtre – which is probably what we were drinking.

Whoops.

'Do you feel all right, Mace?' I asked tentatively.

'Yes – in fact, I feel wonderful!'

'Right. Er . . . Mace, I think Gloria put a little something of her own concoction into the sherry.'

'I thought it tasted unusual – but pleasant. What does she use? I thought it was only liqueurs that had herbs added?'

'I could have been wrong. Or got the glasses mixed up . . .' I mused.

'It doesn't matter, does it? At least now I've got the chance to tell you how beautiful you look tonight.'

The slow-burning-fuse smile made my spine tingle and my toes sort of curl like Turkish slippers . . .

Jessica, who'd retreated to the other side of the room, was giving me the evil eye, and I didn't think she even realised she'd taken a bite of birthday cake. Birthday cakes made by Em have one hundred calories per crumb.

The blissful moment was rudely shattered. 'You made a right cock-up of that, you daft ha'p'orth!' Gloria hissed in my ear like an angry wasp. 'He was supposed to be looking at that Jessica when he drank it, not you!'

'But, Gloria, wasn't that a bit . . . underhand?'

'Never you mind!'

I was about to tell her that I'd had a sip myself, then stopped. It *was* the tiniest sip and couldn't possibly matter . . . could it?

'Still, maybe . . .' She sighed heavily. 'I'll brew him something tomorrow to cancel out the spell – but you can't go against Fate; I should have known better. Time to start dinner.'

'What's the matter? What was she saying?' asked Mace.

'Everything's fine,' I assured him. And it would be once he'd had the antidote and saw me in my usual persona of boring old Charlie, sometime murderess and part-time children's nanny.

Walter beat the gong with enthusiasm, and we all trooped

into the dining room and seated ourselves under the birthday banner, Father at the head of the table, with Jessica sitting smugly at his right like a Borgia bag of secrets.

I don't remember much about the rest of the dinner, except that Mace sat next to me and told me all about his first play, and the one he was writing now, which both seemed to be about guilt, and hasty actions leading to disastrous outcomes. But then, so is life.

Good, dry champagne ran like water, and Jessica drank too much, which is easy to do when there's nothing else whizzing round in your system. She got a bit giggly and excitable. The sticky toffee pudding would have lagged her bones a bit, but she declined with horror.

'Oh, no, I really couldn't eat a stodgy dessert!'

'You can't seem to eat anything at all lately,' Gloria said. 'And when you do it doesn't stay down. Happen you're pregnant – unless it's that bulimia.'

'I have *not* got bulimia!' protested Jessica. 'And I'm certainly not pregnant. I had my tubes tied when I had the twins.'

'Then I hope they were tied good and tight, flower, because there's no knot that can't be undone,' said Gloria grimly.

Jessica stared at her, aghast. 'Have you been putting something in my food? Or Em – she's put a spell on me, so I get pregnant?'

'Don't be silly,' Em said. 'The last thing I want is for you to get effing pregnant and have any excuse for hanging around here.'

'And it's not what goes in your *food* that makes you pregnant,' pointed out Gloria meaningfully.

'Shouldn't think she is,' Anne said, busy surrounding her castle of pudding with custard prior to the initial assault. 'We've all seen the backside of forty.'

'*I* haven't!' exclaimed Jessica.

'That could have been more felicitously put, but you're right, Anne,' agreed Em.

'Ran, I'm not pregnant, am I?'

'How should I know?' he said irritably, looking up from his dinner plate. 'Does it matter?'

'Of course it matters! It took me a year to get my figure back after the girls were born, and I'm not getting married looking pregnant.'

The pause after that statement *was* pregnant, even if nothing else was.

Ran sighed and put down his spoon. 'Well, I was going to save it for the birthday speech, but the cat is out of the bag now: Jess and I are getting married.'

'What for?' asked Anne.

'We love each other!' Jessica declared dramatically.

'Good home and a meal ticket for life, for Jessie,' Em said, looking grim. 'Unlimited sex for ever for Father.'

'Do we have to have this sort of family discussion in front of our guests?' Father asked with some asperity.

Em looked suspiciously at the vicar. 'Did you know, Chris?'

'No, but I think it's a good idea. I think marriage in general is a good idea,' he added meaningfully, trying to hold Em's hand.

She glowered at him, and then absently drained the wine glass Gloria had just refilled, although she's not generally a heavy drinker.

'Yes, congratulations,' Mace contributed. 'And on the baby, too, if there is one.'

'There won't be,' Em said firmly. 'She's too old.'

'I am not too old!'

'If there is, it might not be Father's anyway,' Anne suggested.

'If I had a baby it would be obvious who the father was – unlike Branwell and Charlie,' Jess said. 'Just look at them – they could be *anyone's*!'

'I don't know what you're hinting at, Jessica, but not all children take after their fathers,' Em said.

'Yes, there's no Rhymer family birthmark shaped like a bloody strawberry,' Anne contributed. 'Chaz looks just like Mother.'

'But no one seems to know who Branwell takes after!'

Father, who'd been ignoring the argument, looked up, frowning. 'I can't remember what Maria looked like after all this time – but no, the boy *has* to have got his brains from me.'

'So that's where they went,' Em said.

'Ho, ho,' Father said, glowering.

'I saw this really good programme on TV the other day,' Jessica said brightly. 'About a new test you can get to prove whether you're the father of your children – and lots of men have found that they really aren't. Have *you* heard of that, Mace?'

There was a small silence. I thought Jessica was just trying to get his attention, but it was an unlucky shot in view of what his ex-wife had said.

Mace turned and stared at *me*, like I was some kind of traitor. 'You overheard what Kathleen said? And I thought—'

He stopped abruptly, and turned his head away as if he couldn't bear to look at me.

'No, Mace!' I protested. 'I haven't – I didn't . . .'

'Only I always get *Surprise!* magazine on Fridays,' babbled Jessica, 'and today it says in "Stolen Secrets" that you had an argument about Caitlin with your ex-wife, and Caitlin's quite plain, really, isn't she? She doesn't look like you at all. And then it said Kathleen Lovell hasn't been seen since she visited you, so I wondered . . .'

She petered out in the face of the incredulous silence. Open mouth and insert both stiletto-shod feet.

'Mace, I did overhear, but I didn't tell anyone – no one at all!' I said urgently, putting my hand on his arm. 'It was obviously something she tossed out in the heat of the moment. Caitlin's yours.'

He sort of shrugged me off, like an insect. '*Surprise!* magazine? *Again?* What did I ever do to them to be victimised like this?'

'Didn't you know about it?' Jessica asked brightly. 'There was a picture of Kathleen Lovell – she's gorgeous, isn't she? – but I still think she's lucky marrying Rod Steigland. And a Christmas honeymoon on a Caribbean island, too!'

'I think you'd better get this gossip rag and show the man, now you've gone this far,' Father said, but Gloria had already fetched her own virgin copy and was thumbing through it.

Em, largely uninterested in the face of her other problems, had been having a muttered discussion with Anne from which I'd heard only odd snippets like: 'evicted from my own home' and 'end of the whole effing family' and 'stay to be treated like a servant' and 'bloody invader!'

This time, when Chris tried to take her hand, Em let him.

'Some Birthday Feast this turned out to be!' muttered Father bitterly.

The magazine article was quite short. Father removed it from Gloria's grasp and read it aloud.

'"An anonymous source"—'

'Not me!' I put in hastily.

'—"said dishy but notoriously bad-tempered actor Mace North had allegedly flown off the handle when ex-wife Kathleen Lovell told him he wasn't really the father . . . blah, blah blah . . . daughter Caitlin was still staying at his country retreat, but no one's seen Kathleen since . . . blah blah,"' Father said, editing ruthlessly. He tossed it aside. 'Load of poisonous rubbish.'

Mace looked up, his eyes dark and steely with anger, accusing me.

'If Charlie'd told anyone, it would have been us, Mace,' Anne said. 'And she didn't. Rhymers don't phone up effing gossip columns. Rhymers don't even *read* magazines with gossip columns in them.'

'I do,' Jessica said.

'You aren't a Rhymer.'

'Rhymers seem to be *writing* their own magazines,' Mace said nastily. 'Perhaps I merit a double-page spread of slime in there?'

'Now, now, Mace,' Father said. 'You should read some of the things they say about *me*!'

'Yes, but they're all true, Father,' I said. 'And this isn't.'

'It'll soon blow over. Where's your ex-wife gone, Mace?'

'No idea – she stormed off in a temper. Nearly ran me down. But wherever it is – and I assure you it isn't a shallow grave down in the woods – she'll turn up in a couple of weeks, for the wedding.'

'There you are then,' said Father, losing interest. 'Storm in a teacup.'

He didn't know how true that was.

Then he looked down at Kathleen's picture again and amended, absently: 'B cup.'

I looked at Mace's dark, angry face and wondered . . . and a shiver ran up my spine. I mean, he *sounded* civilised, but he certainly didn't look it, and he *had been* glaring at me a few minutes previously as though he'd like to get his hands around my throat.

'I think I read the leaves wrong,' Gloria muttered in my ear. 'And maybe the love philtre's not working. But everything's all right – no problem.'

'Can you give him the antidote tomorrow anyway?'

'Perhaps I better had.'

It was an oddly segmented party after that. Outwardly it ran its usual course, and after a short birthday speech Father pulled out a ring of Christmas-cracker proportions and rather sheepishly put it on Jessica's bony finger, to her unconcealed triumph.

After that, Anne excused herself on the grounds of fatigue and went to bed, and Em suddenly announced that she and Chris were going out for a little while. 'Chris is going to show me the vicarage.'

'Why? You pass it almost every day on your walks,' Father said, puzzled.

'Yes, but I don't pass *through* it,' Em said. 'Come on, Chris.'

'Don't you worry about nothing here, blossom,' Gloria

told her. 'Walter and me will tidy it away before we go home, and Charlie can help.'

Mace, who'd been perfecting the art of abstracted brooding, now pulled himself together enough to take his leave. 'Thank you for a lovely evening, Ran, and a delicious meal.'

'You won't get none of those when you're married, Ran,' Gloria pointed out.

'Of course I will. Why shouldn't I?' he said heartily. 'Things will just go on as before.'

So like a man.

'You can go out through the Summer Cottage, Mace,' I said, getting up. 'It will be quicker.' *And* give me another chance to try to persuade him that I really didn't grass on him.

'No, don't bother,' he said curtly. He didn't even glance at me. 'I need the fresh air.'

'Mace—'

But he was gone. And after all, why *should* he believe me – and why should I care? In a minute he would be turning the corner of the Parsonage and walking down the track, still thinking I was the sort of person who would do that sort of thing . . .

I got up, said quickly, 'Happy birthday, Father. Congrats, Jess – hope you're happy,' then shot out of the door, down the stairs, through the kitchen where the dogs slumbered by the stove, and then almost fell headlong down the dark stairwell to the Summer Cottage.

Without stopping I ran out onto the track, but Mace must have moved faster, for he was already ahead of me.

There was only one way to catch him: hitching up my skirts with both hands I cut straight across the rough, steep corner, losing my balance and falling headlong down the bank to land on the track at his feet.

There might have been more dramatic ways of getting his attention, but I can't think of any.

The ground was frozen hard, my cheek stung, and my ankle had twisted. It hurt; but then, so did Mace's hands gripping my arms and hauling me upright.

'You fool!' he exclaimed. 'You could have broken your stupid neck running over ground like that in the dark – and you must have known there was a drop down onto the track!' And he gave me a whiplash-injury-inducing shake, my feet dangling in mid-air like a rag doll's.

'I *did* hear what Kathleen said, but I really didn't tell anyone!' I gasped painfully. Then I gave a sudden galvanic shiver; well, I *was* out in December wearing a wisp of chiffon and not much else, being mildly roughed up by a large, bad-tempered man whose wife had disappeared under sinister circumstances.

He stilled and looked down at me, though it was hard to make out his expression in the moonlight. 'Who else could it have been?'

'How should I know who she's told? Perhaps she told them herself!'

Though he could, of course, be convinced she hadn't told anyone because he had after all buried her in a shallow grave in the valley . . .

I shivered again, and he said roughly: 'You're twice a fool: running after me like that when I'm in a rage, and in just a thin dress,' and pulled me inside his warm, downy coat.

'Could you put me down, do you think?' I suggested, struggling weakly. But when he did, my left ankle was too painful to stand on, so he scooped me back up again effortlessly like so much illicit loot, and strode off.

'I don't know what's the matter with me tonight!' he muttered. 'I *want* to be angry with you, but whenever I look at you, I just can't!'

'It's only Gloria's love philtre – it was in your sherry. You were supposed to fall for Jessica, but you looked at me instead. But don't worry – you can have the antidote tomorrow when she's brewed it.'

'You can't possibly really believe in love potions,' he said shortly. 'And you had some too.'

'Only a tiny sip – too little to matter. You drank most of it.'

'OK, so maybe she spiked the drinks with a few herbs, but . . .' He stopped, and looked down at me, his expression unfathomable in the moonlight. 'No,' he said firmly.

'It doesn't matter whether you believe in it or not – Gloria's spells usually work. Maybe all that rage cancelled it out? But what's important is that you believe me now, about my not telling anyone what Kathleen said.'

'I suppose I'll have to, since you nearly broke your neck in the effort to explain it to me.'

'Then do you think you could take me home?'

'No, we're nearly at my place and I want to see what you've done to yourself first.'

'It's all right – Gloria's probably still there, and she will clean my scratches and do something for my ankle. It's only twisted.'

'That does it – I'm not taking you back until she's gone home! And I thought *Em* was the one to watch.'

'Oh, Em just wanted you as a sacrifice.'

'A sacrifice? She was going to *kill* me?'

'Of course not, don't be silly. She just wanted your body, because you have a dark side and could help her get in touch with *her* darker powers. But actually, none of us wants her to try any black magic, because she does tend to throw herself into things so enthusiastically that there's no saying where it will end. So Gloria and I sort of spiked her drink with the love philtre, too, while she was talking to Chris.'

'Does that make Chris the sacrifice?'

'Willing victim, but not to the black arts, which is a relief.'

'So why did *I* get the potion? And why was I supposed to fall for Jessica? No, don't tell me – to get her away from your father and Upvale?'

'Probably. I didn't know Gloria was going to do it until the last minute, so I'm not sure. Or maybe it was because she got the mistaken impression that you were interested in me, and she doesn't like it.'

'Any particular reason?'

'Something in the teacup, mostly.'

'The teacup?'

'The leaves, but she won't tell me what. I expect she thinks you will use me and cast me aside, or something – after all, she's been reading *Surprise!* for years. I've told her I'm not interested.'

'Thanks.'

'Well, it's so silly of her to imagine *you* would be, isn't it? I'm no pretty young girl, and there must be plenty of those interested in you.'

'Oh, yes, I'm a babe magnet, all right,' he said shortly, kicking the cottage door open and walking in with me. 'Fame and money are all it takes.'

I looked up at his distinctive face and said involuntarily, '*And* the rest!' and he grinned, and kissed me like the season for it was about to run out.

After that, I don't know what got into me.

All right, I do – and it wasn't just the love philtre. My secret fantasies about dragging Steve the gardener into the bushes had, at some point, been entirely replaced with ones involving Mace: I just wasn't expecting them actually to *happen*.

Caution prevailed for – oh, maybe three seconds, give or take one or two – and then was tossed away. I mean, so maybe he *had* done away with Kathleen, but did it seem important at that juncture? No.

Or perhaps it was Gloria's potion working in both of us – or all that champagne?

Who cared? It was now or never . . .

'Now!' I said, an abandoned nymph indeed.

Little did Felicity Hake-Hackett know on which illustrious bedroom floor her dress would end up. How much she would have loved to be the one from whose body it was stripped by impatient fingers; in silence. He's a great one for deep, meaningful silences.

Later, drowsily, I let him clean up the mark on my face and convey me (boneless and almost entirely witless, I fear) back to the Summer Cottage.

He deposited me safely in my own bed, kissed me long and hard with one hand planted on either side of my head, and took himself off.

Intense isn't in it.

A note from Gloria was pinned to the side of the bedside cabinet: 'Drink contents of glass the moment you return, to avert evil consequences.'

The contents of the said glass looked like they'd been dredged hastily from the bottom of the nearest cesspool, and the only evil consequence would occur about a second after I drank it.

The other sort of consequences I haven't had for years; I'm a barren vessel, except for the paintings . . . and Flossie.

I *intended* to go and find Flossie, but I couldn't even raise the energy to switch the lamp off before great waves of sleep completely submerged me.

Chapter 18: Absolution

It was very late when I woke the next day, strangely tired, aching and disorientated.

For a few heart-stopping moments I couldn't remember where I was, then my eye fell on the glass of disgusting liquid on my bedside table, now separated out into a layer of sludge topped by clear green, and it all came back to me in Glorious Technicolor, along with my sanity.

Perhaps my vocation in life was to become a hermit and never leave the house, or speak to anyone outside my family, ever again.

Especially Mace.

Not that *he'd* actually said very much last night, as I recalled, after that first kiss – but his actions had spoken volumes (the sort that should be behind locked bookcase doors).

But it was no good; I couldn't hide for ever. Besides, I was feeling guilty about abandoning Flossie, of whom there was no sign.

After a shower I felt a bit better, and apart from a graze on my cheek, a few promising bruises, and a tender left ankle, I didn't look too bad either.

And at least it was a Saturday, so I didn't have to go down and fetch Caitlin, for how would I ever face Mace again after last night's goings-on?

I mean, I was sure they were entirely due to Gloria's potion, probably helped along in Mace's case by enforced abstinence due to being marooned in the country with Caitlin – and there were not many nubile young starlets in Upvale.

I supposed handsome, rich actor/playwrights had casual sex all the time usually, though, so he would not think any more about it once he'd had the antidote.

I had no excuse for my actions (except for the enforced abstinence bit) because I only had one tiny sip. It was just irresistible lust and champagne.

However, had I known how good sex could be, Fidelity wouldn't have been my middle name all those years. Either Matt was not very good at it, or Mace was a master of the art. I suspected the latter.

The previous night had been wonderful (in a 'my God! Did I *really* do that?' sort of way) but it mustn't happen again. Gloria would just have to find a way of giving Mace the antidote to the love philtre *fast*.

I dressed in jeans and jumper and went upstairs, where I found Flossie curled up with Frost; quite sweet, really. I decided that was where she'd spent the night, so we were both loose women.

Em was sitting quietly at the table – the whole house seemed strangely silent – and the only place still set for breakfast was mine.

Unusually, she wasn't doing anything, just dreaming over a cup of coffee.

'Well, madam!' Gloria said, appearing in the doorway and

surveying me with her hands on her hips. 'Here's another one who was up to goodness-knows-what last night. It's to be hoped you drank what I left for you, because you need some powerful magic to oppose the likes of that one!'

'It's all right, Gloria,' I assured her, although, I feared, I had poured the disgusting stuff down the loo. 'I – just went after Mace to try and explain that I hadn't told anyone about what his wife said when they quarrelled.'

'Takes a long time, that sort of explanation,' she said drily. 'You don't fool me – I know what I saw in the teacups!'

'Well, whatever you saw, it wasn't entirely Mace's fault. You shouldn't have given him the potion.'

'It would have worked fine except for your meddling.'

'I'm sure I've lost my powers,' Em sighed. 'When I look inwards I can't see anything except Chris's face. Isn't that odd?'

Yes, that was pretty odd. I tried closing my eyes for a moment, and immediately saw a dark, strongly boned face as clearly as if he was— I snapped them open again, to find Gloria looking thoughtfully at me.

'I thought sex was supposed to enhance your powers, Em?' I said hastily.

'Only if she did it as part of the rites,' Gloria said. 'In a place of ancient power. Not just flinging herself headlong between the sheets with a man of the Church.'

'I didn't! We just talked – all night,' protested Em. 'Gloria, you didn't put anything in *my* drink, did you?'

'Of course not, my blossom,' Gloria assured her. 'It must be love.'

'White witchcraft and the Church are not incompatible,' Em said dreamily.

'Obviously.'

'Traditionally, the one has been absorbed into the other. Chris and I think our beliefs can co-exist within a relationship of mutual respect.'

Gloria and I stared at her.

'Have you got one of those, then?'

'Yes, but I'll have to make allowances for the Dickens, and he'll have to make allowances for the ways of Wicca.'

'Are his intentions honourable, though, Em?' I asked.

'I effing well hope not!' she said, sounding more like herself.

'You could get married,' I suggested, examining the covers on the hotplate and heaping a plate with slightly dried bacon, egg and mushrooms. Suddenly I felt absolutely ravenous.

'I don't know – we'd have to find a form of service we could both be happy with. But Chris says vicars aren't supposed to live with someone unless they're married to them.'

'You're going to live with him?'

'I don't know,' she said, going off into another trance.

'I'll make you some fresh toast,' Gloria said to me. 'And some coffee – or maybe a cup of tea?'

'I don't feel like tea,' I protested, but that's what I got, and she stood over me until I drank it, too, then sat down and spent a long time examining the bottom of the cup.

She sighed heavily.

'What?' I said, eating buttered toast.

'It's still there. I knew he was trouble, but what will be, will be. And it might not have been the potion, not if he already loved you,' she mused.

'But he doesn't love me, and I don't love him – as will

become quite clear when you give him the antidote. Last night didn't mean anything to either of us. For me, it was just a quick last fling before I become a middle-aged artistic recluse.'

'Out with a bang?' Em suggested helpfully, becoming more alert.

'Thank you, Em. And . . . do you think you could take Caitlin back to Mace later?' I asked cravenly. 'Maybe with the antidote, if it's ready?'

It would be easier to treat the whole thing as if it hadn't happened if a bit of time elapsed before I had to come face to face with him.

'Only I promised Vaddie I'd take my new pictures over to the gallery today.'

'You needn't worry about Mace being there,' Gloria said, seeing through this. 'He's gone, and Caitlin with him.'

'Gone? What do you mean, *gone*?' I asked, stunned.

'To London,' Gloria said. 'That's the sort of man he is, even with a full dose of love philtre inside him! Chancy.'

'Mace collected Caitlin early this morning,' Em explained. 'He phoned first . . . I'd just got back. Chris walked me home,' she added, going into another trance.

'Em!' I said sharply.

'Oh, yes – he said he was coming to get Caitlin, and take her to his mother's house in London, because the press had started phoning him at dawn, and they'd be turning up on his doorstep in droves any minute.'

'Didn't he leave any message?'

'He said to tell you he had to go away for a few days, and he'd let you know when they were back.'

'Kind of him. Was that it?'

'Yes, except that he asked to speak to Jessie. What *was* all that last night about Caitlin? Isn't she his?'

'Of course she is!'

And if he could ask to speak to Jessica, he could have asked for me – if he'd wanted to.

'There you are then, Gloria. Love clearly doesn't come into it. He's probably forgotten last night already.'

Em looked at me severely. 'I hope you took precautions.'

'Em, I haven't conceived for years and I'm the shady side of forty; I'm barren.'

'And I left her a brew last night, in case,' Gloria added. 'So that should be that . . . if she doesn't do it again.'

'I've no intention of doing it again!'

'Yes, but it won't stop her getting Aids or anything, will it?' pointed out Em helpfully.

'Mace has *not* got Aids!' I said crossly.

'He's put it about a bit, according to *Surprise!*' Gloria said.

'I'm not convinced you can believe anything it says in there, and I'm sure Mace isn't the sort of man who would have . . . who would have put me in danger of that kind!'

And I was, too: instincts of a barbarian, manners of a gentleman.

Gloria looked doubtfully back into the teacup. 'I'd better get that anti-love potion brewed – he's coming back soon.'

'I really don't care, though I'll miss Caitlin.'

'Perhaps he's gone to find what happened to Kathleen?' suggested Em. 'And did I tell you that Father and the Treacle Tart went with him? It was an impulse, but Father's delivering his manuscript to his agent, and Jessica wanted to shop.'

'But the girls . . .? It's term time.'

'Anne offered to look after them. She's taken them out somewhere.'

'Let's hope she remembers to bring them back, then!'

'They're not bad girls,' Gloria said.

'No, I'm getting quite fond of them,' I admitted. 'And Caitlin.'

'Well, I'm not getting fond of Jessica,' Em said firmly. 'One of us will have to go.'

'Yes, but Father's going to *marry* her, Em, so it looks like she's here to stay. We might *all* have to go – she won't want the whole family round her neck, too.'

Gloria had been out of the room, but now returned and began to smear a cold green paste over my grazed cheek.

'Gloria, I can't go over to York looking as if I'm daubed for battle. Vaddie's expecting *me*, not the Last of the Mohicans.'

'It'll soak in. And you were limping – you can't drive like that. Better stay home, and let me put a compress on that ankle. What did he do to my little chicken?'

Her expression boded ill for Mace, should he ever return. I said hastily, 'He didn't hurt me. I fell down – and it won't bother me, driving. Do you want to come, Em?'

'No. I'm taking Chris up to the standing stones on Blackdog Moor. He hasn't been there yet and it's a powerful spot . . . I'll take a flask of something hot, and a few sandwiches.'

Thank goodness it's too cold for anything *else* on the

stones besides a chilly picnic, because I don't think Chris has the power to resist Em.

'Where's Bran?'

'Finishing off his manuscript before it goes off to be typed up by some poor creature at the university.'

'Oh, well, I'll take Flossie, then. She will enjoy the drive.'

But even Flossie declined to come with me, and retired downstairs to her igloo. Perhaps she is miffed that I left her in the Parsonage kitchen all night.

Skint Old Motoring Tips

The car is not a household god, it is a motorised biscuit tin, and need have only the same attributes: dry, roomy and convenient.

For once, it was actually quite good to be driving over the moors to somewhere away from Upvale.

A day away would let me push my confused feelings about Mace behind a locked door. It would also give me a chance to turn over in my mind what was likely to happen if Father did indeed marry Jessica.

From what he had said about nothing changing it was clear he hadn't thought it through. The day he married Jessica, it would be like shaking a kaleidoscope: the parts would be the same, only they'd all be in entirely different places in relation to each other, some not even touching.

Nothing was *ever* going to be the same again.

Vaddie fell on my paintings with cries of great joy. She loved what by now had become the *Jessie Down the Well* series, and when I told her that the first one would be on the cover of *Skint Old Northern Woman* she ordered a personal copy in advance, and said she'd like a whole stack to put on the desk, sale or return, under the actual picture featured.

I'd decided not to sell that one, but give it to Father and Jess as a wedding present, assuming she actually managed to pull it off.

Vaddie said I looked totally different, and actually my change of hair colour and clothes made me look years younger and twice as pretty, which was kind of her. She had a cheque for me from the last lot of paintings she had sold – she didn't part with money unless you went to her in person and demanded it – and after that I went out and bought myself a turquoise cashmere tunic sweater and then, as an afterthought, a rose-pink and silver nightie and dressing gown.

Definitely Pisces and slithery, although I wasn't sure about the rose colour.

I popped in to see Miss Grinch on my way home, and told her about Angie, and my melon catharsis, and in return she told me all about the goings-on of the new people who'd moved into my house.

They sounded like they were providing a lot more enter-tainment for her than I ever did.

During my absence, Gloria had found a chewed document addressed to me in Frost's basket, which proved to be the final bit of my divorce: I had absolution.

I didn't know how long it had been in the basket, and nor did I really care.

I had absolution already.

Divorced Skint Old Northern Woman?

The Should I?/Shouldn't I? Dilemma: Some Common Questions Answered

1) Will I be lonely?
Answer: Yes, but probably not any lonelier than you were before the divorce. Buy a dog.
2) I'll never be able to understand the paperwork, the tax returns, the bills . . .
Answer: The running costs of an accountant are much less than a husband.
3) Will my married friends still invite me round?
Answer: No.
4) Will all my 'happily' married friends' husbands suddenly make passes at me?
Answer: Yes. You now have 'Divorced and Desperate For It' stamped across your forehead in a special ink only they can read.
5) Will I ever have sex again?
Answer: Only if desperate. (See question 4.)
6) Will I ever find a new partner?
Answer: What are you, some kind of masochist?

Chapter 19: Nuts

We settled down to quite a pleasant and normal week before Father and Jessica returned (by train). Pleasant and normal by Rhymer family standards, that is.

Perhaps searching the woodland nearest to Mace's cottage for signs of freshly dug earth *was* a trifle on the bizarre side, but I only truly accepted this when I bumped into Anne and the twins doing the same thing (except the girls thought they were looking for acorns).

Besides, we were quite high up there, and the ground had been frozen underneath ever since I'd moved home, even when the surface seems to have thawed out. (Just think of Upvale and the surrounding Blackdog Moor as being in a sort of snow dome, with its own ecosystem. Hence the early snow when other people were having Indian summers.)

I'd been spending almost all the daylight hours painting minute barbarian warriors on horseback being sucked into vortexes of savage greenery, like warped Persian miniatures.

It was very enjoyable. And no, I was not going to think about the significance at all.

Anne seemed happy looking after the girls, although Em

took over one day when Red showed up in order to abase himself.

Once he'd grovelled enough they vanished upstairs. Anne was saying as they went, 'So what's the matter with sodding war wounds? Seen them before, haven't you? One battle's the same as any other bloody battle, isn't it?'

I assume their *entente* was *cordiale*, since although he would now be away until the New Year on an assignment, they were to resume their semi-attached state of shared flat-dwelling when Anne was back in London after Christmas. Her treatment was to finish just before, so she would be fully revitalised after one of our family celebrations.

It could be the last, for everything was bound to change when or if Father married Jessica. The kaleidoscope would shift permanently and we would all be cast to the edges.

The family circle had expanded already to include Chris – since the picnic at the standing stones he and Em seemed mysteriously to have become one entity.

Indeed, they were spending so much time together, it made me wonder if he ever did any vicar stuff at all – not that I knew what they were supposed to do anyway.

Still, Em's powers seemed suddenly to have returned to her with a vengeance: she was very practical when I told her about my dark thoughts regarding bodies in woods. Having borrowed from Gloria a copy of *Surprise!* containing a photo of Kathleen Lovell, she called in Freya, Xanthe and Lilith and sat down to discover the actress's whereabouts.

The unanimous result was that Kathleen was certainly alive, somewhere far away from Upvale. And they all felt that Kathleen was . . . well . . . *dwindling* was the way they put it.

I hoped she had not succumbed to some wasting disease? But no – surely she would have told someone?

It was certainly a relief not to have to look for the body any more.

Lilith, Freya and Xanthe seemed quite resigned to Em not joining their coven after all. I didn't think it would affect their friendship.

And speaking of friendship, Freya had managed to strike up an acquaintanceship with Angie, and invited her to meet the other two at the pub tonight to, as she put it: 'direct her out of her present circle of hate, and into a more profitable frame of mind that will take her orbit elsewhere.'

Mars would be good.

On the Tuesday Branwell finished his book – or, at least, stopped scribbling and took to staring at the pile of manuscript as though he couldn't remember how it got there.

He was extremely averse to the idea of its being taken away so we could post it off to the poor woman at the university whose job it was to type up this scrawl. In the end Em had to lure him away to visit a second-hand bookshop, while I had the whole thing photocopied and returned to his room before he realised it had been removed. Then I sent the copy off; it was clearer and darker than the original, anyway.

Of course, when we got the computer printout back he'd scribble all over it again, but the end was in sight.

When I returned from the post office I found Walter arranging a plant delivery in the veranda. There were six coconut palms, one almost touching the roof.

I knew only one person who could afford this kind of

extravagant gesture – whatever sort of gesture it was – for there was no message, unless it was something to do with nuts.

I supposed it could just be a final farewell from Matt, in lieu of ducks? But I didn't think he had the imagination, and anyway, he appeared to have forgotten about me entirely.

So it must be Mace. But what did it mean? Nuts to me? You're nuts? What's got a coconut in every bite?

Friday's copy of *Surprise!* contained what could only be construed as an abject apology and retraction about their alleged Mace and Kathleen item. Of course, when you have only hinted at something it's very hard to hint that really your *first* hint wasn't true, but they did their best.

I expected that having Invasion of the Kalmucks in their office did wonders for their powers of retraction.

Father was abstracted when he and Jess got home. I feared inspiration for the next character assassination had struck, although we didn't know yet who the victim was to be.

I wondered if perhaps he would surprise us by proving that Dorothy actually wrote all Wordsworth's poetry for him, in a literary about-turn; but then again, maybe not.

Jessica was, I think, miffed that the girls hadn't missed her more, though they were delighted to see her back, and quite polite about the gifts she'd brought them.

They had had a busy week, and we hadn't found them any trouble at all: Anne did the school run and subverted them, they'd painted with me, and learned to cook with Em, been for dug-earth-spotting expeditions in the woods, played with the dogs, learned to whittle with Walter and helped Gloria coat every wooden surface in the house with home-made beeswax and turpentine polish.

Clo was showing an interest in photography, and she and Anne had set up a darkroom in an unused back pantry.

They were perfectly happy, just as we all had been, growing up here in Upvale. We're adults long enough – why start too soon?

Indeed, why start at all?

Jessica found solace in having increased the contents of her wardrobe and shoe collection by about half, which, while lifting her spirits, must have stretched Father's credit card until it bulged at the seams.

> Sit in the sun and
> hold out your hand.
> How heavy the world feels
> in your palm.
> From 'Words from the
> Spirit' by Serafina Shane

Jessica was trying to assert herself around the house already, the engagement ring flashing on her bony finger.

Of course it didn't *get* her anywhere, but it was a sign of what was to come.

Walter was spending much time in the small sitting room constructing Christmas presents, and Gloria continually thrust cups of tea into people's hands, especially mine, and fussed after me so much that I'd even taken to shutting the door at the bottom of the Summer Cottage stairs and ramming a chair under the handle (only I was continually having to remove it to let Flossie in and out).

There was still no word from Mace, unless you counted the nuts, so it looked like the potion had worn off all on its own.

'The vicar just asked me for Em's hand,' Father said on the Saturday, wandering into the kitchen and pouring himself a cup of coffee. 'I told him he could have any of her he fancied.'

'He already has,' muttered Gloria.

'What?'

'You didn't really say that, Father, did you?' I asked.

'Of course he bloody did,' Anne said. 'He hasn't realised the implications yet – too full of himself.'

'What implications?' Father looked surprised. 'Em won't get married. She's a natural spinster.'

'Thank you,' Em said. 'But as so often in your life, you're entirely wrong.'

'But are you *really* going to marry the vicar?' Jessica exclaimed.

'I might. We've worked out a reasonable compromise about the service. His bishop probably won't like it, but everyone round here will be fine about it. Anyway, Chris says he doesn't want to rise in the Church, he just wants to stay here, with me.'

'Implications?' muttered Father, looking slightly dazed. 'And what do you mean, stay *here*: is he moving in?'

I thought he'd pretty well done that already. I was surprised Father hadn't noticed.

'No, I meant staying in Upvale. He's got the Vicarage – I could live there.'

'Well, I think you're doing the right thing,' Jessica said warmly. 'When are you going?'

Em gave her a look. 'It's not decided yet, but after Christmas – so you can keep your nose out of everything until after that, since it'll be the last real Rhymer family Christmas. Then the place is all yours.'

'What do you mean, all yours?' Father said, finally getting to grips with the situation. 'You *can't* go, Em! I mean, who's going to run the house, and cook and . . .?' He stopped and stared at her.

'Your *wife*, of course, silly!' Jessica said brightly. 'With Gloria's help, of course – it *is* a very big house for just us. But I expect we could shut some of it off, and install central heating, and showers, and a microwave, and—'

'How can we shut it off? We use it all,' Father said, looking bewildered. He dislikes change nearly as much as Bran.

'She means after Em leaves, and Anne doesn't come home any more, or Bran – though it might be difficult to stop him – and I vacate the Summer Cottage.'

'But why would you all want to do that?'

'Wouldn't be home any more, would it?' Anne said.

'The Vicarage bungalow isn't very big, but Chris says we can squeeze everyone in, and my family is his family,' Em said.

'Tell that to Bran,' I said. 'He'll just turn up in his old room whatever you do.'

'Me and Walter go where the girls go,' Gloria said firmly. 'Big changes are coming: I saw it in the teacups. It's started, and nothing can stop it now.'

'Oh, is that all, Gloria? You had me worried there,' I said.

'That was just the general overview,' she said grimly. 'And you're going to need me the most, Charlie; mark my words. Troubles and changes! And it's all since that Mace North came to Upvale.'

'That's quite unfair, Gloria,' I said. 'You can't blame everything on Mace.'

'Yes I can – I knew he was trouble. He's the dark agent of change!'

'What, like a catalyst?' Anne asked, interested.

'I thought he was an *actor*,' Jessica said, bewildered. 'Ran, isn't he an actor? Only he writes plays now, too?'

'Shut up, Jess, don't let them sidetrack me,' Father said. 'Of course the family stays here. If Em does want to go – well, that's her own funeral.'

'Wedding,' Em said.

'Jess will keep things going here just the same. There's no need for anything to change.'

Not quite: I thought a healthy, fat-free diet would pall on Father quite soon, but perhaps the girls would take over the cooking when they'd learned a bit more from Em? After all, she'd started running the household when she was younger than they were.

Jessica was looking alarmed and thoughtful, but Father, having comfortably decided that things could go on as before, minus Em (the linchpin of the whole house), simply put it out of his head.

Bran hadn't taken it into his head in the first place. Em was deep in thought – probably thinking about the practicalities of cooking in the Vicarage kitchen – and Anne was looking like she was starting to miss her nice, spartan London flat.

'Bloody battlefields!' she said, getting up and walking out; but at least she had a place of her own to go to. I'd sort of got settled in my cottage, but I was sure Jessica would want us all to go.

Father, who'd been calmly eating his breakfast now he thought he'd settled things to his satisfaction, looked up. 'I've invited Mace and Caitlin for Christmas dinner,' he announced.

'But what about Caitlin's mother?' I began.

'Her mother's going to be on honeymoon in the Caribbean until the New Year, and Mace said his own mother doesn't celebrate Christmas – she always spends it quietly in a hotel in Bath.'

Bran looked at him and beamed. 'Christmas?' he said happily. 'Brandy snaps? Snapdragon?'

'Of course, Bran,' Emily said. 'Don't we always?'

'Mouse Hunt? Hunt the Thimble?'

'Yes, this time, but it will be the last Christmas as we know it.'

'Oh, come on, Em!' Father protested. 'Where else would you all go? I don't believe you really mean to marry the vicar!'

'I do.'

'You wouldn't be happy and neither would he. It would finish his career.'

'He doesn't want a career. He wants to stay here, in Upvale with me.'

'Just as well – he won't have any option, once word gets round about who he's marrying. I can't think what's got into you.'

'You shouldn't go inviting single men round to the house, then, you great lummox,' Gloria told him shortly. 'Especially men like that actor. Christmas dinner indeed! He's trouble and change. I saw it in the tea leaves – and more!'

'Speaking of Mace, I nearly forgot,' Father said, feeling in his pocket and producing a slightly mangled envelope. 'He sent you this.'

I took it eagerly, but then he added, 'It's your wages for looking after Caitlin.'

It was, too – nothing else. 'Was there any message?'

'No. He said he'd already sent you one.'

'Caitlin looks forward to seeing you again soon. She's staying with her granny until after the wedding, then Mace is bringing her home,' Jessica said kindly. 'I expect you'll see her then.'

'I don't want his money,' I said shortly, stuffing it back into the envelope. Father looked faintly surprised.

Jessica said: 'Is it because he thought you'd told *Surprise!* magazine about stuff? That's all sorted out – he's not angry with you any more.'

'Big of him. And I don't *need* his money. I'm selling paintings again.'

'*And* we've got advance orders for *Skint Old Northern Woman*,' Em said.

'Told everyone I know to buy one,' Anne agreed. 'And Em's book, too. Christmas reading. Presents.'

'Not using *my* telephone, I hope,' Father said. 'Some of your friends live on the other side of the world.'

'Bloody skinflint.'

'Advance copies should be here next week,' Em said.

'Good. Drum up some more sales.'

Father nodded at the envelope: 'You did the job, didn't you? Take the money, and if you don't want to do any more, tell the man when he gets back tomorrow.'

'Tomorrow?' I echoed, looking down at the envelope and

feeling like I'd been paid off. Was I worth the money? He'd probably had better, but maybe not so easily.

I decided I wasn't keeping it.

Skint Old Beauty, No. 2: Hair Today

More bristles than a toothbrush? Finding a solution to the moustache problem.

1) *Professional treatment at a salon – but if you can afford that, what are you reading this magazine for?*
2) *Plucking. This is excruciating, gives you a pink upper lip, and the hair doesn't even give up and stop growing back, like eyebrows do.*
3) *Shaving: not unless you are sure you never want to kiss anyone ever again.*
4) *Cream. This one has a built-in Catch-22: if you leave it on long enough to work, you get a rash.*
5) *Bleach. This gives you a white bristly moustache and also, sometimes, an interesting rash. (See also no. 4.)*
6) *Wax strips. This leaves hair and wax behind on your upper lip, thus giving a whole new meaning to the phrase 'stiff upper lip'. However, excess wax can sometimes be used to shape the hair into a pleasing handlebar moustache.*

Chapter 20: Returns

I spent most of Sunday painting more small, mounted infidels in the veranda.

Just as the light was starting to fade in the afternoon, Mace's low, dark car slid past down the track, with lowdown dark Mace in it.

It didn't stop.

Not that I expected it to, of course – and I *wasn't* watching out for it. It was simply a coincidence that Flossie gave the one sharp yap that was her summons for me to open the door and let her out just as he went by.

Three seconds later the door opened again, and Em walked in, followed by Chris, tastefully (and tastily) attired in motorcycling leathers and dog collar.

'Close the door, you're letting all the warm air out,' I said, putting the brush down again. It really was too dark now to see tiny barbarians . . . or even whopping great big ones.

'Mace is back,' Em informed me, patting Flossie, who'd followed her in.

'I know.'

'Hi, Charlie,' Chris said. 'Hope we're not interrupting you?'

'Not at all,' I said politely. I might block the door down

from the Parsonage kitchen to keep Gloria out, but it didn't stop anyone walking in the front. My house was like a railway station.

'Did Mace call in on the way down?' Em asked.

'No.'

'The bastard!'

'Why? Were you expecting him?' asked Chris, looking puzzled.

'No!' we said in unison, and he recoiled slightly.

'Chris's bishop wants to see him,' Em told me.

'Perhaps he's heard about the engagement, and is going to congratulate you?'

'Someone must have told him about us, but I'm not too sure about the congratulation bit.'

'I expect he'll get used to the idea,' Chris said calmly. 'He'll have to.'

'We've been to buy a betrothal ring – look,' Em said, flashing a large, strangely set yellow stone in my face.

'Lovely,' I said. 'Where did you get it?'

'Chris had it made for me – a friend of his near Huddersfield has a jewellery workshop.'

'Ah, Huddersfield – cultural Mecca of West Yorkshire,' I said nostalgically. It was ages since I'd been over there.

'I'd better go and start dinner,' Em said. 'See you later. Come on, Chris.'

Flossie followed them out and upstairs. She clearly saw the Parsonage kitchen as her spiritual home now, to the point where I was thinking of moving her igloo up there.

Gloria seized her chance to descend with tea and dire warnings, before leaving by the veranda door, her basket over her arm.

I assumed she was going home early, and went up to see if Walter was still about.

Chris was standing by the Aga stirring something and reading *Hard Times*, so even love hadn't yet cured him of Dickens.

Walter was still there, so I asked him to fix a bolt on the door at the bottom of my staircase.

He didn't ask me why, just did it, regarding his neat handiwork at the end with a pleased smile, while passing a pink hand over his shiny pate.

Apart from Father's study, and Anne's bedroom, Rhymers didn't lock doors on each other, but I wanted to be able to if I felt the need . . . Or *didn't* feel the need for yet another cup of tea.

Before I got the chance to use it, Anne and Em trooped past me, saying they were going out for some fresh air before dinner, which I thought was very odd, especially since they didn't ask me to go, too. Em said Chris was watching dinner, so not to worry.

'It's cold out there,' Walter said, gazing after them worriedly. 'Especially without a hat.'

'Yes, but they've both got lots of hair,' I pointed out.

After that we went upstairs and he showed me the walking sticks he'd been carving for the little girls for Christmas – including one for Caitlin, which was a nice thought. Then he hid them away in the cupboard by the fireplace and locked the door, before putting the key under his wig on the stand.

There were shavings neatly brushed into a little heap on the carpet; but then, there usually were shavings around Walter.

Em and Anne couldn't have had much of a walk, for they

were already back. Em was talking in a low voice to Chris by the stove, while stirring something into the big cauldron (probably the Dickens). Anne was sitting at the table with a glass of whisky in her hand, marking possible Christmas gifts in *Extreme Terrain: The Catalogue*.

'Drink?' she asked.

'No, thanks – I'm just going back down to stretch another canvas for tomorrow.'

'Dinner in one hour,' Em said over her shoulder.

'Where are the girls? It's very quiet.'

'Out at a friend's. So's Jess. Bran's doing a jigsaw puzzle in his room, and Father's in the study, snoring.'

I went down, resolutely picked up the envelope of money, put on my coat, and set off down the track in the dusk to throw it back in Mace's face – metaphorically speaking.

Or maybe even literally speaking, for I was still angry enough: laid off and paid off.

By the time I got there, though, I'd remembered Mace's scarier aspects, and my nerve for a confrontation had pretty well ebbed away, though the money still lay like lead on my heart.

So I sat down on his doorstep and scribbled on the envelope with a stub of pencil I found in my pocket: 'I don't *want* your money . . .'

I couldn't think of anything else to say, since that pretty well summed it up, so I quietly lifted the flap of the letter box and slid the envelope through the rectangle of yellow light.

As I straightened up, the door swung suddenly and silently open. Backlit in the doorframe stood Mace like the Demon King, the envelope in his hand.

'Oh no, you don't!' he said, and, reaching out a long arm, yanked me inside and closed the door.

Still gripping me with one hand he glanced down at the envelope. 'Terse,' he said. 'Admirably to the point. But why not?'

'I – just don't,' I said lamely.

'Why? I'm not paying you off for services rendered, if that's what you think,' he said sardonically. 'I just owed you your wages for looking after Caitlin, and I thought you might need them.'

'Well, I don't. I'm selling paintings again, now I'm over Dead Greg.'

'Is it because I didn't write?' he said, gazing at me, brows knitted. 'But I *did* send you a message. Didn't you get it?'

His beautiful mouth quirked up at the corners.

'The coconut trees?'

'Of course.'

'To say what, exactly, Mace? Nuts to you?'

'No, to say I'm nutty *about* you. Isn't it evident?'

'No, it isn't. I think my first interpretation was right – it was a "thank you and goodbye" present: but you needn't have bothered. I don't think Gloria really needs to bother with the potion she made for you now, either,' I added.

He frowned. 'I don't know what you think you're talking about.'

'The other night – you don't need to feel guilty about it, it was just the love philtre. But I'm sure the effects have worn off now, so we need never mention the whole unfortunate episode again.'

'Guilty? Why should I feel *guilty*? And I told you – I don't believe in magic potions, or Sabrina the Teenage Witch, or the Tooth Fairy, or—'

'You don't *have* to believe in them, they work anyway. And just look at me. *I* only had one sip and I did something totally out of character.'

'I'm glad to hear it.'

'What, that I only had one sip?'

'No, that you don't jump into bed with every passing man.'

'Oh? Well . . .' I looked at him uncertainly. 'You may not believe in it, but perhaps you ought to have the antidote, just in case?'

'Have *you* had it?'

'No – I didn't tell Gloria I'd had any love philtre in the first place and, anyway, it was just a temporary blip in my sanity. It's worn off.'

'Has it? So, let me get it straight: *you* only slept with *me* because Gloria'd spiked the sherry with a bunch of herbs picked naked by the light of the full moon?'

'Something like that,' I agreed. 'But not naked; she'd catch her death.'

'Why do I not feel too concerned about that?' he asked himself aloud.

'I love Gloria! She's been like a mother to me.'

'I think we have a different understanding of the word "mother",' he said wryly. 'So you believe that *I* only slept with *you* because I'd had a mega-dose of the brew? And you only had a tiny bit, so it's worn off: but if I still fancy you, mine hasn't? Right?'

'Er – yes.' I found his expression very disquieting . . . And the way he was standing so close to me, looking down thoughtfully, even more disturbing.

'So, darling, does that explain why the bottle of whisky your father just sent me, delivered with suspicious cheerfulness by your Gloria, had its seal broken? I thought maybe she'd just had a swig and topped it up with water.'

'Gloria wouldn't do that!' I said indignantly. 'She can help herself to any drink she wants, she doesn't have to sneak it.'

'Including your father's single malt?'

'Yes, of course,' I said, astonished. 'But if Gloria was nice to you – and she brought the whisky down herself . . .'

'As a thank-you for giving Ran and Jessica a lift to London. Mind you, I could have done with it before I set *out* for London, to dull the sound of Jessica's non-stop twittering.'

'Her voice is a bit high-pitched,' I agreed. 'But you're right about Gloria – she must have wanted to give you the anti-love philtre she's been brewing as soon as possible. It won't do you any harm.'

'All's well that ends well?' he said sardonically. 'So, I drink the whisky and what? I think you're an absolute dog, and never look at you again?'

'Yes,' I said coldly.

'But how do I know it isn't some insidious poison that will send me white-haired and raving?'

'Because she wouldn't do anything like that,' I said, with more conviction than I actually felt, because there *were* situations where I was pretty sure Gloria would . . . but I was certain this wasn't one of them. 'You'd better drink it.'

'I already have, and so have your sisters. And if it's so harmless, you can prove it by having some too.'

'What – Anne and Em? *When*?'

'Just after Gloria left; that's why I haven't been up to see you yet. My visitors have been arriving in shifts since I got home. Here,' he added, handing me a tumbler of neat whisky.

'A likely story,' I said coldly, and defiantly drank the contents of the glass. 'And why would Anne and Em visit you?'

'Em said she was seeing things clearly now, and she felt Gloria was putting the wrong interpretation on the leaves. She stared at me a long time, but she didn't say much.'

'Strangely enough, her powers have increased since she fell in love with Chris. Did Anne say anything?'

'Not a lot, just implied that she'd break every bone in my body if I hurt you in any way. But I told her that was the last thing I wanted to do – and then we all had some whisky.'

'You all had it? I hope Em . . .' I thought about it. 'No, it won't affect her, because she was falling in love with Chris before she drank the love philtre, so she won't fall out of love with him now. It just sort of hastened things on. And Anne didn't have any in the first place, so it won't affect her, either. But you—' I broke off and stared at him. 'What are you doing?'

'Pouring the rest of it down the sink.'

'But what a waste of good whisky!'

'I like to know exactly what I'm drinking,' he said shortly, tossing the empty bottle into the rubbish bin. 'Right, that's that. So now I'm just my usual self, and you're *your* usual, highly irritating, self, and we start again?' He raised an eyebrow quizzically.

'Yes. Only I'm not going to look after Caitlin,' I said, edging towards the door.

'I don't see why, now you're not afraid I'm going to jump on you. Though of course, there's no guarantee that the real, untampered-with Mace might not want to jump on you anyway. And Caitlin's going to miss you.'

'I'll miss her, too – but I expect she'll be coming up to see the twins, won't she? We're bound to see each other then.'

'Charlie – I'm sorry I suspected you of having told everyone what Kathleen said about Caitlin,' he said unexpectedly.

'That's all right. *I* thought you'd buried Kathleen in the woods.'

'I've had that test done – the one Jessica was going on about – to see if Caitlin is mine. I couldn't decide if I really wanted to know. Even if I wasn't really her father – well, I don't think anything could alter the way I feel about her. I'm waiting for the results.'

'I never thought she wasn't yours for a minute, and I don't suppose Kathleen did, either; it was just something hurtful to say. Has she turned up yet?'

'No, there's no sign of her.'

'I wonder where she's got to?'

'I don't know. And I haven't managed to get hold of Rod Steigland, the man she's going to marry, yet either. He's still in the States, but he'll be flying over soon for the wedding, so wherever she is she's bound to surface some time. She called a friend just after she tried to run me down, that's where *Surprise!* got the information, so she drove off under her own steam.'

'I really did search the woods,' I confessed.

'Why? Do you think I'm that kind of man?' he asked incredulously, and I looked away.

'Well . . . Gloria told me about your first wife's accident, and that you had to marry Kathleen when she refused to get rid of the baby . . .'

'Bloody magazines! They take a particle of truth and blow it out of all proportion!' he said angrily. 'It's true I had an argument with my first wife – we married young, and we fought all the time – and yes, she slammed out in a temper and crashed the car. I'll always feel guilty about that, just as I expect you'll always feel guilty about being the cause of Greg's death. Is that what you want to hear?'

'But Gloria says you argued because she found out about all the other women.' (And she'd said his reputation with women stank, but I didn't repeat that; his temper looked balanced on a knife edge as it was.)

'There weren't any other women, Charlie. I'm strictly a one-at-a-time man, believe it or not. The magazines don't tell the truth, the whole truth, and nothing but the truth – and what they said about Kathleen was a damned lie! We had a short affair, and I married her simply to stop her aborting the baby. She didn't want Caitlin, she wanted a career.'

I looked at him – it all seemed pretty sordid to me. Maybe I'd led a sheltered life?

'I don't know what to believe. It's all a totally different world from the one I'm used to. And I don't know what kind of man you are, either – except it isn't my kind.' I turned to go.

'Charlie,' he said softly.

'Yes?'

'Tell Gloria not to give up the day job, because her concoctions don't work: you still look pretty good to me.'

I closed the door with a slam and set off up the track in the darkness, engrossed in my thoughts . . . until the night was shattered by the deafening roar of a car engine right behind me.

The headlights were turned full on, pinning me in their twin beams like a frightened rabbit – except that I wasn't a rabbit. I leaped sideways into the ditch just in time, and slid down to the icy bottom.

The car roared past, then pulled up with a squeal of brakes. As I clambered out, a door slammed.

'I *thought* I would have felt it if I'd hit you,' Angie said regretfully, picking her way towards me in her stilettos. 'Pity. And it's a pity no one round here wants to know anything about what you're really like, not even the local paper. What *is* it with the Rhymer family? Some sort of rural Mafia?'

I got to my feet, gingerly. 'No, the family came from round here originally, so when Father moved back we weren't incomers: we belong. The churchyard's full of Rhymers.'

'I was hoping to add one more!' she said viciously. 'I—'

But that was all she had time to say, before I realised the car tail-lights behind her weren't stationary but slowly moving back, and I pushed her into the ditch before landing on top of her.

The car slowly careered onto the rough verge and stopped at an angle, one wheel hanging over us.

'You didn't put the handbrake on properly,' I said, hoisting myself up without being careful about kneeling on her ribs.

'Oof!' gasped Angie.

I climbed out of the ditch for the second time. Angie was still spread-eagled down there. She started to lever herself slowly up.

'The car!'

'I think you've cracked your headlight. If you walk to the farm, Madge's dad will get the tractor and tow you out – for a price. And by the way, I think I just saved your miserable life,' I said, and left her.

I washed and tidied myself up, then went belatedly up to dinner.

'Sorry I'm late,' I said, taking my place. 'Angie just tried to run me over.'

'Women drivers,' Father said absently.

Em stared at me. 'Something will have to be done about that woman,' she said severely.

'Better do it bloody quick, before Gloria hears, or she'll be doing something herself – permanently,' Anne advised.

'I'll phone Freya, Xanthe and Lilith after dinner,' Em promised. 'Bran, lift your book up. It's in the soup.'

> On the hill
> the bracken burns;
> the red flower feeds
> off beauty.
>> From 'Words from the
>> Spirit' by Serafina Shane

Chapter 21: Home Comforts

Food For Thought

Men are from Mars . . . so, if some of them make chocolate, they can't all be bad.

I tossed and turned all night, then dropped off with the dawn and was the last for breakfast; Jessica was just leaving for school with the girls as I arrived.

Father had finished – he and Em are early risers, no matter how late they go to bed – but he must have received a parcel in the post, for he was carefully examining the contents of a small box.

As I sat down with a plateful of calories, he got up and approached Bran with a cotton bud held out before him like a scalpel.

'Open your mouth,' he said.

Bran looked at him with amicable blankness, but on having the tip of the cotton bud pressed to his lips obligingly opened his mouth and then closed it again firmly as though he'd been offered a thermometer.

'Open again,' Ran ordered. 'And keep it open!'

Obediently Bran did so, and Father gave the stick a quick twirl and withdrew it. We watched in some surprise as he placed the bud into a little stoppered tube and wrote on the label.

'Father, what are you doing?' I asked.

'Never you mind – it's just an experiment,' he said slightly furtively, then snapped impatiently: 'You can close your mouth now, Bran!'

Picking up another cotton bud he advanced on me. 'Right, Charlie. Your turn.'

'No way!' I began, pushing my chair back, but I'd have done better to keep my mouth shut instead, for he dexterously popped in the stick.

'Really, Father!' I said, when I was able. 'What on earth do you think you're doing? You might *ask* before you do that sort of thing!'

'I don't know what all the fuss is about,' he said, adding my stick to a tube in his strange collection box. 'It's just a little experiment.' Then he advanced again with yet another fresh cotton bud.

'Emily.'

Em and Anne shared a glance and said in unison, 'Absolutely not.'

Then Em rose, one finger marking the page in the book she'd been reading at breakfast (*Pagan Origins of Christianity in Britain* by Florisande Cote-Gibbon), and stalked out in silent disgust.

'Don't even effing think about it,' Anne warned, helping herself from a dish of kidneys at the sideboard.

Father sighed: 'Well, you girls aren't as important as Branwell.'

'Already bloody know that, don't we?' Anne said coldly.

He went out bearing his little box, and didn't mention the experiment again, so I don't know what all that was about. He did do odd things from time to time. I didn't let it put me off my breakfast.

Later, Em gave me a set of five power bracelets, each one made of a different semi-precious stone. There was clear quartz for peace and wisdom, amethyst for intuition and intelligence, rose quartz for love and the healing of past hurts, garnet for creativity, and hematite for stability and peace.

She said that should cover all the angles, whatever Gloria thought she saw looming in the tea leaves, and it was a nice idea. Had she given me one as a wedding present, my life would probably have taken an entirely different turn.

'I'm absolutely shattered!' Xanthe Skye exclaimed, sinking into the nearest comfortable chair. 'Freya, Lilith and I spent pretty nearly the whole night helping that poor, tortured soul, Angie.'

'Tea?' asked Em. 'Or one of Gloria's restorative herbal brews?'

'One of Gloria's, but not the nettle. The nettle is too robust for my delicate nature.'

Em put the kettle on, and I said gratefully, 'It was very kind of you all to go and sort out Angie.'

'Actually, we quite enjoyed it – there's such an odd assortment of people up at Hoo House that the vibes can be quite wild! You wouldn't believe the results with the Ouija board sometimes – but *gloomy*, always gloomy.'

'I'm not surprised. Did you use the board last night?'

'Yes – we formed a circle, just us three and Angie. Her husband came through; he told her clearly to let go of her anger and move on.'

'Did he? Where to?'

'Freya tried the crystal, later, and she thinks a cruise is indicated – a long, long cruise. But first she must be purged of all dark thoughts, in order to reap good fortune. And Lilith said she thought her heart line showed a new love interest entering her life before too long.'

'I believe cruise ships are hotbeds for that sort of thing – and to afford a cruise, Greg's insurance money must be coming at last, don't you think? That would be the good fortune.'

'It seems likely,' agreed Xanthe placidly, taking a teaglass of disgusting straw-coloured liquid from Em. 'But, as we told her, only if she closes one door behind her will the next door open into a bright new future.'

She sipped from her glass with apparent relish, then crunched up a peanut butter biscuit with her strong white teeth. 'She was wavering . . . then Lilith read her leaves. She's not as good as Gloria, but she saw the Two Ways clearly and it's up to Angie now.'

'Oh, she'll take the money and the man every time,' I predicted confidently.

She drank the last of her evil brew and sat back. 'That's better. And so is your aura, dear – not quite golden, but *better*. Would you like me to see what your future holds for you? I have my Tarot with me.'

I shuddered. 'No, thanks. I'll just take it as it comes, one disaster at a time.'

Widows: Unexpectedly Single

While a widow has much in common with being divorced (see page 9: 'Divorced Skint Old Northern Woman – Some Common Questions Answered') this is singleness without blame or stigma.

In fact, being a widow is so terribly respectable it can be played as a sympathy card in tricky situations. For example, while your friends' husbands will still perceive you as 'available', they will not persist once you make it clear your heart was buried with your husband.

Of course, your heart may *have been buried with your husband, in which case you have my very deepest sympathy.*

However, many widows go on eventually to make an enjoyable life for themselves (some even start it from day one) and it is surprising how many perfectly happy and liberated widows there are who take on a new lease of life once the shackles are off.

Provided the life insurance and mortgage angle are fully covered, Skint Old Widow may also be a contradiction in terms.

For the down side, many of the answers to the Divorce article apply here too. But always remember: while there is gin and chocolate, there is life.

Later, a truculent Angie walked into my veranda as I was painting, without so much as a knock on the door – or even a quick graffiti scrawl.

She planted herself in front of me and said aggrievedly, 'I've got to say I'm sorry, and I'm going to forgive you. I'll be leaving Upvale soon and going on a cruise.'

'Good for you,' I said, relaxing my defensive grip on the palette knife. 'I hope you have fun – a lot more fun than trying to run me over, anyway.'

'Sorry I called you a whore. Sorry I called you a murderess. Sorry I tried to kill you,' she reeled off, as if reading down an internal list of Twenty Apologies for the Obsessed.

'That's all right,' I said. 'I'm desperately sorry I killed Greg, and I always will be. Is that it?'

She examined her conscience – nicotine yellow, ragged edges – and found it reasonably clear. 'Yes, I think so. Well, that's that done!'

She shifted tack, looking over my shoulder at the small canvas. This is something I am not terribly keen on, even with people who haven't recently tried to kill me.

Something about the painting seemed to strike a chord. 'You having it off with that gorgeous actor, then?'

'No, I've just been looking after his little girl in the mornings,' I said coldly.

'Only he seemed so protective of you, down at the cottage – play your cards right and you might get a consolation prize for losing Matt.'

'Could any compensation possibly be enough?' I said sarcastically, but it just passed her by.

'Sort of getting your own back, though, after him ditching you for that nurse in Saudi,' she suggested.

I turned and stared at her. 'Which nurse? He said there *wasn't* anyone else!'

'Well, he would say that, wouldn't he? But I thought you knew. He asked you for the divorce because she got pregnant, and he's going to marry her – if she can still fit in a wedding

214

dress. God, is she huge! Perhaps it's twins, she's big enough for . . .'

I could sort of vaguely hear her voice going on and on, alarmed and rising, but it sounded far away, probably because I was on my knees on the cold stone flags, and some poor woman was howling, 'No! No!'

It sounded like me.

'Poor old Charlie,' part of me said sadly. 'She's having a bad day, but I wish she'd shut up.'

'Charlie?'

Someone scooped me up, rigid and resisting, and held me in strong, warm arms. 'Charlie, what's the matter?'

'We were just talking, and then she went mad!' Angie said.

'What have you done to her?' Mace's voice demanded angrily.

'I haven't done anything! I only came to apologise.'

'You must have said *something*!'

'Only that her ex-husband was getting married again – his girlfriend's pregnant. I suppose that upset her, because she never had any – kept miscarrying all the time. But I didn't know she'd carry on like this!'

'Didn't you? Well, I think you've done enough. Get out before I throw you out!'

'There's no need to be like that when I came round here in all good faith to apologise. And after all, she *did* kill my husband!'

There was the tapping of high heels and a slammed door, but it seemed to be happening somewhere else, beyond all that awful sobbing.

I cried myself out, curled up on the bed in Mace's arms,

215

while he stroked my hair, and murmured soothing things . . . and eventually I stopped sobbing on a hiccup, and lay there, feeling exhausted, but much better.

After a while (and a lot of nose-blowing) he brought my flannel and washed my face with cold water, as though I were the same age as Caitlin. Then he fetched a bottle of champagne (which he must have brought with him) and two glasses, and we lay on the bed and drank that, as the afternoon light faded into dusk.

It was terribly cosy: the lion *shall* lie down with the lamb.

'What are we drinking to?' I asked after a bit. My voice was interestingly husky – quite sexy really – but I didn't suppose it would last.

'The test results – Caitlin's definitely mine. I wanted you to be happy with me.'

'Oh, Mace, I'm so glad! And I'm sorry about that scene. I think I must have been bottling lots of things up for too long, and they all sort of exploded at once. I didn't mean to cry all over you.'

'I'm just glad I was here for you.' He tightened his arms around me. 'Charlie, as well as the good news about Caitlin, I also came to swallow my pride and tell you I think I love you.'

'What do you mean, *think*?' I demanded before I could stop myself.

'Well, I've never felt quite like this before,' he said, sounding puzzled. 'I don't know what it is about you, but you've somehow managed to get right under my skin, so now whenever I think of the future, you're there, too. But it's also been slowly dawning on me that if I marry you, I'm going to have to take on board the whole Rhymer clan as well. It's a big commitment.'

216

Marry me? Is the man mad?

'That's all right,' I assured him soothingly. 'I'm not going to marry you.'

He relaxed his hold a bit and gave me one of his smouldering stares. 'You're *not*?'

'No, of course not! It wouldn't work – I don't want to live in London, and also I simply don't think I could take all the effort involved in trying to look good all the time for the role of Mace North's wife. Too boring and exhausting. There was a Regency dandy who killed himself simply because he couldn't take any more of the buttoning and unbuttoning. I think I'd feel just like that.'

'But you *do* look good all the time. You're a beautiful water sprite, come to drive me mad. Besides, I'm going to spend most of my time in Upvale, though my house in London is very nice, with a big, private garden. You'll like it.'

'I'm not going to see it,' I said firmly. 'I've done the marriage bit, and now I'm going to stay here where I belong, and paint, and maybe run the magazine, if it takes off, and be happy.'

'You could marry me and still do all that – and we can share Caitlin,' he offered, persuasively.

'But would I be happy as the third wife of the actor Mace North? I don't think so!'

'Better the last than the first, darling,' he pointed out.

'Really, Mace, you must be mad wanting to marry me! I wonder if you could be impervious to Gloria's antidote because of your Tartar blood? But then, if it was that, I suppose the love philtre wouldn't have affected you in the first place.'

'My Tartar blood is about to rise to the boil if you don't

217

say you love me . . .' he muttered, kissing me. 'Or maybe it's rising anyway.'

'Cooee!' called Gloria down the stairs. 'Are you there, Charlie? Would you like a nice cup of tea, my little chicken?'

Mace sprang up from the bed with a muffled curse, kicked the door to the bottom of the stairs shut, then shot the bolt.

'Mace, Gloria will think—'

'Gloria will be quite right,' he said, advancing purposefully.

Mace stretched his muscular frame out to straighten the kinks left by my little bed.

He always looks so gorgeously graceful I still expected those camera trolley things to whiz in and out at odd moments. Mind you, it would have been pretty disconcerting if they'd done that during our recent odd moments – if we'd noticed.

'I'll have to go,' he said reluctantly. 'Tomorrow's the opening night of my new play in London, and I'll have to be there. Then I can bring Caitlin home – but right now I'm going to go straight back to the cottage and finish writing the last act of my next play, even if it takes me all night!'

This man clearly has his own private energy source, because I feel as limp as a boned herring.

'And the first batch of *Skint Old Northern Woman* is coming sometime this week!' I remembered, feeling even limper. 'We've got lists of advance orders already, and Chris is coming round in the morning to help us get everything organised – we're a bit amateur.'

'I'd come and help too, if I didn't have to go to London.

218

Still, at least I'm sure now that Kathleen will turn up for her wedding, because Rod phoned earlier from the States and said the wedding organiser would know where she was.'

'Of course – *someone* must be in charge of it!' Weddings don't arrange themselves, after all.

I sighed as he got up, and said wistfully, 'Do you have to go home now?'

'Afraid so. Besides, it'll give you a chance to think about me while I'm gone, and maybe miss me. There are advantages to marrying me you may not have thought of yet, too: like if your father's marrying Jessica, couldn't you marry me simply to get your hands on my cottage?'

'That would be mercenary,' I said, shocked. 'Besides, I could go and live with Em in the Vicarage if it came to it, only it's awfully small. I can't really imagine Em being happy in such a little kitchen.'

'Well, my cottage isn't huge, but it's bigger than the Vicarage. You think about it.'

The cottage was likely to be way down the list of his assets I thought about while he was away.

He pulled a fleecy dark top over his head, then picked up a heavy leather coat lined with rather outrageous fake fur.

'What happened to the duvet?'

'Nothing – I'm just having a change. Do you like it?'

'On you, yes. On anyone else, I'd say they were a raging queen.'

'Well, I'm not.'

'Evidently.'

'I think I'll leave by the Parsonage and make my peace

219

with Gloria,' Mace said thoughtfully. 'Maybe have a word with Ran, too, if he's in. What would be the best way to make an impression on Gloria? The sort that doesn't involve being transformed into a toad?'

'Say you've come specially to take the super-strength love-potion antidote she brewed up at home last night, and if she asks you to drink a cup of tea after that, do it.'

'And it definitely won't be hemlock?'

'No – though I wouldn't mention . . . well, what we've been up to.'

'I don't usually issue bulletins. But I thought I'd tell your father my intentions are honourable, in case Anne and Em try to kneecap me.'

'He won't know what you're talking about – he doesn't even realise you've ever had any *dishonourable* intentions. And when you've drunk this new version of Gloria's concoction, you probably won't,' I added firmly.

'Don't bank on it,' he said, kissing me.

He opened the stairway door and came face to face with Flossie, who was sitting on one of the steep steps, trying to remember whether she was going up or down.

'Hello!' he said, and she got up wagging her tail, licked his face, and went back upstairs ahead of him.

He didn't come back down. Gloria probably ushered him firmly out after he'd spoken to Father – *if* he spoke to Father; for surely he must have been joking?

After a while I dozed off.

When I woke up again it wasn't as late as I thought, and after washing my face – which looked normal, if a trifle feverish – I went up to the kitchen.

Em was there alone, though I could hear Gloria belting

out 'Three Little Maids from School' in Father's bedroom, and Walter's 'heh, heh, heh' laugh from the small sitting room where he was watching children's TV.

'Where's the body?' I asked.

She looked up and grinned. 'He took the cup of poison from Gloria with his own hand, and drained it in one.'

'Did anything happen?'

'Well, he didn't suddenly smite his forehead and exclaim, "Yes, I see it now – she looks like the backside of a donkey, and has the intelligence of a cushion." In fact, he looked exactly the same, only more so.'

'More so?'

'Sort of determined on a course of action. He said he was off to see Father next, but Gloria gave him a cup of tea first. She told him she'd put bromide in it, but she was only joking – I think. You haven't been at it again, have you?'

'You needn't make it sound like I'm a rabbit. I had a rather traumatic visit from Angie, and Mace was just comforting me.'

I told her what Angie'd said. 'And I don't know why it should upset me so much, because I thought I was over all that: I mean, I accepted I wasn't going to have a baby years ago. But Mace was so sweet, and just held me for ages, and wiped my eyes, and hugged me and—'

'Spare me the rest. There was something very significant about the way he slammed closed the door to the stairs.'

'You heard that, did you? Yes, there's something significant about all his actions – it's because he's an actor, I think, but also he's just sort of naturally graceful.' I sighed.

'He's not coming back for dinner later, is he?' Em asked. 'Just so I know how many to cook for – I'm doing individual syllabubs.'

'Coming back? No, of course not. He's suddenly got over his writer's block, and he says he's going to finish the last act of his play tonight, no matter how long it takes, because he's due back in London tomorrow. It's the first night of his latest play, then the wedding, so he'll be able to bring Caitlin home after that – assuming Kathleen turns up, and agrees to it.'

'So he does mean to come back to Upvale?'

'He did. I don't know how he'll feel after a bit more time in his own theatre world – or about me, after the potion kicks in.'

'*If* it does.'

'Em . . .'

'What?' she said, sieving sugar in glistening cascades.

'You know the five power bracelets you gave me?' I asked. 'Well, the rose quartz one exploded spontaneously, and there are tiny beads all over the place.'

'Probably the heat,' she said drily.

'But that's the one for love!'

'Precisely.'

'Do you think it's significant?'

'Yes, but like Gloria and the tea leaves, I can't decide which way. I'll get you another one.' She set out a row of little glass dishes, and spooned syllabub into them. 'I must put two of these in the fridge for the twins to have later – I promised, because they're going to a birthday party after school.'

Then she picked up a small packet and read: '"Super-Lite Mousse: The No-Calorie Dessert."'

'Is that the Treacle Tart's?'

'Yes, she's bought loads of them, and Super-Lite Soup, and

I'm to serve her one instead of my fat- and calorie-laden concoctions.'

'Is that what she said?' I watched as she emptied the packet into a bowl, poured in double cream and began to whisk.

I examined the packet. 'It says water here, Em, not cream.'

'I know.' She added a bit of sugar, poured the mixture into a little dish, and garnished it with angelica to distinguish it from the rest.

'There. It looks almost as good as the real thing, doesn't it?'

Em was ladling soup by the time Father came in, looking baffled: 'They're all at it! Mace just waltzed in and asked me for Charlie's hand in marriage. Have they all been reading Jane bloody Austen? Is your Red going to turn up next, Anne, singing "White Wedding"?'

'Not effing likely.'

'What about you, Bran?'

Bran looked up questioningly.

'Going to get married, are you? Got a girl?'

'Isis.'

'You can't have a relationship with a figment of your bloody imagination!'

'Language!' said Jessica primly. We all looked at her.

'Isis Cadwallader. Student. Postgrad.' Bran looked from one to another of us as though trying to pick up faint and fuzzy signals. 'Speaks eight languages.'

'In bed?' asked Anne, interested.

'Yes,' Bran said. 'Miss her a bit,' he added thoughtfully.

'Well, as long as she doesn't turn up and ask me for your hand,' Father said.

'She's got two of her own,' Bran replied seriously, propping his book up against the recumbent figure of Mr Froggy and losing interest in the conversation.

'Mace must have been playing a joke on you, Ran,' Jessica said. 'He couldn't possibly be interested in Charlie – he could have anyone!'

'He probably has,' Gloria muttered, hacking viciously at a crisp new loaf.

'No, he seemed serious – said he found her compellingly irresistible.'

Everyone turned and looked at me.

I shrugged. 'We haven't found a cure yet. Gloria's won't work, for some reason, though perhaps the new one will, in time.'

'What do you mean?' Jessica interrupted. 'What cure? And have you been having it off with Mace, you dark horse?'

It forcibly struck me that poor old Jessica is always bobbing along on the surface of our lives like a cork, and she is, and always will be, one sub-plot short of a novel.

'You're such a romantic,' Em said to her sarcastically.

'And you've got it the wrong way round,' Gloria told her. 'He's after my Charlie – but he's only good for one thing, you mark my words, blossom.'

'Bet he's good at that, though?' Jessica said enviously, then caught Father's eye and subsided.

'He's a bold one!' Gloria said rather admiringly. 'Said he'd come for the cup of poison and drank the anti-philtre right down in one go. Then he took a cup of my special tea to take the taste away, smiled at me, said a handsome dark stranger had just entered my life bringing change, and then off he went to see Ran.'

'So, what did you say, Father?' Em asked.

'I said to ask me again when his last wife had turned up safe and sound, and he said he would. Providing she's not in bits, I've no objection, I suppose. But I thought Charlie would have had enough of all that marriage stuff. Have you been dosing the poor man up with love potions, you lot?'

'*I* haven't. And thank you, Father, but your gracious approval won't be necessary – Mace drank one of Gloria's love philtres by mistake, but he's resistant to the antidote. We think it's the Tartar blood or something. Shouldn't the new antidote have worked immediately, Gloria?'

'Yes. He's impervious.'

'Load of rubbish,' Father said uneasily. 'Er – you didn't give any of it to anyone else, did you, Gloria?'

'Oh, do they work?' asked Jessica eagerly.

'No,' Gloria said flatly to both, and slamming down the bread knife, went out muttering.

'Oh, well,' Jessica said, disappointed. 'I expect it's just a temporary infatuation then, Charlie. You should marry him while you can!'

'No point. I won't leave Upvale ever again, but he will soon tire of it and go back to London permanently. We come from two different worlds,' I added tritely. 'We've nothing in common.'

'If pagans can marry vicars, artists can marry actors,' Em said. 'Marry him, and bend him to your will – we'll all help you.'

'Come on, does he look bendable to you? And name me an actor who's been married to the same woman for more than five minutes.'

225

There was a long, thoughtful silence.

'Anyway, I don't want to live *his* life, I want to live my own. I'm going to stay in Upvale, and paint, and maybe the magazine will sell so many we can publish it regularly – say six issues a year or something. I'll be happy and successful, which is the best sort of revenge on Matt that I can think of.'

'Reminds me,' Anne said. 'Jen rang. The first five thousand copies of the mag. are arriving tomorrow.'

'Five *thousand*! Don't you mean hundred?'

'No.'

'My God – where are we going to put them?'

'Anywhere except my study,' Father said firmly.

'How about the back sitting room? The one we don't use because of the little poltergeist thing?' Em suggested.

'Do you think she'll mind?'

'Probably glad of the company. I'd sit in there myself sometimes, except she's always so bloody miserable and restless.'

'Which little poltergeist thing?' Jessica said, looking scared. 'I thought you said that room was never used?'

'Oh, it's used, all right, just not by us.'

'Have to get organised: promotion, packing, labelling,' Anne reeled off efficiently.

'Chris is going to help. He's coming round tomorrow when he's seen the bishop, and he's bringing his computer. He says he can print out the address labels on it, and he's going to do the book-keeping,' Em said.

'What if his bishop sends him away?'

'He won't go – he belongs here in Upvale now, with us.'

'There!' Father said with satisfaction to Jess. 'I said

everything would go on as usual. The bishop will defrock Chris, and he can come and live here with Em. There's no need for her to leave: problem solved!'

'Not with the Treacle Tart as stepmum, it bloody well isn't,' Anne said.

Chapter 22: First Cuckoo

Mace arrived just after the first batch of *Skint Old Northern Woman* was delivered, strode in like a conquering emperor, and kissed me right in front of Em, Anne and Walter, who were all helping to shift the magazines into the back room.

Bran had been helping, too, but had wandered off with a copy and hadn't come back. Probably analysing it.

Mace was wearing the fur-lined leather coat, with a checked cotton Arab *keffiyeh* tied around his neck. Instead of looking poncy and affected, he gave the impression he'd just dismounted from his shaggy pony and parked his scimitar at the door before popping in for a quick tea-and-ravage.

'I've finished the play – three o'clock this morning – now I'm on my way to London,' he said, favouring me with one of his intense 'slow fuse heading for the dynamite' smoulders. 'This is just to remind you that I'll be back.'

He released me and, while I tried to reinflate my lungs, began moving cartons of magazines himself, rather faster than we had. 'I'll take a box of these with me, if that's OK. I'll settle up for them when I get back: if you trust me?'

'We'll bill you,' I croaked, then cleared my throat and added, hardening my heart: 'In case you decide *not* to come back.'

'Oh, I'll be back, darling – count on it.'

'Do you want to be nude centrefold in the next one?' asked Anne hopefully. 'Give your services for free?'

'I always do,' he said, grinning. 'And I'll think about it.'

'Heh! Heh! Heh!' laughed Walter, seeming to find this amusing, for some reason. 'If he don't want to do it I could be your pin-up,' he offered generously. 'I've got no bodily hair whatsoever.'

'Well, that would certainly be *alternative*,' Emily said. 'Or how about Chris, in just his dog collar and motorbike boots?'

'Too kinky – the Church wouldn't approve,' Anne said seriously.

'I don't think the Church are going to approve of his marrying me, either,' Em said.

'Chris has been summoned to see his bishop this morning,' I told Mace, as he stacked the last of the boxes. 'We don't know why, but we think he must have heard rumours about Em.'

'Them ones about sacrificing chickens and funny crosses are all lies,' Walter said stoutly. 'Our Em never would hurt a fly.'

Well, she wouldn't hurt a dumb *creature* . . . though dumb people were another thing.

'If Chris and I can work out a form of marriage that respects both our beliefs, I don't see what the Church has got to stick its nose in for,' Em said mutinously.

'Perhaps you and Anne could hammer out some form of agreement for Charlie and me?' Mace suggested. 'A peace treaty, so we could live adjoining lives, like friendly territories, overlapping at the edges here and there. The odd little border skirmish . . .' He reached out and ran a finger down my cheek until it reached my lips, which quivered suddenly in a very Sue Ellen way, all on their own. 'Meanwhile, I'm off to London, where hopefully I'll discover Kathleen all in one piece, so satisfying Ran, at least, that I possess the qualities of a potential son-in-law.'

'We already know Kathleen's all right,' Em said, looking thoughtfully at him. 'We've seen it – by various means. But if the Treacle Tart marries Father, we *all* might be looking for a new home: so marry Mace, Chaz, and we'll come and live with you.'

'I don't see why *I* have to sacrifice myself so the family can stay together!' I protested.

'Oh, thanks!' Mace said. 'Don't mind me.'

'Yes, but Mace is probably filthy rich,' Anne pointed out. 'Aren't you, Mace? You could afford to buy a bigger house, with room for us all?'

'I could, but . . .'

'This *is* the only really big house in Upvale,' Em said.

'Well, he could have an annexe built on his cottage,' I suggested. 'And everyone probably won't want to come at once anyway, unless it's Christmas or something.'

'So, are you going to marry him?' Anne asked.

'No, of course not. What would I do that for?'

They turned as one and looked at Mace.

'Pretty obvious reasons, I should think,' Em said, after a minute.

'Bloody right,' Anne agreed.

Gloria came in with a tea tray, and gave Mace a scathing head-to-foot inspection. 'It's you, is it?'

'It was last time I looked,' he agreed. 'I'm off to London, though – I've a first night to attend – but I'll be back after Kathleen's wedding, with Caitlin.'

'Why bother? You've played your part,' she said sourly.

'Life's a play, and all the men and women in it but the players . . .' he misquoted cheerfully, his pretensions not looking particularly depressed. 'I refuse to be First Villain – I'll be back. Would anyone like any shopping done in London? Christmas presents?'

Em felt in her dungaree pocket. 'If you want a challenge, I've got Bran's Christmas present list here.' She looked down and read: '*Three Hundred and Fifty-Nine Definitions of Meaning* by Gottfried Flauncy Gresham. Published in 1959, probably had a print run of five copies.'

'Hasn't Bran put anything easier on the list?' Anne demanded. 'We'll never effing find that!'

'Jelly beans? *Harry Potter*? Liquorice smoking set and chocolate cigars?'

'That's more like it.'

'I might as well give the book a go,' Mace offered, and scribbled down the details before giving me another look of extreme (if blistering) intensity and striding off, his shorn black locks ruffled by an invisible hand.

'You lay off him!' I said to the air, which quivered sulkily like a heat haze – only in this case, a *chill* haze.

'You can't blame her for trying,' Em said.

'Yes I can.'

The window shutter banged twice, rather petulantly.

Unfortunately, Chris's bishop did not want to congratulate him on his intended pagan/Christian nuptials with Em, instead merely pointing out the gaping gateway to Hell grinning at his feet.

After that, Chris said, he fully and frankly expressed his

231

own feelings on the matter to the bishop, which is probably how he got sent to Upvale in the first place, it being The Land Time Forgot.

'I'm taking early retirement, just as soon as they find a temporary replacement,' he told us as we sorted out our magazine dispatch depot. 'I won't have remarks like that made about the woman I love.'

'Oh? What did he say?' Em demanded eagerly.

'My lips are sealed,' he replied firmly, looking resolute under his Wyatt Earp moustache.

Seeing Em was considering unsealing them with the paperknife, I said hastily: 'But won't you have to move out of the Vicarage, too, Chris?'

'I'm afraid so. But not out of Upvale. I have a modest private income of my own, enough to buy a small cottage. But I hate to reduce Em to that level, after being used to all this space.'

'Oh, anywhere that hasn't got the Treacle Tart in it sounds wonderful to me at the moment, Chris,' Em assured him. 'And you can move in here with me until we sort things out.'

'Not until we're married,' he said firmly.

'But—'

'Bloody straight-laced vicars,' commented Anne.

'He is not!' Em said hotly. 'He—'

'Em,' Chris said, and she stopped and looked at him.

'Oh, all right.'

'The attics?' I suggested. 'There are lots of them empty. Or why not get married quickly, if you've worked out a compromise ceremony?'

'We could, if my friend can get away for long enough to officiate,' Chris said. 'Em doesn't feel she can come any further into the church than the front porch, so we can have a simple ceremony there, and then we can all go up to the standing stones and Em's friends can say a few words.'

'Yes – just a general sort of blessing, you know – nothing *extreme*,' explained Em, which relieved my mind a little.

'And then we can have a party!' Anne said.

'If we did it just before Christmas, we could combine the celebrations with that,' Em suggested.

'But what will your father say if I just move in?'

'Nothing,' Anne said. 'You're here most of the time now, anyway, aren't you? He's got used to you.'

Skint Old Bookworm, No. 1

Never trust a biographer: they read other people's letters.

'Ran said he had no objection to us marrying now, Em, providing you didn't die in childbirth,' Chris said, returning after bearding the lion in his den. 'Has he always had these morbid ideas?'

'That was bloody *Charlotte!*' Anne said. 'Honestly – you wouldn't think he'd written a book about the Brontës, would you? If anyone was going to die in childbirth it would be Charlie, not Em.'

'But I'm not the one marrying a clergyman.'

'And I'm not having effing children,' Emily stated. 'Date stamp's up.'

'That's all right, I don't want to share you,' Chris said.

'Why not? I share you with your effing motorbike!'

'Are you jealous of my motorbike?' he asked, pulling her close and kissing her.

A small avalanche of magazines cascaded down behind them like a waterfall.

'She doesn't like it, Em,' Anne warned.

'Who doesn't like what?' asked Chris, confused.

'The poltergeist thing. She never likes it when you're happy. She's a miserable bugger.'

'Oh?' He looked a bit taken aback. 'Should I say a prayer, and see if it feels any happier – or goes away?'

'If you like,' Em said unconcernedly. 'If you say one every time you come in here, she might get fed up and leave voluntarily, but she's not doing anyone any harm.'

'Right,' he said uncertainly.

Skint Old Fashion Victim, No. 3

Some time around forty, our fashion sense withers away to a whimpering pinprick, and we make major clothes-buying mistakes.

Although we can see in the mirror that we don't look the same as we did at twenty, somehow we still expect the same clothes to suit us.

This is the time when we buy sheepskin jackets that double our bulk (and the only thing that looks good in a sheepskin is a sheep), glitzy ankle socks, and diamanté Alice bands.

Due to gravitational pull, our bums and boobs have begun their slow but inexorable continental drift south-wards, so leggings and boob tubes are out.

However, you will slowly start to forge a new and unique personal dress style once you've overcome this initial catastrophic phase.

You will know you are over the worst when you buy something thinking: I don't give a stuff if that's fashionable or not – it's just so comfortable.

Since Chris found out about the invisible occupant of the sitting room, I had caught him in there once or twice muttering and sprinkling water about. And actually the atmosphere did seem to be warming up, so maybe she was gradually vanishing from the scene. Or perhaps she simply didn't like all the new technology: Chris's humming computer, and the printer doing the labels, not to mention the packing of magazines into slithery plastic postal packets, which had all been going on pretty well non-stop.

I didn't know how Madge had done it, but it seemed like every WI member in the country had ordered a copy for a start, and all Anne's friends and acquaintances had too. (Probably too frightened not to.)

I simply didn't have time to think about Mace more than thirty or forty times a day . . . and night. It was exhausting; he was certainly such stuff as dreams are made on.

In fact, now he'd gone it did just feel like I'd had a really, really wonderful fantasy involving some gorgeous but unattainable person, who you knew really wouldn't behave in the least like that to you in real life (and it would petrify you if he *did*, anyway).

I expected things were settling into a more familiar perspective for Mace, too, now he was back with his rich and famous friends, in his posh London town house. I thought a few more days of drinking London water would flush even the most resistant love philtre out of his system.

He hadn't totally forgotten us, though: a reporter and

photographer from one of the Sunday papers turned up to do an interview – and who else could have told them about *Skint Old Northern Woman*?

Father was a little aggrieved that they hadn't come to interview *him* this time, and insisted on at least being in on the photograph. Jessie did, too, but we drew the line there since she'd done absolutely nothing to help: I mean, even Clo and Feeb had been putting in time packing magazines into packets.

Other than this, there had been no *word* from Mace, though on the first day of Christmas, my new love sent to me – a banana tree.

Figure that one out.

One morning, after the usual brief tussle with Frost, Father retired to the end of the table to read his mail, muttering darkly, though I thought it was very clever of Frost to realise that the post belonged to us at all: nobody had trained him to fetch it in.

There was only one thing in the post for me, and Frost had to drag that in separately – a stiff envelope like you send photographs in, containing – yes, photographs.

I puzzled over them, for most seemed to be photos of the Parsonage interior . . . especially my bedroom before Jessica seized it, and the little triangular bathroom off it with the fireplace, and roll-top bath with lion feet.

There was also one taken inside what looked like a tropical house at Kew, and a note from Mace: 'This is my London house – thought you might like the way I'm re-modelling some of the interior rooms. The workmen have put the conservatory up, working literally night and day, which hasn't pleased my neighbours . . .'

I looked up. 'It's from Mace. He's making part of the inside of his London house look like the Parsonage . . .' I looked down again, frowning. 'But he can't have done all that since he got back, can he?'

'And why would anyone *want* to do that?' Jessica said, puzzled. 'He's got one of those lovely, huge old terraced houses in a quiet square; I've seen it in a magazine.'

'He borrowed a book of photographs of the Parsonage interior, ages ago: mentioned it to him in the pub one night,' Father said. 'The one that peculiar American did. *Ranulf Rhymer: In His Place*. I expect that gave him the idea.'

Em passed the photos round to Anne. 'I expect he's just doing one or two of the rooms up to make you feel at home, Chaz.'

'What do you mean, feel at home?'

'So you're happy there, when he has to be in London,' she explained. 'We had a little chat when he came up to see Gloria. He told me he ordered the work done last time he was in London, after the Birthday Feast. Then he had the conservatory remodelled, and he says the garden is very lush and quite private, with a gazebo and a big pond with fish.'

'But that means he was expecting me to . . . I mean, all that time ago when I—' I broke off, confused. I'd accused him of treating me as an easy lay, when all the time he'd been turning his London house into a home from home for me? I looked at the photos again.

'I can see now it's *not* the Parsonage – it's sort of Essence of Parsonage meets . . . well – Comfort, I suppose.'

'Yes,' Em agreed. 'He said he wasn't going to sacrifice central heating in the interests of authenticity.'

'Don't bloody blame him,' Anne said. 'Got it in my flat.'

'I like chopping wood and stoking fires,' Walter said. 'It keeps me nice and warm. I feel the cold, I do, because I've got no bodily hair whatsoever.'

Em said, 'I told him we'd have central heating if we could afford it, only Father always spends too much on tarts and booze – but we'd have open fires, as well. And real sockets for the electricity, not two-pin ones with battered old adaptors, like we have now.'

'Yes, aren't those dangerous?' Jessica said. 'The ones in my room look like Bakelite.'

'They *are* Bakelite. The whole place is a deathtrap,' I said.

'Yes, but I'd know if it was going to burn down,' Em said. 'And it would show up in Gloria's tea leaves pretty spectacularly, too.'

'I've never seen a fire in the tea leaves,' Gloria said. 'Not unless you count what Charlie's lit under that Mace, what can't be put out with any potion I can brew.'

'The whole house wants so much spending on it, it's ridiculous,' Jessica said. 'It would be much better to sell it, and have a cosy little modern house in the valley with all mod cons and a built-in kitchen. The show house on the Mango estate is lovely.'

'Sell it?' echoed Em.

'Better for bloody who?' Anne asked.

'Ran, why don't we have the house valued, just out of interest, to see what . . .?' she began to wheedle, but then stopped and stared.

Father, a strange and interesting shade of ash, was gazing down at his letter as though transfixed.

Then he looked up and gradually focused on Bran as though he'd never seen him before.

'You're not my son,' he said slowly, in a strange voice. 'I sent the cotton buds away for analysis, and you're not my son!'

'I know,' Bran said, dribbling honey onto his toast.

'What do you mean, you *know*? How can you know? I didn't know till this minute when I read the letter!'

'Mother told me.'

'Mother? Which mother?'

'I only have one of those,' Bran said patiently. 'Maria Podjecki. Professor Podjecki.'

Father's mouth opened and closed silently, like a rather handsome halibut. 'Professor?' he managed to say eventually.

Bran nodded. 'Anthropology. Came to see me in my first term. Pops in sometimes if she's over for a conference. Smoked salami and schnapps. Don't like the schnapps,' he added.

'You never mentioned it!'

'No? Sorry,' he added vaguely, since we were all looking at him. 'Should I have done?'

'But – I've been supporting you all these years, and you're not even my son!' Father dropped his head into his hands and groaned.

'You mean that's what your little experiment with the cotton buds was about? Having us tested out to see if we were the genuine article? Well, I wonder where you got *that* idea from!' Em looked unlovingly at Jessica.

'Devious old sod!' Anne said.

'It does rather make a mockery of your "Breed Your Own Brontës" experiment, Father,' I said.

'Unless he's one of the Nurture rather than Nature brigade,' Em suggested. 'In which case, it doesn't really matter, does it? It doesn't matter to me who Bran's father is either – he's still my brother.'

We all agreed with that except Father, who was still staring down at the letter, turning it over in his big hands as though there might be a retraction on the back: 'Ha, ha! Fooled you!'

'I thought it was odd that Bran didn't look like the rest of you. I mean, Em and Anne are the *image* of their father, but Charlie and Bran—' Jessica broke off. 'Are you all right, Ran?'

'Oh my God!' Father said. 'I missed the second page – the second result – Charlie!'

'What?' demanded Jessica avidly, leaping up and peering over his shoulder. 'Oh my God! Oh, no! I can't believe it!' She looked up, transfigured with excitement. 'Guess what? Charlie isn't Ran's either!'

'I want to speak to Lally Tooke,' I said into the receiver for the tenth time, tracking my impossible mother across the American continent.

'Well,' said a voice doubtfully. 'She's vury, vury busy just now. May I ask who's calling?'

'Her daughter.'

That's one thing I can be sure of, anyway.

'Her daughter in England, Europe?'

'Has she got any anywhere else?'

'I don't rightly know, ma'am, but if you hold on, I'll go see if I can put you through.'

After several interminable and expensive minutes (at the expense of the man formerly known as Father) Lally said, 'Hello? Which one of you is it?'

'Charlie. But don't ask me my surname, because I don't have the slightest idea *who* my father is.'

There was a pause. The line hissed like a muted python. 'You know . . .? Does Ran know?'

'It was he who told me. He got some kind of kit and tested me and Bran.'

'Bran?'

'Bran turned out to be not Father's either. Funnily enough, he already knew, but it just hadn't registered as being of any importance. His mother's been in touch with him for years – she's Professor Podjecki now.'

'Oh, I knew that – I took an interest, because of thinking Bran was your half-brother. And actually, we met once in Prague.'

'Mother, who *is* my father, if Ran isn't?'

She paused. 'I wasn't sure if you were Ran's or not. Either way, you were a mistake, because I was about to leave when I fell pregnant, and I had to put it off until after you were born.'

'So who was my father?' I repeated. I didn't want to go into her reasons for abandoning us again, although acute selfishness and enlightened self-interest become something totally other in Mother's books.

'Have you heard of Brendan Furness?'

'The *poet*? It wasn't!'

'Must have been. He rented a house nearby, to get back to his roots because he'd hit a writer's block, and he was quite a bit older than me, but terribly, terribly sexy, with big, sad dark eyes, although politically *totally* incorrect on women's issues.'

'Yes, Maria thought he was attractive, too. That's who she told Bran his father was.'

241

'The old goat! He had a heart attack and died the year after you were born – and no wonder!'

'This is my father we're talking about!'

'Yes, but he didn't know it, and he'd have run a mile if he did. And he was terribly clever and famous, so I don't know what you're worrying about. Look, I'm giving a reading in ten minutes, I'll have to go and get ready . . .'

'Don't you want to know how Ran's taking this?'

'You just let me know if he throws you out,' she said, 'and I'll send you a cheque. How is your divorce settlement doing?'

'Ducked,' I said, but I was talking to the air: she'd slithered off.

Mother is a Pisces, too.

'Did you get her?' asked Em, who was heading the crisis meeting taking place down in the kitchen.

'Somebody bloody well should,' Anne said. 'Bran, I can't believe you never said anything!'

Bran smiled, but that might have been because of the hot chocolate topped with whipped cream Em had just put in front of him.

There was one each; clearly this was a time for desperate measures. Flossie had a blob on the end of her black nose, and was trying to get her tongue out far enough to lick it off, her eyes like colliding planets.

'Yes, I got Mother, eventually,' I said, sinking down onto a chair and wrapping my strangely cold hands round the glass cup. 'Bran, you and I have the same father.'

'He's dead,' Bran offered. 'Dead Poets Society. Only we can't keep society with dead poets – except through their poetry.'

'Quite,' Anne said. She wrinkled her brow: 'So, you and me and Em have the same mother, Charlie? And you and Bran have the same father . . .'

'It means Charlie's related to all of us by blood. Bran's related to Charlie through their shared father, so . . .' Em paused, thinking.

'We're all still family,' Anne finished.

'Of course,' Em agreed. 'It doesn't matter who fathered who now, does it? We are *one*. We are the Rhymers.'

'Like a tribe,' agreed Anne.

I was feeling better. They were right.

'But poor Father – I mean, Ran?' I asked.

'Shut himself in his study – shut the Treacle Tart out, and serve her right, the interfering bitch,' Anne said.

'He must be terribly upset.'

'His *theories* are terribly upset. For the rest – well, he'll get used to the idea.'

'But he might not want to have Bran and me here any more.'

'We'll just have to wait and see. And it might be immaterial, anyway, since the Treacle Tart doesn't want *any* of us here any more. He's going to find himself playing effing Bungalow Bill in Mango Valley if he doesn't put his foot down.'

Skint Old Health

For reasons that should be obvious, never leave lying about those alarmingly suppository-like waxy-pinkish plastic corks from cheap wine bottles.

Their inadvertent application would mean an

embarrassing trip to the nearest Accident and Emergency
department and possible entries in both The Lancet *and*
the Guinness Book of Records.

Father looked dreadful the next morning, but that was
mostly because he'd been shut up in his study on a bender
since the previous day's postal revelations. He let Jessica in
sometime, though, because she wasn't round to wake the
girls up for breakfast. Anne went and fetched them down,
in the end.

However, when he did finally emerge, he kissed my forehead, patted Bran on the shoulder, and said heavily, 'Well,
well – you're still my children, after all; but it's been a shock.
And if that old sod Brendan Furness was still alive, I'd have
his balls.'

'Ran, please – not in front of the girls!'

Feeb and Clo giggled into their porridge.

'Ran and I are going to look at the show house together
on the Mango estate, this morning,' Jessica said brightly.

She'd found time to polish her surfaces and attire herself
in a skimpy top and short, tight skirt, though I always think
those bras that push up the skin of your chest and then
slam it together in the middle are a mistake. From the side
she looked like a narrow-chested pouter pigeon.

We all stopped eating and stared at Father.

'What does it matter to *me* where I live?' he said, sighing
heavily. 'I'm a broken man, with no son to carry on the
family name . . . no grandchildren of my own . . .'

'Jessica had better have her tubes unknotted then, and
you can try again,' Anne suggested.

Gloria stuck her head out of the pantry: 'I know what

244

I know!' she said, which was neither illuminating nor helpful.

'You can't sell the Parsonage!' I said.

'Why not? He'd get lots of money for it, because it's so big!' Jessica said brightly. 'He can't really afford to keep it up – *or* to keep all of you . . . but then, he doesn't need to, does he? Em can go and live with Chris, Anne's got a London flat, Bran's away at his university – he could live there, he doesn't have to keep coming back – and Charlie can marry Mace: I mean, I know it wouldn't last if she did, but she can get a big settlement when they divorce and buy her own place. Or maybe she'll get the cottage.'

It was amazing what went on in that tricky bundle of wires she called a brain.

'I'm not going to marry Mace, not even for purely mercenary reasons! I'm going to be happy and successful on my own,' I declared.

'Without a *man*?' she asked incredulously.

'Yes,' put in Em. 'And she doesn't have to marry Mace to have a home. She can always live with Chris and me, and so can Bran.'

'Not when they defrock Chris and turf him out of the bloody Vicarage, though,' Anne pointed out.

'De-leather,' I corrected. 'And he said he would buy a cottage – though I thought you were trying to persuade Chris to move in here, Father, so you didn't lose Em?'

'I don't know what I want any more,' Father said brokenly, although I noticed he'd managed to put away a gargantuan breakfast as usual. 'I'm a broken reed.'

He went out with Jessica and the girls, so they could

visit the new estate after they'd dropped Clo and Feeb off at school.

I wondered if that house in Passionfruit Place was still for sale.

Chapter 23: To the Bone

'I've found Kathleen,' said Mace's deep, knee-quiveringly beautiful voice. 'Or rather, she's turned up.'

The line crackled like Cellophane. Em, who'd just handed me the receiver, struck a 'be still, my beating heart' pose, hands to her palpitating bosom.

'Shove off, Em,' I said, and she grinned and went back upstairs.

'What? Can you hear me, Charlie?'

'Just about, Mace. Em brought the cordless phone down, but it doesn't work very well here. Did you say you'd found Kathleen?'

'Rod found the wedding organiser, and she gave us the phone number, but by then Kathleen had turned up at Rod's place anyway.'

'But where had she been?'

'Some sort of fat farm, trying to lose nonexistent weight – and funnily enough, it turned out that Caitlin knew all the time, except I'd kept it from her that we were worried about where her mother was.'

'Of course!' I exclaimed. 'She was going on about losing weight to get American film parts when I met her at the cottage, don't you remember? And the coven did say she was dwindling! I bet she's not as thin as Jessica, though. We're thinking of using *her* rib cage as a dish rack.'

'I haven't seen her, just spoken on the phone. Rod said she looked great, but then, half the actresses he works with these days are walking skeletons, so his eye for normality's warped.'

'You are used to being with thin, immaculate women too,' I pointed out. 'And *I've* no intention of reducing myself to emaciation point – or going in for liposuction, facelifts or even bikini waxing – I'm staying *au naturel*.'

'You don't need to lose weight – you go in and out in all the right places – and I like you just as you are, *especially au naturel*,' he assured me, and I could hear the wicked smile in his voice. 'I wish you were here now, so I could show you how much. And I'm not the only one who misses you: Caitlin talks about nothing but Upvale and the Rhymers. She's dying to get back as soon as the wedding's over and she's done her bridesmaid's act – and so am I.'

'Will Kathleen let you bring her back, though, without a fight?'

'Yes, under certain conditions. It's all been a bit tricky. She was mad with her so-called friend for passing on to *Surprise!* magazine what she'd told her in confidence about our custody argument, because now the newshounds have got their eye on her. But I got together with Rod, who's a really nice guy, and he's persuaded her that she should do what's right for Caitlin – whatever Caitlin wants. And Caitlin's made it abundantly clear that she wants to come back to Upvale. She'll see Kathleen as often as possible, of course, but she can do that in the holidays and when Kathleen's over here.'

'How awful for Caitlin to have to make the choice, though: her mother or her father!'

'Oh, there wasn't any real contest, darling, though it wasn't the thought of living with *me* that swung it, it was life with the Rhymers.'

It didn't seem quite the right moment to tell him that actually, technically speaking, I wasn't a Rhymer any more.

'Kathleen's been offered a major part in Rod's next film, which has focused her small attention span on other things. She loves Caitlin in her way, but her chief worry if Caitlin stays with me is what the press will say about it. So she's come up with a solution – a PR exercise: she wants *you* to come to London and bring Caitlin home to Upvale straight after the wedding.'

I nearly dropped the phone.

'Me? Why *me*? I thought *you* were going to bring her?'

'I'll drive her home, yes, but Kathleen wants to show the press that she's reluctantly letting her make her home with me and her beloved nanny—'

'I didn't know she had one,' I interrupted, astonished. 'It's the first I've heard of it!'

'She means you.'

'*Me?*'

'Yes, you.'

'But you're making me sound like an old retainer!'

'That's the whole idea. A touching scene after the reception, where she hands Caitlin over to Nanny. "I only want what will be best for my little girl," says film star Kathleen Lovell . . . Well – you can see how it will be.'

'You're very cynical!'

'I've been around long enough to know the score, that's

all. What I didn't tell Kathleen is that soon you'll be looking after Caitlin permanently in your capacity as Mrs North.'

'The third?'

'And last.'

'There's no guarantee of that, though, is there? If I was mad enough to marry you, one day you'd wake up and see boring old Charlie Rhymer and trade me in for a new model. I've already done all that stuff; I'm not going through it again.'

'If you're still waiting for the magic potion to wear off, forget it. You've got so far under my skin you're now part of me, and I want you for keeps. And better to be the last Mrs North than the first, don't you think, darling? Did you get my message?'

'Yes – I'm bananas.'

'*I'm* bananas about *you* – I have to be or I wouldn't have turned my house into Homage to Haworth via Upvale Parsonage. Did you get the photos? I walk into some of the rooms and forget where I am; and the conservatory is like a chunk of Kew. Do you want a fountain and fishpond in there, as well as in the garden?'

'You're wasting your money,' I said severely, thinking what a long time it seemed since breakfast and Revelations One – and an even longer time since I'd seen Mace . . .

'When you come down to collect Caitlin you'll see it, and you can tell me what you think,' he suggested enticingly.

Just as well he couldn't tell what I was thinking at that moment.

'I've got some coloured brochures from a tropical plant supplier full of things like pineapple plants and palms, and I don't know what to order,' he added, my very own private serpent in Eden.

'I'm very busy with the magazine,' I said, weakening. 'We've been working till all hours packing and labelling, and a Sunday paper came and photographed us, and they're doing an article about it. Was that your doing?'

'I may have mentioned it to one or two people. And I'm sure Em and Anne and Chris could manage without you for a couple of days, when they know I need you to come and fetch Caitlin. She's dying to get back, and if you don't do what Kathleen says, she might change her mind – she's very mercurial – and whip her off to America instead.'

'But if my photo's in the paper with a caption saying something like: "Charlotte Rhymer, daughter of biographer Ranulf Rhymer, pictured in the office of her new alternative women's magazine *Skint Old Northern Woman . . .*" and then I suddenly appear in *Surprise!* or somewhere in the guise of a nanny, aren't people going to notice?'

'Dark glasses and a nanny-type felt hat,' he said. 'I'll arrange it. And take it from me, Kathleen will be occupying centre stage in any pictures, while you'll be firmly relegated to the background.'

'Yes, but what if they find out I'm really Charlotte Fry, the Pan Murderess?'

'It was a domestic accident, and no one except the local paper reported it at the time, did they?'

'Well, no.'

'So, how would they find out?'

'Only if someone told them, I suppose . . . and Angie's gone home to pack for her cruise.'

'So, what's the problem?'

I dithered.

251

'Mace, I *do* miss Caitlin, but I'm sure Kathleen could find someone else to bring her here, and—'

'No. She said you or no deal. She took a fancy to you, for some reason. You don't want me to tell Caitlin that you won't do it, do you?' he added persuasively.

'Well, no. We all want her back here. I just don't— I mean, I've never been to London.'

'I'll send a car, and you can stay here overnight; you'll feel at home, because I've recreated your old Parsonage bedroom. Then my mother will have Caitlin's things sent over – she's off to her usual hotel for Christmas – and when you've collected Caitlin in a taxi from the reception, I'll drive you both back. Bring that green dryad dress and I'll take you to see my new play. It seems to be a success.'

'Congratulations,' I said rather absently, my mind racing. Did I want to spend a night alone with Mace in London? (Yes! Yes!) Did I want to be seen at the theatre with a well-known actor and playwright, wearing a chiffon nightie from a jumble sale? (No!)

And if he took me to the theatre he was bound to see at last just how much of a fish out of water I was among his sophisticated friends ... so perhaps I'd better do it, and sooner rather than later? Gird my loins in floaty sea-green and prepare to disillusion him?

I wavered. 'You just want me to see you crowing on your own dunghill, don't you?'

'I'd rather be Cock of the North,' he said cheekily, but I thought he was shaping up to that quite nicely already.

In the end I gave in and agreed to stay one night, but more because he was showing signs of being about to drive all the way back up here just so he could drag me out and carry me off personally (not that this idea didn't have a certain attraction too).

I decided to tell him when I arrived about my not being a real Rhymer after all, though unlike Matt, who set such store by it, Mace had enough fame for both of us.

It was odd to realise I now didn't have a right to any name except, I supposed, Matt's, should I get the mad urge to start calling myself Charlie Fry at this late hour. And even that was not really my own, and forever now connected with Dead Greg.

Looking down, I discovered I'd covered the notepad in front of me with 'Charlotte North' in big loopy writing.

'You big, loopy pillock,' I told myself severely.

Chris's temporary replacement had arrived (so amazingly quickly they must have been convinced he'd thrown his lot in with the Devil and was about to hold satanic rites in the parish church), so he was devoting himself instead to the running of *Skint Old Northern Woman*, at which he was very good.

If it became a regular thing – and I felt it just might – perhaps he could become the editor?

The *Skint* team certainly didn't need me at that moment, and Anne and Em positively urged me to go to London to see Mace on his own ground.

'After all,' Em pointed out persuasively, as she sewed a button onto her dungarees while still wearing them, 'he's shown he's serious about you, doing all that work to turn his house into a home from home. You could give the man a chance.'

And even Gloria said I might as well go – it would make no difference now.

Well, in the end I thought: what the hell? Feel the fear and do it anyway, if only to stop the arrival of ever more banana trees! I'd need a veranda annexe at this rate, and would be entitled to call myself Charlie Del Monte.

I was waved off in a large car, the back of which was bigger than the Parsonage pantry, though I was divided from the driver by an impenetrable wall of glass (not that this wouldn't be a good idea for the pantry, too, when Gloria or Em were in it brewing potions).

Anne loaned me a large rucksack, into which I packed my green Hake-Hackett outfit, turquoise cashmere sweater and the pink and silver nightie and dressing gown purchased in York and as yet unworn: my encounters with Mace having so far been of the spontaneous kind. (He was clearly the kind of man who started first time without the choke out.)

Jessica loaned me a pashmina to go over my green dress, but otherwise I didn't have many clothes, so jeans would have to do. I hoped they were acceptable nanny garb, but I couldn't help thinking they were going to look very odd with a felt hat and shades.

I took a bottle of Father's best whisky as a present, undoctored this time. Em gave me a picnic hamper, and a huge cold box full of food for Mace, in case no one was feeding him properly down there. She said he needed his strength keeping up, but she didn't say for what.

She also affixed a little silver Chinese good luck charm to the zipper of my handbag and made sure I was wearing my power bracelets, including the new, much chunkier rose quartz replacement one she'd bought me.

Jessica insisted on spraying me liberally at the last minute with her Happy perfume, so I left in such a fug I had to have the windows right down for the first hour, and it must have seeped through the partition too somehow, because the driver kept coughing.

Still, it's reassuring to know that whatever happens to the rest of me, my wrists and handbag will be enjoying a really good time.

Skint Old Bookworm, No. 2

It is a little-known fact (because no one ever mentions it) that the Brontë sisters were all midgets. A visit to the Parsonage museum at Haworth, where some of their clothes are on display, reveals that they were not much bigger than the Tooth Fairy.

Chapter 24: Strange New Powers

Skint Old Fashion Victim, No. 4

Those in the know get their footwear from the sort of discount shoe warehouses where they string them together in pairs like kippers and toss them over racks.

For the persistent, there are good makes at market-stall prices, and you can build up an Imelda Marcos-sized collection for the cost of one pair of Jimmy Choos.

There is, though, as always, one snag: discount devotees can always be recognised by the two tiny punched holes in the heels of their shoes where the string was threaded.

The driver, Trevor, was quite friendly once I'd persuaded him that opening his little glass partition and all the windows for a short while would be the quickest way to get rid of the eye-watering perfumed fug.

When we stopped for lunch he declined to share my picnic, preferring a burger meal in the motorway café, but afterwards he showed me photos of his four children and serenely smiling wife (though don't ask me how you can look serene with that many offspring).

After this I fell asleep in the back of the car, due to a potent combination of perfume fumes, exhaustion from not having slept much the previous night, and over-indulgence in food from Em's picnic hamper. Oh, and the half-bottle of red wine she'd thoughtfully included might have had something to do with it, too.

By the time I woke up it was dusk.

'Primrose Hill,' Trevor said, jerking a thumb at what I'd taken to be a stretch of countryside, then turned down a street of little shops and into a square of big, terraced houses set round a garden, and we were there.

'What was that perfume called again?' he asked as we pulled up. 'Only I quite like it now it's faded a bit, and I thought I'd get some for the wife.'

'At last I have you in my power!' hissed Mace melodramatically, curling the ends of an imaginary moustache and leaning against the closed front door.

I smiled nervously – but the house *was* very quiet. I stood in the hall among my varied luggage, feeling like the new governess in one of those Gothic romances.

'We're not alone here, are we?'

He straightened and smiled, looking more like himself, which was just as alarming in its way. 'Yes. Did you think I'd have a retinue of servants lined up to greet you on the steps, with Mrs Danvers at their head? A cleaning service comes in on Mondays, and that's it. I can cook, too,' he added, 'even if I'm not in the same league as your sister Em.'

'She's sent you some food – it's in the large hamper and the cold box, and there's quite a lot of my picnic lunch left in the small basket. Oh, and there's a bottle of father's whisky, too. Not doctored this time,' I added hastily.

'Just as well – what I've got's incurable, and I'd hate to waste another bottle of good whisky. I thought you had rather a lot of luggage for one night, though,' he added. 'If you tell me which ones you want, I'll show you your room first, so you can tidy up and come down when you're ready.'

Ready for what? I wondered. After all, I'd agonised about spending the night with him and now here I was, alone and in his power, and so far he hadn't even kissed me! Didn't I deserve some compensation for being about to make a fool of myself in front of his friends?

I followed him upstairs, and he paused in front of an open door and said, 'This is mine . . . should you happen to want me for anything in the night.'

'Unlikely,' I said coldly, but I peeped in as we passed.

Mace's room had a sort of Moroccan palace look to it, something to do with the rich colours and canopied bed. It suited him anyway; as I suppose my little replica Parsonage room suited me, like a shell round a snail.

On closer examination I found it a little odd, because it was like – and yet not like. Everything was softer and thicker and more luxurious, and the bathroom off had a shower over the little bath, and a heated towel rail, and radiators.

'It's amazing,' I said, wandering around touching everything as though it might suddenly vanish like fairy gold.

'I just wanted you to feel at home, Charlie. I thought it might tempt you to come here with me sometimes.'

'But Father said you'd borrowed that book about the Parsonage interior ages ago, long before you met me.'

'Yes, he mentioned the book and I realised it was just what

258

I needed for the stage sets for my first play – sort of austere but functional, old-fashioned but with the odd modern convenience standing out like a sore thumb, you know?'

'I certainly do,' I said, back in the bedroom, fingering a satin eiderdown like a lilac cloud while my feet sank into the carpet.

The colour was all it shared with the rough cord matting in my old bedroom.

There was soft lighting, and a little desk as well as the rather Shaker-style white painted furniture. I opened the wardrobe and discovered a long, navy gabardine mac with a belt and back pleat, and a polystyrene head sporting a mouse-brown bobbed wig, a navy felt hat like something out of a wartime film, and a pair of round-lensed tinted spectacles.

'I think I've found your dressing-up clothes, but your secret's safe with me,' I said politely.

'*Your* dressing-up clothes – it's your nanny outfit. I borrowed the coat and hat from the props department, but the glasses and wig I bought. I thought they'd give you just that air of drab efficiency you might otherwise have lacked.'

'Thanks.'

I closed the door, and turned to look at him, feeling puzzled and rather touched. 'Mace, you've gone to a lot of trouble – and it might have been for nothing.'

'But I liked imagining you here, and I was vain enough to think I could persuade you. And I want you to feel happy when you are here,' he said.

'Actually, it's more like home than home is now that I've lost my room to Jessica. Aren't you afraid I might take up residence?'

'No,' he said seriously. 'No, I'm not afraid of that.'

Our eyes met, and he gave me one of his more ravishing smiles; but he still made no move to touch me and I was feeling . . . well, *piqued*, I think you might say.

'I thought you might like to see my play tonight. An old friend's invited himself along, too, with his wife, but we can shake them off afterwards, and come back here for a late supper from Em's hamper.'

'That sounds lovely,' I lied. I expect I might have enjoyed it, too, but not dressed in my jumble-sale finds, and with his London friends. But still, wasn't that part of the point of my coming, to show him how incongruous I was in his usual setting? That it wouldn't work? 'I'm looking forward to seeing your play.'

Well, at least that was true.

He looked pleased. 'Are you really? Then I'll leave you to get ready while I stow away that mountain of food and drink Em's sent. There's lots of time before we have to leave. And by the way,' he added as he turned to leave, 'note the door does lock, and the key is in it!'

I looked out of the window at the dark, quiet square, where the big trees filtered out the streetlights into filigree patterns on the damp pavement, and puzzled over what Mace had said and done – or not done – since I'd got there.

By the time I'd unpacked and had a leisurely shower I'd come to the conclusion that for some strange male reason, because I was alone in his house with him, he'd decided to behave like a perfect gentleman.

I admit, that's not quite what I had expected.

Alternatively, he was playing hard to get.

Adjusting the neck of the green dress to a point where it strained modesty, I picked up Jessica's pashmina and went down to see what the lion was doing in his den.

Walking into the theatre on Mace's arm, wearing my jumble-sale wisp of chiffon, I wondered if I was in a dream or a nightmare.

Mace, six-four of immaculate dark suiting, *was* a dream, but his friend Gavin's wife, Krystal – a tall, beige tapeworm of an ex-model – had given me to understand that I was hopelessly out of fashion to the point of being bizarre, without actually putting it into words.

However, when we got inside I could see that my dress wasn't any weirder than a lot of the other outfits, and then Mace introduced me to several of his friends who didn't seem to see anything amiss either. Most of them were really nice, and quite ordinary. This may have been because they *were* ordinary, but since I didn't know who was famous and who wasn't I just treated everyone the same, which seemed to work perfectly well.

The only dodgy moment came when I was left briefly alone with Krystal and another woman came up to talk to her, trailing a man with her like a fashion accessory.

'Sonya – and Alistair! How lovely!'

'Krystal, darling – all alone?'

'Yes, but only for a minute – Gavin and I came with Mace North.'

Not only did she not introduce me to them, the two women talked to each other like I wasn't even there.

I've never been snubbed before.

After a minute I looked across at Alistair, a tallish, slightly vacuous-looking man with a rather nice, pudgy face, and smiled and he smiled back.

I got off to a good start with him, and it was *amazingly* easy: he moved nearer and said he hadn't seen me around, had he? He was sure he wouldn't have forgotten me. I said no, I was Charlotte Rhymer and usually lived in Yorkshire, but I was there for the evening with Mace North, and we were just getting on like a house on fire when Mace, with no more than a brusque 'Excuse me!' reappeared and dragged me away.

'What do you think you were doing?' he demanded, crossing his arms and glaring down at me. 'He's a married man – where's your sense of ethics? Or were you just trying to make me jealous?'

'I was only flirting!' I protested hotly. 'And I wouldn't have done it if his wife and Krystal hadn't snubbed me – though he has got a rather nice, teddy-bear sort of face,' I added provocatively.

'Unlike me?'

'You're more Conan the Barbarian than cuddly toy.'

'I don't know if that's good or not,' he said, frowning, 'but I do know that if you flirt with anyone else, it's over the shoulder and back home.'

I bet he would, too.

'We Rhymer girls know how to deal with caveman tactics like that,' I said with dignity.

'Charlie . . .'

The bell went, and people suddenly started to move. 'Come on,' he said, slipping his hand around my waist and almost sweeping me off my feet. 'The curtain's about to go up.'

We were in a box, which made me feel as if I was on

show, although I don't suppose anyone was interested in the rest of us with Mace there; he was definitely worth looking at.

My God, he was beautiful when he was angry.

Once the play started I forgot anything else for, as well as his more obvious attributes, he could certainly write: it was sharp, witty and completely engrossing.

I was still bound up in it when we left the theatre, so I didn't notice the photographer until a series of bright lights went off right in my face. I stopped dead, blinded, but Mace kept right on walking, taking me with him.

I only hoped the green dress didn't come out in a revealing Lady Di manner, though perhaps they would airbrush me out, or something, because I wasn't anyone.

When we stopped to let Gavin and Krystal catch us up, Krystal was looking furious, but I don't know if that was pique because she missed being in the picture, or because I flirted a little bit with Gavin in the interval, just to see if it worked on him, too.

We parted outside. Mace excused us from going on, saying I'd had a long day (although Krystal didn't seem that enthusiastic about Gavin's suggestion that we all go on somewhere together, anyway), and whipped me off in a taxi, which he seemed to conjure out of thin air.

'So,' he said, sitting back with a good foot of space between us. 'Is flirting something you make a habit of Charlie?'

'I wasn't asleep,' I said, snapping my eyes wide open again. 'And no, I didn't even realise I could flirt until tonight.'

'Of course you can do it. You had them eating out of your hand, and Krystal and Sonya are probably giving their husbands hell at this very moment.'

I yawned. 'It was their own fault, they should have been nicer to me.'

'Just how nice did you want them to be?' he snapped.

'I meant Krystal and Sonya should have been nicer, not the men,' I explained, 'but I'm sorry if they've got into arguments because of it . . . they were nice. Most of the people I met tonight were nice.'

'Well, I don't know why you should sound surprised about it!'

'Mmm . . . but some of them were quite well known, weren't they? And I'm not anyone, really. I don't fit in your world.'

'Why not? The theatre world's full of oddballs.'

'Thanks.'

'And if you don't fit into my world, I'll make it fit around you.'

'But, Mace, everyone will think you're mad! I think you're mad! I'm not anybody. There's no reason . . .'

'Of course you're somebody – the artist daughter of famous biographer Ranulf Rhymer, editor of a new alternative magazine – the article's coming out in the paper on Sunday, by the way – beautiful, unusual, maddening . . .'

'I still don't think people will know what you see in me; and neither do I. I must have the charm of novelty, but it'll wear off.'

'No it won't. It's not love philtres or infatuation or senile dementia or anything else: it's love. And it doesn't matter what other people think, does it?'

'I suppose not, though I thought it did before tonight. But I suppose people are just people when you get down to it. Some are nice, some are boring and some are swollen-headed and full of themselves.'

'I hope that last one wasn't aimed at me?'

'No – you seem surprisingly normal, considering.'

'Considering what?' he demanded, but fortunately we'd arrived home, and the first thing I did was kick off my sandals and head for the kitchen.

I might be exhausted – it seemed like a century had passed since this morning – but I was also ravenously hungry. Mace set the table with candles, and opened champagne, and we demolished a large part of Em's supplies, after which I felt like a new woman (but not necessarily a better one).

Mace was a very champagne sort of man, I thought: dry, crisp and given to the odd occasional explosion.

I was more like the peaty single malt whisky we had afterwards; though actually, as it turned out, a blended one would have been closer to the mark.

'I'm glad you've stopped being all dog-in-the-manger about my flirting,' I told him, sinking into a rather billowy sofa and tucking my feet under me. 'Because I've got something I want to tell you.'

He stared at me for a moment, then threw himself down next to me and pulled me into his arms. 'I'll show you dog-in-the-manger,' he muttered, kissing me.

I kissed him back with some enthusiasm, which might or might not have been due to the combination of champagne and whisky, but after a minute he stopped and frowned down at me. 'I really wasn't going to do that.'

'Well, stop doing it, then; I did say I'd got something I wanted to tell you.'

'But is it something I want to hear, like "I love you, Mace"?'

'No, it's something I found out recently – about myself.

But I think you ought to know and . . . well, I want to tell you about it.'

He settled back with me in his arms, and all the lights suddenly dimmed to a romantic glow.

'How did you do that?' I demanded, sitting up.

'Magic,' he said, pulling me back.

I was glad of the dim light, actually, because telling him all about Ranulf not being my father, and all the rest of it, upset me much more than I expected, and Mace had to comfort me in the way he does best.

One thing sort of led to another, but had I behaved like a lady I'm sure he would have carried on behaving like a perfect gentleman, for whatever weird masculine reasons he was doing it.

However, he was pretty perfect just as he was.

Chapter 25: Much Travelled

Skint Old Philosophy

We are probably the first generation capable of choosing not to become our mothers.

Mace found me planning out the conservatory next morning wearing only his dressing gown, and had there been more ground cover I don't suppose I'd have been wearing that for very long, either.

'Mace,' I protested, fending him off with a tropical plant catalogue, 'the neighbours can see us.'

He released me reluctantly. 'Then you'd better order enough plants to turn the place into an impenetrable jungle while I go and find some breakfast.'

'Maybe I'll go and put some clothes on first. I only meant to have a quick look in here in the daylight, but I got carried away.'

'I'd like to get carried away, too, but it's late, and I've got to go and collect Caitlin's things from Mother's house before you do your nanny act at the Savoy.'

'Oh God – is that where the reception is?'

'It's all arranged. Someone will show you where Kathleen and Caitlin are, there'll be a couple of quick photos, and then you get back in the taxi and come here.'

'And then we can all go home?'

'Then we can all go home,' he agreed, smiling. 'But first, we've got to go to Mother's.'

'*We?*'

'She just phoned up. She wants to meet you.'

I don't know about *meet* me – it was more like I'd been granted a short, royal audience.

Mace's mother was a tall, strong-boned woman with cropped white hair and the same slightly slanting dark blue eyes. She was wearing cord trousers tucked into short laced boots and a jumper that had seen better days.

'Well,' she said, surveying me doubtfully through the first of a series of rank cigarettes, 'you're a shrimp, aren't you? Still, at least you're not skinny – and they do say size isn't everything!'

I looked helplessly at Mace; all he'd told me about his mother was that she'd always spent at least half the year travelling abroad, wherever the fancy took her, both before and after she was widowed. He hadn't told me what she was like.

'Go away, Mace,' she ordered. 'Put Caitlin's stuff in the car, and I'll send Charlotte down to you in ten minutes.'

'So,' she said, as soon as he'd gone, 'Mace has told me all about you. Met your father – man's a handsome fool.'

'He's not really my father,' I confessed. 'I've just told Mace that actually it was someone else.'

'Oh?' She lit a fresh cigarette from the stub of the first

and blew smoke rings. I hoped they spelled out SOS and Mace would come back and rescue me. 'Does everyone know?'

'Only the family, and we've only just found out. My brother, Branwell, has the same father: Brendan Furness, the poet.'

'Mmm. Know the family, and at least he's dead, so no messy ends. So, has it broken you all up? Destroyed this strange Rhymer clan Mace's been going on about, and Caitlin's itching to get back to? Speak up!'

'No,' I said slowly. 'No, if anything it's made us closer. Stronger.'

'Good, because it's attractive to Mace, this family business,' she said, striding about the room. 'He never had one. I travelled, did my own thing – wasn't fashionable, but hell, you only get one life! Hubert – Mace's father – did his own thing too. Handsome, boring man – big mistake. I should never have married, though the money was useful. Mace had a nanny.'

That explained a lot.

'He wants a family – that's why he married that actress when she got pregnant – she trapped him nicely! But now he seems to want you, too.' She looked at me again. 'So, do you love him?'

'What?' I stammered. 'Well, yes, but – I mean, I didn't want to. I don't want to get married again, either. And anyway,' I added, becoming indignant, 'you obviously didn't want to do the homemaking wife bit so you should understand that neither do I. I've already had one go, and I didn't like it. It wastes too much time and I've got other fish to fry.'

'He's got money,' she said abruptly. 'He's got fame, he's got looks. All he wants from you is for you to be yourself and let him love you. You go away and think about that. Maybe I haven't been the perfect mother, but I'd like him to be happy now – and you seem to be what he wants.' She turned away abruptly. 'There, I've had my say.'

As I was leaving she added, over her shoulder: 'By the way, Mace gave me a copy of *Skint Old Northern Woman*. Liked it.'

'I'm so glad,' I said coldly. 'I like it too, and I think my readers might think it a bit of a cop-out if the editor suddenly married your son, don't you?'

'No,' she said thoughtfully. 'Having met you, I think you're dyed-in-the-wool skint old northern woman all the way through, and nothing's going to change you.'

Kathleen looked vaguely at the mac, round glasses, and fringe of mousy hair sticking out from under the hat. 'Charlie? You look different.'

Caitlin, after an amazed scrutiny, threw herself at me, giggling hysterically. She was clearly overtired, overexcited and overwrought, so I picked her up, meringue dress and all. Her little face pressed against mine felt worryingly hot.

'Just a few quick snaps,' murmured Kathleen, arranging us with a series of small tugs. 'Now, if Caitlin leans forward towards me . . .'

As Mace predicted, Kathleen was centre-front to the camera lens, kissing her daughter in a fond farewell.

The photos should be deeply touching, though, because Caitlin's raised, flushed face was running with tears – only

270

I knew they were really overexcited tears of hilarity at Nanny's appearance, not regret.

'Can we go now, Charlie?' she demanded after a few minutes of this. 'Mummy, is that it?'

'Yes, darling,' Kathleen said. 'The whole wedding was a *Hello!* exclusive. Now, give Mummy a kiss goodbye – I'll have to get back to the party.'

'No,' Caitlin said firmly. 'There's been too much kissing already.' And she turned her head away.

'She's tired, Mrs – Mrs Steigland,' I said, just remembering in time who she'd married. 'It's been an exciting day for her. Shall I take her away, now? In fact,' I said, looking cautiously down at Caitlin's suddenly sober, and slightly awry expression, 'I think she's going to be sick!'

Kathleen took a step back: 'Oh, darling – I told you not to eat two lots of crème brûlée! Yes, do take her away, Nanny, and – er, Mummy will phone, darling . . .'

Fortunately there were no photographers to see when Caitlin threw up behind a convenient pillar outside, only a disgusted doorman and two arriving guests, and although the taxi driver was reluctant to let us get into his cab, I assured him that should Caitlin feel that she had to chunder again, she could do it into my handbag.

Well, maybe it wasn't strictly speaking *my* handbag, but the staid clasp-top leather job Mace had borrowed with the nanny outfit.

Fortunately this extreme measure didn't prove necessary, Caitlin having recovered her colour, but not her bounce, by the time we got to Mace's house. He carried her in, half-asleep, and put her straight on the sofa for a little nap.

She looked like a rather flushed and dishevelled cherub.

'She'll probably feel better by the time we're ready to go,' Mace said.

'I think she felt better as soon as she'd thrown up,' I said. 'Too much excitement for one day, but at least she doesn't get car sick, and she looks tired enough to sleep most of the way there.'

I yawned, and itched under the wig. No wonder Walter never wears his! 'I'll go and change out of this awful outfit.'

'Do you want any help?' he offered, a gleam in his eyes. 'Only you look pretty grim in that uniform, and I'd enjoy helping you remove it.'

'No, thank you,' I said primly. 'Caitlin might wake up.'

I sincerely hoped he didn't have a nanny fixation, after practically being brought up by one, because I had no intention of ever donning that get-up again.

Chapter 26: Dazed and Confused

Back in the Parsonage kitchen with Anne and Em, Flossie on my knee, I described my adventures.

Well, *some* of them – the ones that didn't need an X certificate.

It was late, and Mace had dropped me at my door and gone straight on down to the cottage, with Caitlin fast asleep in the back of the car in her child seat, tucked up in a bunny rug. She was still wearing the crumpled meringue dress, but at least she hadn't been sick again.

The house was quiet; Chris was staying down at the Vicarage, Father and Jess had gone out, and the twins were in bed. Bran was quietly sitting at the far end of the kitchen table, doing a big jigsaw puzzle of an Alpine scene.

It had been an action-packed trip in more ways than one, and I felt exhausted and sort of stunned by the experience. Jet-lagged. It was good to sit there with a mug of cocoa in my hands and a plate of Em's macaroons in front of me, fondling Flossie's silky ears.

'So how's Mace, Chaz?' Anne asked. 'Is he absolutely shattered too?'

'He's not the man I took him for if he isn't,' Em remarked.

'Mace behaved like a perfect gentleman,' I said evasively, not mentioning that unfortunately *my* behaviour hadn't reached the same standard.

'Bad luck, Chaz,' Anne said sympathetically. 'Maybe the potion's worn off then?'

'No it hasn't. He still wants to marry me, though I don't know why. I mean, things are all right as they are, aren't they?'

'Apart from the fact that you may not have a home of your own much longer,' Em said. 'Jessica and Father must have seen every house for sale in Upvale.'

'Have they? But I'm sure he can't be serious – he wouldn't really sell the Parsonage?'

'Jessica's been working her wiles on him. He's started to say how cosy it would be with just the two of them, and the girls, presumably, in a little home of their own.'

'That doesn't sound like Father. And it can't be that small, either, because of all the books, and a study so he can work.'

'And a big bedroom, with lots of effing wardrobes,' Anne added.

'Let's not think about it until after Christmas,' Em said. 'We'll make this the best Rhymer family Christmas ever, and Chris and I are getting married the day after tomorrow.'

'Oh, Em! Is it all arranged?'

'Three ceremonies in one day – register office, church porch blessing and then a little rite up on the moors with Xanthe, Freya and Lilith. Chris says he wants to be sure he's covered all the angles.'

'I think that should do it. Is it just family?'

'Mace and Caitlin can come if they like, and I don't mind the twins. That Jessica will come whether I want her or not.

Then Chris is moving in here with me while we look for a place of our own – but not an effing Mango Home.'

'Oh, Em, if only you and Anne hadn't put all that money into *Skint Old Northern Woman*, you'd have much more to spend on a cottage now!'

'It's taking off. Going to be a cult thing, I think,' Anne said thoughtfully. 'Get our investment back.'

'Yes, and it could give Chris a job too, in case he's at a loose end now he's retired. And then Charlie can concentrate on writing the articles for the next one, and her painting – and Mace.'

'It will certainly be good to get back to my painting again: I've got an idea, a new theme.' It was the combination of Mace, and the lush greenery in that outrageous conservatory . . . 'I met Mace's mother. She's mad.'

'Well, we can't effing talk,' Em said. 'What was Mace's house like?'

'You'd like it, Em. Parts of it are just like the Parsonage, only comfortable, and the conservatory has a little domed glass roof, and a fountain. Oh, and the garden is long and surrounded by trees and bushes, you could be in the country!'

'So you quite liked it then?' Anne said drily. 'What about London?'

'Mace's part is more like a village, with a little shopping street, and a park. We didn't go anywhere else except the theatre – someone took our photo coming out – and he introduced me to lots of people. Some of them looked a bit familiar, so I expect they were actors and stuff,' I said vaguely. 'They were all quite friendly and sort of ordinary, except for a couple of women who snubbed me, so it was all right. If they don't delete me from that picture of Mace, though, you'll probably be able to see right through my nightie.'

'If so, let's hope it says who you are,' Em commented. 'It'll give the magazine a bit more coverage.'

'If you can see through Charlie's dress, she'll probably get lots of effing coverage,' Anne said. 'What's in the carrier bag, Charlie? Prezzies?'

'One present – for Walter.'

I fished out the bobbed nanny wig, looking like a flaccid ferret, and the polystyrene head. 'Mace got the wig to go with the nanny disguise, in case anyone recognised me – the article on the magazine's about to come out. He didn't want it back, so I thought I'd gift-wrap it for Walter for Christmas. What do you think?'

I arranged the wig on the head, and they studied the effect.

'It's quite Good King Wenceslas, isn't it?' Em said. 'He'll love it. I tell you what, I'll make a wreath of gilded artificial ivy and berries to go round it. That will finish it off.'

Bran, who'd been slapping jigsaw pieces into place with great speed, now looked up and said: 'Finished.'

'So it is,' Em said. She looked at her watch: 'One hour and twenty minutes, Bran. I think that's a record. Are you going to turn it over and do the other side?'

'No. Might go up to the pub.'

'Well, Ran and Jess are there, and Walter.'

Bran went off to find his coat, and once he was out of earshot I said, 'Mace managed to find a copy of that book Bran wanted – I don't know how. It's in America, but it's coming Federal Express, or something.'

'Well, bugger me!' Anne said.

If the bestseller charts and the literary prizes were judged on the actual numbers of books sold by the authors, Mills & Boon writers would probably occupy most of the top places. However, these can safely be left out of the equation, since they are only writing for women, a mere half of the world's population.

Em had a white wedding. It snowed.

Fortunately it was just a light sprinkling, enough to make everything look pretty, but not stop Chris's friend, another motorbiking vicar, from getting here to officiate.

Em looked lovely in the tawny velvet gown, with a dark cloak for warmth, loaned for the occasion by Freya – very *Wuthering Heights*, although actually Em is more Heathcliff than Chris is.

Love kept her warm; the rest of us dressed like Nanook of the North or Hell's Vicars – or teddy bears, in Caitlin's case.

We drove in a small procession from venue to venue, ending with the bumpy track up to the standing stones, then we all retired back to the Parsonage, where Gloria and Walter laid out a buffet prepared by Em, and had a party.

I think I made rather an impression with the visiting vicar, using my newly acquired flirting skills, until he noticed Mace glowering at him and sheered off; but it was quite encouraging, what with that and the two men in London, because at least *they* hadn't had any love philtre and yet still obviously fancied me.

Perhaps the love philtre didn't have anything to do with it, and Mace really did fall for me. Only when I looked at him, tall, dark, handsome, brooding and way out of my league, I just found it very hard to believe.

Later, Father, Chris and Mace got their heads together in a corner, having what looked like a very serious conversation: but being men it was just as likely to be about something totally trivial, like sport. Or the pros and cons of marriage – Jessica had gone distinctly orange-blossom and yearning as the day wore on.

'That Mace!' Gloria said, bobbing up beside me suddenly like a cork as I watched the three little girls chasing each other around the room, flushed and overexcited, their home-made wreaths of gilded bay leaves slipping over their eyes. 'He wasn't the dark man with the child, bringing trouble and dividing the family, like I saw in the leaves – I don't *think*. It must have been that Brendan Furness. He was dark, and he brought trouble, turning out to be your dad, and all.'

'He hasn't broken up the family, though, has he?' I pointed out. 'We're still together. If anyone breaks us up, it's clearly going to be Jessica, because Father's putty in her hands; and since he found out about Bran and me he seems to have lost all power to resist her.'

'You must all stay here in your place; not let that Mace lure you off to London with him again.'

'*He* seems to want to stay here too, and marry me, but I don't see the point of marriage any more. I don't really see myself housekeeping in his cottage either, do you? Such a waste of time when I could be writing magazine articles and painting!'

'I need to read your leaves again,' she muttered thoughtfully. '*And* his.'

*   *   *

'Gloria just made me drink one of her disgusting cups of tea,' Mace complained later. 'It hardly goes with champagne and good brandy, does it? Then she said I was "a great streak of nowt", and went off with the cup.'

'Oh, good. I'm glad she's getting to like you, now she knows you better.'

'*I* wasn't glad to see Chris's friend getting to know *you* better,' he said darkly, putting his arm round me and pulling me close. 'I'm jealous as hell. Is that what you wanted?'

'No, of course not,' I assured him, though actually it was still an enjoyable novelty. I wondered if that extreme Goth look had frightened men away before. Or perhaps it was just that I hadn't thought to try flirting. 'I don't see why either of you finds me interesting. I'm not young or particularly pretty, or sophisticated, or—'

'Don't fish for compliments; you're beautiful in your own strange way – and unique – that's why I love you. You aren't like anyone I've ever met before.'

'I don't suppose Em or Anne are like anyone you've ever met before, either.'

'But I haven't fallen in love with either of them – only you. You're what I've been searching for always, only I didn't know it until I found you,' he said poetically.

I was putty in his hands. A voice that beautiful could make baked beans sound like the food of the gods.

Caitlin panted to a halt in front of us and stared from underneath her lopsided festive wreath.

'Daddy, you've got your arm round Charlie!'

Mace put his other arm round Caitlin. 'It's because I'm trying to persuade her to marry me.'

Caitlin peered across him at me, her eyes wide. 'Are you going to marry Daddy?'

'I don't know.'

'I think you ought to,' she said firmly. 'Then Anne and Em and Bran and everybody will be *my* family too, won't they? And I'll belong here.'

'Yes, but wouldn't you mind my marrying your daddy?'

'Not really – he won't love you as much as he loves me, but he does like you a lot, really.'

She bestowed a kind smile on us and skipped off.

I stared after her. 'Isn't the stepmother/stepdaughter relationship supposed to be excruciatingly difficult?'

'Only when they hit adolescence, I think, and then they're so awful it hardly stands out against the rest. Anyway, now you've received royal dispensation, are you going to say yes?'

'No – I still don't think it would work long-term, Mace, so there isn't any point.'

'Why not? What do you really *want* out of life, Charlie?'

'To stay here in Upvale, and be successful with the paintings and magazine – which it looks like I'm going to be – and for the Parsonage to stay the same, with my family around me. Only nothing ever does stay quite the same, does it?'

'No. Your family's changing already, now Jessica and Chris are becoming part of it. And what about *me* now you've turned me upside down? Do you want me?'

'You know I do, but . . . well, I want to live *my* life, not be a minor satellite orbiting yours.'

'I think it's the other way round – *I'm* the one being sucked into orbit around Planet Rhymer, and there's no escape now.'

'Daddy,' Caitlin said, reappearing. 'We have to come back on Christmas Eve, Em says, for dinner and Snapdragon and

Hunt the Mouses. And I can come tomorrow too, and help Feeb and Clo and everyone bring in the holly, and the ivy and mistletoe, and make decorations, and do the tree.'

'Snapdragon?' he queried, looking down at me, eyebrow raised. 'Mouses?'

'You'll see,' I told him.

'Time to go home to bed,' Mace said, picking Caitlin up. 'You've got a busy day tomorrow – you've got our tree and decorations to put up too, don't forget.'

'I'll get lots of holly,' she said sleepily.

When everyone had gone I retired to my chaste couch, and there discovered an early Christmas present, tied up in gay wrapping paper and gold cord.

The label on it was from Gloria: 'Open this first thing tomorrow: not before, not after.'

Another spell?

Chapter 27: Present Magic

After I opened Gloria's present next morning, as per instructions, her magic had such a powerful effect on me that by the time I shook off the spell and went upstairs with Flossie everyone had had breakfast and gone, except Anne and Em.

Anne was still sitting lazily over a cup of coffee, since she's finished her course of treatment and so doesn't have to rush out every day to the hospital, and Em was making Christmas stollen at the other end of the table, hence the delicious, spicy aroma that greeted me.

'We'd given you up,' Em said. 'Thought you might have gone down to Mace's, or something.'

'No. I was a bit . . . a bit occupied,' I said distractedly. 'And I'm not very hungry so I'll just have some toast.'

'You'll have more than toast,' Gloria said, suddenly popping her head in from the scullery. 'You need to keep up your strength. Am I right?'

'I don't know how on earth you knew, when I had no idea,' I told her.

'No idea about what?' Em demanded, looking up.

'Gloria gave me an early Christmas present last night – a pregnancy test kit. And I've just done it, and it's positive.'

'Bloody hell, Chaz!' Anne exclaimed.

'Well! And you asked *me* if I knew about safe sex,' Em said. 'How pregnant are you?'

'I've no idea. You know how erratic my periods have always been – probably why I've always found it difficult to get pregnant. It seems ages since my last one, but I sort of thought I was heading into an early menopause.'

'Not yet, my chicken,' Gloria said. 'You're much too young for that.'

'But aren't I a bit old for pregnancy? And I don't even feel pregnant. I wonder if the test was wrong?'

'No, it's right,' Gloria assured me. 'I could see it in the leaves.'

'Oh, well,' I said, sitting down. 'There's no point in getting excited. I expect I'll just lose it like the others.'

'Not this one you won't,' she assured me.

I looked at her hopefully. 'It says I'll have the baby in the tea leaves?'

'Yes – it was there all along, only when it came out about that Brendan Furness being your real dad I got confused and thought he might be the dark stranger bringing trouble and a baby, and nothing to do with Mace. But I kept looking again, and it's still there.'

'You'll have to tell Mace, it's only fair,' Em pointed out.

'I can't! He only married Kathleen because she was pregnant! I don't want him to think he has to marry me.'

'Since he wants to marry you anyway, that doesn't matter, does it?'

'I don't think he really does – I'm just a whim. I seem to have some sort of novelty value for him, though I don't know why, and it can't last.'

'You're a bloody expensive and long-lasting whim, Chaz!' said Anne. 'Face it – the man *loves* you.'

'And he could have anyone, but he's chosen you,' Em pointed out. 'Is it because he's been married before? Anyone can make a mistake.'

'Mistakes – he's had two previous wives, don't forget.'

'*You* were married before, too.'

'But only once!'

'Well, you aren't operating a "two strikes and you're out" policy, are you?'

'No . . .' I agreed. Everything just seemed too much to take in at that moment. 'Let's just keep this to ourselves for a few days – I'm finding it all hard to get my head around. And until I get over the three-month stage I'm really not going to believe it's going to happen.'

'All right,' Anne agreed.

'You must tell Mace on Christmas Eve, though,' Gloria insisted. 'That's the right time.'

'Is it?'

'Yes,' confirmed Em, looking up with that familiar, far-seeing, 'the lights are on but there's nobody home' expression. 'Mace is going to make decisions on Christmas Eve that will affect us all.'

'Changes are coming,' agreed Gloria.

'They certainly are,' I said, looking disbelievingly down at my still-flat stomach.

I mean, if they call mothers over thirty elderly, what are they going to call *me*? Geriatric?

'Hurry up and eat your breakfast,' Anne said. 'The girls will be down in a minute, ready to go for the Christmas tree. We're picking Caitlin up on the way.'

'Yes,' agreed Em. 'There's lots to do. I've got all the sugar mice to make for the hunt later, and I need some string for the tails, and more silver balls for the eyes. Oh – and Bran says will someone take him shopping for his Christmas presents?'

'I'll do that then, and get the stuff for the mice,' I offered.

Bran may be last-minute with his present-buying, but he solves it by going into one shop and buying the same thing for everyone.

The year it was a cobbler's and we all got small shoe-cleaning kits in tins, was particularly memorable, but the year of the chemist was even more so.

'He's on the phone,' Em said. 'Can't you hear him shouting?'

There was a far-off bellowing going on, now I came to think about it, but I'd just sort of thought it must be Father, as usual.

'Won't hold it next to his ear in case the bloody demons pop into his head,' Anne explained.

'I thought that was just mobile phones?'

'So did I, but it seems we were wrong. His girlfriend phoned up.'

'Isis? You mean she's *real*?'

'Sounded real. They started talking some weird language or I'd have left the door open so we could have had a listen.'

'I'd better put her on the present list,' I said. 'Let's hope Bran chooses something easy to post this year because it'll have to go straight off.'

'Done all mine,' Anne said complacently. 'Order one day, arrive the next. Sorted.'

'Speaking of orders, I'd better just see how the magazine's doing,' I suggested.

'It's OK – Chris has it in hand,' Em assured me. 'You'd better start writing issue two: it's taking off.'

A strange letter arrived from Matt, who had apparently been sent all the magazine cuttings of me in London with Mace, and the newspaper article about setting up the magazine with Anne and Em.

Angie must have sent them as a last spiteful gesture before setting off on her cruise.

Matt seemed to be insinuating that I'd been underhand and devious in being happy and successful without telling him, and I should be paying maintenance to him, or something.

However, as I'd learned recently, what I actually signed was a clean-break divorce agreement, giving me no further right to Matt's money and vice versa. Not even a duck.

There was something deeply satisfying about Matt knowing that not only had I set up a successful business without him, but I was going out with a man who was so far up the desirability ladder he's fallen off the end. Had I wanted revenge, this was surely the best sort.

He also included a threat to tell Mace (and the newspapers) that I'd killed Greg, so I sent him a 'publish and be damned' note back: Mace knows, and no one can say it was anything other than an unfortunate domestic accident – or not without being sued by my personal Barbarian Horde.

Now, had anyone noticed that the mousy little nanny hovering in the background of one of Kathleen's wedding feature photographs was me, that might have been a different kettle of fish. But even I couldn't recognise me in that outfit.

When buying lemons for gin and tonic, buy large unwaxed ones, slice them thinly, and freeze. This way when you add them to a drink you get both ice and lemon instantly, and it is economical since you never have green-furred lemon halves on saucers at the back of your fridge.

Christmas seemed to hurtle towards us, a whirl of activity and excited children; and excited me, too, nursing my secret to myself.

It was just as well Chris was now running the magazine efficiently, for after the article about *Skint Old Northern Woman* was published, with a photo of 'the three daughters of Ranulf Rhymer, the biographer' ('Botticelli's *Three Effing Graces*,' as Anne put it), we were swamped with orders and enquiries. People wanted to subscribe regularly, so we were having to do a bit of long-term planning. I'd started writing articles for the next one.

I was also painting like mad, too: a London gallery had seen the article, and wanted to show my work, though what they would make of my current *Adam and Eve* series, goodness knew. Still, thank goodness for Chris's managerial skills.

It felt like Chris had always been one of us – he just naturally fitted in, and Em looked terribly happy. We were all doing an ostrich thing about what would happen to the family after Christmas, because it looked increasingly like the unthinkable was going to happen and Father would sell the Parsonage and move into a smaller place with the Treacle Tart.

Mace and Caitlin were here every day, too – in fact if you took a film of the Parsonage and the bit of track leading to Mace's cottage, and speeded it up, it would probably look like an ants' nest. Sometimes Caitlin went off with the girls, and Mace and I got a bit of time together. It was difficult otherwise, because I wouldn't spend the night at the cottage with Caitlin there, and he couldn't leave her and come to the Parsonage. But he hadn't mentioned marriage for days.

He'd probably seen how impossible it would be, and decided to settle for what he could get – which I was afraid in my case was almost anything he asked for. And he'd already given me the best Christmas present in the world, even if he didn't know it.

Why did everyone insist that I had to tell him? He'd start going on about marriage again, even if he *had* changed his mind. It seemed a pity . . .

We had a delirious postcard from Angie, who'd flown out to the Caribbean to start her cruise, and a birth announcement from ex-spouse and wife number two, but no duck. (Still, there were no veiled threats either, this time.) It didn't upset me as much as Mace thought, but I let him comfort me again in the way he does best.

Nobody does it better.

The Christmas landslide swept us all along to Christmas Eve, and paused for that still moment when even the house seemed to be holding its breath on the edge of something momentous.

The Parsonage was garlanded, bedecked and scented with fir and spices. Presents were wrapped and piled under a huge tree, and Walter stoked every roaring fire in rotation, because there was no skimping on firewood at Christmas.

The night before Christmas Eve we all went down to Mace's cottage to add some finishing touches to his decorations (and, from Em, some edible gifts to his larder) so it now looked, and smelled, like an extension of the Parsonage.

Chris had closed the magazine office for the holiday, leaving the diminishing little poltergeist thing as caretaker, and was down at the church helping his temporary replacement with the celebrations.

Em communed with her kitchen, performing traditional rites of her own, and on Christmas Eve manufactured an excuse to get everyone out of the house for an hour while Gloria hid the sugar mice.

Then six o'clock came, and the Rhymer family and guests assembled for what we all knew in our hearts to be the last Christmas in the Parsonage.

Chapter 28: Snapdragon

As always, one of the oddest things about the Christmas Eve party was seeing Walter with a flossy white beard, eyebrows and hair; but then, bald Father Christmases are not traditional.

He had to take the beard off to eat his dinner, and on one memorable occasion his eyebrows kept dropping off into the food.

Mace and Caitlin were to go back to their cottage after dinner followed by the Mouse Hunt and Snapdragon, but come back next morning. Mace wanted me to stay, too, but I wouldn't: this Christmas morning it should be just Mace and Caitlin, the stocking, and three million presents.

Not that she didn't seem to have a lot of presents under our tree, too.

While we were all drinking mulled wine and eating a Christmas cake depicting Stonehenge under snow, with Druids, set in a garland of gilded oak leaves, the girls ran in and out shouting out how many presents they had under the tree, and begging to open just *one* now.

'Mouse Hunt!' Father announced loudly, putting his empty glass down. 'The one who finds the most wins the chocolate mouse. Come on, Jess!'

He seized her hand and she looked surprised. 'But isn't it just for the children, Ran? I mean—'

'Children? No – why should they have all the fun?' Dragging her with him he rushed out into the hall and flung open the door of the grandfather clock.

'Aha! One!'

'Come on, Mace,' I said. 'Not finding any is a true mark of shame.'

'Don't you Rhymers have an unfair advantage? You'll know where they all are from previous years.'

'Oh, Em and Gloria always find more new places – and this year there are fifty, because there are more of us to find them.'

The others, swept along by Father's enthusiasm, had left the room on his heels, but I tarried long enough to remove a green mouse from the music box on the mantelpiece, and two more from behind the fire dogs.

Mace, getting into the swing of things, beat me to the slightly warm one in the light fitting.

We had a good number by the time we passed Em in the kitchen (there never are any in there – it's too under her feet) and descended the stairs to my cottage.

'Will there be any down here?' Mace asked.

'Not usually, but there might be this year,' I told him, resolutely bolting the door at the bottom of the stairs. 'There, that should hold the others off if they think of it.'

'Oh?' he said, a gleam in his eyes. 'Isn't that cheating, or did you have something else in mind?'

'I've got a couple of things to say, Mace.'

'And I've got something to say to you, too, darling – or

break to you before dinner, when your father tells me he intends to spill the beans.'

'Spill the beans?' I echoed, forgetting my own news. 'About what?'

'You first,' he ordered. 'And this had better be a confession that you're dying to marry me after all!'

'No-o . . .' I said, avoiding his dark eyes. 'No – I – it's . . .' I took a deep breath and took the plunge. 'Mace, I'm pregnant.'

Mace stopped lounging elegantly against the table and stared at me. 'Pregnant? My God! Charlie – but you told me you couldn't – that you were—'

'Barren? I know. And I'm sorry, Mace. I did think I was.'

He strode across the room and seized me. 'Sorry? What the hell are you sorry about? It's wonderful! Aren't you pleased?'

'I'm still stunned. I can't believe it, or that it will be all right. But Gloria and Em both predicted it, and that the baby will be fine.'

'Darling, of course it will be all right!'

'It's not only that I'm afraid of losing it like the others, whatever Em and Gloria tell me; but I'm past forty now, which is old for a first baby. And there's a higher risk of something being wrong with it.'

'There's more chance of everything being *right* with it.' He looked searchingly down at me. 'My secretive little Undine! So, how long have you known?'

'Only a few days,' I assured him hastily. 'Gloria knew first, and she bought me a pregnancy test. I still don't feel any different from usual, which is partly why I didn't want to tell you yet. Only, Em and Gloria both seemed to think I should tell you *tonight* for some reason.'

'Not tell me? Of course you should bloody tell me! I'm the father, aren't I?' he demanded hotly, his arms tightening around me.

'Of course, but you *had* to marry Kathleen, and I didn't want you to think I was trying to force your hand.'

'But, Charlie, it's the other way round this time – I want to marry you, and you won't even stay overnight at the cottage with me!'

'Because of Caitlin. It wouldn't be fair to her to suddenly appear in your bed one morning – and then disappear when you got tired of me.'

'Which would be never – so she's going to have to get used to it. In fact, when we're married she's going to think it pretty odd if we *don't* live together.'

'I don't know what to do any more,' I said helplessly, putting down my handful of hot, sticky sugar mice.

'Just as well I do, then. Let me tell you *my* news: I've bought the Parsonage from your father, lock, stock, barrel and Rhymers. I'm moving in, and the only people moving out are Ran, Jessica, and the twins – and then only as far as my cottage. We've done a sort of house-swap.'

My knees buckled slightly and he held me up, close against him, which made it even harder to concentrate on what he'd just said. 'You and Father have been plotting this behind our backs? How could he do this to me? The devious old sod!'

'Tut, tut,' Mace said. 'Is that any way for a dutiful daughter to speak about her father?'

'He isn't strictly speaking my father; and how can you expect the rest of us just to fall in line with your arrangements?'

'Why not? Isn't it the perfect plan? The Parsonage continues being everyone's home, just like before, except I thought Em and Chris might like a private suite in the attics, so they can be on their own when they want to be.'

I pushed him away as much as I could (which wasn't very far) so I could look up at him. 'Is this just a negotiating move? You can't *possibly* want to take on the whole clan!'

'It's more of a coup. Think of the advantages, Charlie – we can turn the Summer Cottage into the *Skint Old Northern Woman* offices and Chris can run it full time. Em continues her reign over the household, but they'll have their own private spaces too. You can write for the magazine, paint in your veranda, and generally continue leading your odd Charlie Rhymer existence, and Anne and Bran can come and go as they please. The twins will be near, which Caitlin will like, and even Ran can use the house as a bolt hole if Jessica gets too much for him. What do you say?'

Not a lot – the ground seemed to have been efficiently and ruthlessly cut from beneath my feet, and if I didn't grab Mace I was going to fall an awfully long way . . .

'What about Gloria and Walter?' I said weakly.

'I included them in with the family – they will stay here, won't they, if you all do?'

'But, Mace . . .'

'I do have one condition, though: you have to come with me to London sometimes, because then I'll have you all to myself. I have a fantasy about you and me in the conservatory . . . all that lush, tropical greenery . . . the hot, steamy air . . .'

The air seemed to be getting a bit hot and steamy *now*. But it was interesting that it wasn't just me who fantasised about dragging people behind bushes.

'So what do you say, darling?'

'I think I've been overwhelmed by superior fighting forces.'

He was just overwhelming me again when the veranda door burst open, letting in a cold blast of air and several people.

'Cheats!' Anne said. 'We had to run round in the cold and get the key out of the frog!'

She unbolted and threw open the door to the stairs, and the girls rushed down followed by the two dogs.

There was a crush of bodies in the little room, and then it emptied just as suddenly again – including, I noticed, of the mice I'd put down on the table.

'Oh dear. I'm going to get the booby prize for Least Mice,' I said ruefully.

'Which is?'

'I have to wear the reindeer headband and fluffy tail all through dinner. But I can take the flashing nose off to actually eat.'

'I can hardly wait,' Mace said.

Party Games: Snapdragon

Snapdragon is an old English custom that well deserves reviving, since it is highly dangerous but still legal. It makes an exciting finish to a Christmas meal, the adrenaline rush aiding digestion.

Involving the same technique as igniting the Christmas pudding (and there is something so deeply symbolic about setting light to the finale of a meal the woman of the house has spent the entire day producing) you simply pile a great heap of raisins onto a fireproof dish, pour alcohol such as brandy over the top, and set light to it.

Everyone then tries to snatch a raisin without burning their fingers or setting fire to themselves.

Tip: have a lid large enough to cover the whole plate, a fire extinguisher, and a fire blanket to hand, for those unforeseen moments.

Father won the Mouse Hunt, which put him in an excellent mood for dinner, though everyone except me was laden with sugar mice anyway.

Mace said I looked cute in the reindeer headband, but I noticed his lips kept twitching whenever he looked at me. Personally, I was still in a state of numbed shock from his deviousness (and Father's), and so was everyone else when we got to the sherry trifle and Father told them all about his and Mace's plans.

I've never known a family gathering be so silent for so long. Then Em and Anne turned as one and looked at me.

'I know – Mace just told me downstairs.'

'Bloody good tactics, Mace!' congratulated Anne. 'Surrounded and out-manoeuvred, Chaz.'

'Mahomet came to the effing mountain – nice one,' agreed Em. She looked thoughtfully at Mace. 'That seems . . . very satisfactory.' Then she turned and gave Chris a poke in the ribs with her elbow, and he choked on his wine. 'But don't you ever hold out on me again, Chris, or I'll be wearing your guts for garters. Right?'

'Right,' he agreed, his eyes watering. 'But I was sworn to secrecy, because Mace wanted to sort it out and then tell Charlie first. It seemed to me the perfect solution all round.'

'*I'm* to live in Mace's cottage?' Jessica said slowly, as she caught up with the plot.

'You said you wanted somewhere small with all mod cons,' Ran pointed out. 'Well, the cottage has it all – and a study for me. But I'm warning you, Jess, if you don't let Em teach you how to cook, the wedding's off!'

'Cook? I *can* cook!'

'You can wash a lettuce leaf – but I'm not a bloody bunny! You learn to cook, I'll set the date for the wedding.'

'If it means getting her out of the house, I'm game,' Em said grimly.

'No, don't, Mummy! We want to stay here too,' wailed Feeb. 'We don't want to go and live in a cottage, it isn't fair!'

'No,' agreed Clo. 'Em doesn't mean it. She's only joking, aren't you, Em? Please say we can stay here!'

'No, you can't,' Jessica said rather snappily. 'You're my little girls, and you'll live with me and Ran.'

'The cottage is lovely,' I told them. 'There are two tiny bedrooms tucked into the roof, and you can come and stay here in the Parsonage whenever you want to.'

'Yes – keep your attic rooms here – share you out,' agreed Anne. 'Come and go as you please.'

Caitlin, who'd been nodding off into her trifle, her lap full of mice, said, 'Daddy? Where am *I* going to be?'

'Here, of course, with me and Charlie, and everyone.'

'Oh, good! So you're going to marry Charlie? And I can be a bridesmaid again?'

I said 'No!' just as Mace said, 'Yes.' We looked at each other.

'You better had, Charlie,' Ran said, 'after all this swapping over and stuff. The man's gone to a lot of trouble for you.'

'Yes, but—'

'Haven't you told Mace your news yet?' demanded Em.

'Can we get down now?' interrupted Clo. 'We're all full, and we think there are some mice we haven't found.'

The children vanished, while everyone looked at me like I was about to produce a rabbit out of a hat.

This was not an announcement I ever expected to make – and especially not while dressed as a reindeer.

'I'm – well, *Mace* and I are—'

'Charlie's having my baby,' Mace announced proudly, like I'd just accepted a particularly lavish gift (which I suppose, in a way, I had).

Even Bran was staring at me, the string tail of a sugar mouse dangling from his lips.

'Em and Gloria don't think I'll lose it this time.'

'You certainly won't, my chicken!' Gloria said from the end of the table.

'Freya said she saw you with a baby ages ago, in the crystal, but she didn't like to say anything,' Em added.

'Yes,' agreed Anne. 'And you said Lilith predicted happy outcomes to old issues in the cards, didn't you? She's certainly having an issue!'

'Did anyone happen to see *me* with Charlie and the baby?' enquired Mace with suspicious meekness. 'Or don't I come into it?'

'You already came into it – nothing but trouble, you are!' Gloria said. 'It said so in the leaves all along.'

'It must have said something else, too. Like: "they lived happily ever after"?'

'Yes – bound to have,' enthused Anne. 'Jane Austen said a large income was the best recipe for happiness she ever heard of, and Mace is bloody rich! So didn't it mention that in the leaves, Gloria?'

She sniffed. 'It might have: but I didn't want my Charlie taken away from Upvale again, with her child that should be born here.'

'I'm not going to take her away, or not for more than a couple of weeks at a time, anyway. You know she can't stay away for long – she wouldn't be happy: I understand that.'

Gloria sniffed, and gave him a dour look; but she was starting to like him, I could see.

'In fact,' Mace went on, 'the only trouble *I* seem to have caused is through you trying to avoid the trouble *you* think I might cause.'

We all looked at him: and actually, when you thought about it, he was quite right.

'Isn't it all in the interpretation of what you see? I hope Charlie was troubled by me – she certainly drove me mad. And I went to a lot of trouble to win her. Isn't that trouble enough, Gloria? Aren't there any "happy ever afters" in there?'

'There might have been,' she conceded reluctantly, then got up. 'You'd better have a nice cup of tea. And Charlie.'

'I've suddenly gone off it,' I told her firmly.

'Champagne!' announced Ran. 'Walter, fetch it in, there's a good man. And we haven't had the fortune cookies or Snapdragon yet!'

Mace and Chris exchanged a startled look across the table. 'You don't think we've had enough excitement for one day?' suggested Chris tentatively.

'It's Christmas Eve,' Father said, as if that were an answer. 'We always have fortune cookies and Snapdragon. The champagne was for toasting the house exchange, but we can toast the baby too.'

'Time for Snapdragon?' asked Bran hopefully.

'Bran, take that string out of your mouth before you swallow it,' Em said. 'And save the rest of the mice for tomorrow, or you'll be sick, like last year.'

'Have you Rhymers ever thought of doing things the same way as everyone else?' Chris asked despairingly.

'No, what would be the fun in that?' Em said, astonished. 'This is our way – and yours, now, too. After all,' she added, 'you and Mace and Father have worked out what *you* want, and now you'll just have to go along with the family way of doing things.'

My fortune cookie said that my *chi* was flowing in a creative direction, but it's a bit late with the message, because it's already done that.

When the lights went out and the raisins in brandy were lit, I missed my turn, because Mace took the opportunity of pulling me to the back of the room and kissing me until I was breathless. But then, I'd been burned already.

We found Caitlin asleep on the bottom step of the stairs, and Em went to find a soft blanket so that Mace could carry her home without waking her.

'So what happens on Christmas Day?' he asked me, looking slightly apprehensive.

'We get up, have breakfast, and open our presents. Then you and Caitlin come up and we play Hunt the Thimble for an hour or so, to work up an appetite for Christmas dinner, which is at about two. And we have the works, with a flaming pudding afterwards, and home-made crackers. Then we take the dogs out for a walk, and come home, and play some quiet games. Then it's a sort of tea-cum-supper, and by then we're all usually exhausted and go to bed early. Only Gloria and Walter go home after Christmas dinner and have another Christmas dinner at their house and watch TV.'

'It might take me a year to recover from all that – and *you* shouldn't get too tired either.'

'Tired? I'm not tired in the least!' I said indignantly.

He smiled, and hoisted Caitlin into his arms. 'I am and I've still got a Christmas stocking to stuff.'

'At least she's asleep,' I consoled him. 'I'll let you out downstairs.'

I kissed her flushed cheek, tucking the soft blanket around her.

'Good night, you devious actor, you,' I said, giving him a kiss over Caitlin's head.

'I'll tell you something, darling,' whispered Mace confidentially on the doorstep. 'I prefer you as a reindeer!'

And he strode off, laughing, into the night.

I'd forgotten I was still wearing the headband and fluffy tail.

After he'd gone I went and looked Undine up in the dictionary, and apparently I am a water spirit that has obtained a human soul by bearing a child to a human husband. (Either that, or I have a preoccupation with running water, especially urine – but I think not.)

Next morning Caitlin ran past me into the house squealing with excitement and trailing a pillowcase full of presents behind her: not that there weren't a sackful more waiting for her.

She thundered off up the stairs to the Parsonage, while I closed the veranda door before letting Invasion of the Infidels sweep me into his arms.

301

'Mace, if I marry you, you must promise me one thing,' I told him seriously.

'Anything,' he agreed, with one of those devastating smiles.

'Then just don't turn into an alien, like my first husband did.'

'Did he do that? Must have been a defence mechanism.'

'What do you mean? Are you insinuating that I—'

'You're an impossible woman, but I'm not turning into anything except a devoted – and probably jealous – husband. If that's alien, you'll just have to get used to it.'

'I think I can live with that.'

'I'm not giving you an alternative, darling,' he said, pulling me even closer and kissing me again.

What could I do? I'd done my best to resist, but clearly in a situation like this it was every woman for herself!

With a sudden staccato rattle, a cascade of rose quartz hit the flagged floor and ricocheted against the windows like hailstones.

'What the hell was that?' he exclaimed, raising his head.

'Oh, nothing important,' I told him dreamily. 'Just my love beads exploding again.'

Recipes

Treacle Tart

When I was growing up my mother made treacle tart by simply spreading treacle, sometimes mixed with breadcrumbs, over a shortcrust pastry base. This was served with either condensed milk or custard, and you could make brown treacly swirls in it with your spoon.

Imagine my surprise (and disgust) the first time I was served treacle tart away from home and it proved to be a sweet, pallid object made from golden syrup!

So here is my recipe for the real thing, though you can always educate your tastebuds slowly by replacing first one, then two tablespoons of golden syrup with treacle . . .

Ingredients
6oz/175g plain flour
3oz/75g lard or cooking margarine (you can use butter, but it
   does make the pastry crumbly and difficult to roll)
Cold water

A pinch of powdered ginger
2oz/50g fresh white breadcrumbs
3 tablespoons treacle

Method
Preheat the oven to gas mark 6/400°F/200°C and grease a shallow enamel plate, tart tin or pie tin, eight or nine inches across.

Rub the fat into the flour to a breadcrumb consistency and add a little cold water to make shortcrust pastry.

Roll out the pastry on a floured board and line the plate or pie dish with it. Trim the edge, keeping the offcuts for decorating the top. (I like to pinch the edges of mine into a wavy pattern, but it's not compulsory.)

Warm the treacle gently in a pan, stir in a pinch of ground ginger, and then mix in the breadcrumbs.

Spread this mixture over the shortcrust base and then make a lattice of crisscrossed strips of leftover pastry over the top.

Bake for about thirty minutes until the edges are a pale golden brown.

Can be served hot or cold, with custard, cream or ice cream.

Treacle Scones

While we are on the Treacle Trail, try this variation of the traditional scone – lovely eaten warm with butter in winter.

Ingredients
8oz/225g plain flour
1½oz/38g butter
½ level teaspoon of each of the following:
Baking soda
Ground ginger
Ground mixed spice
Salt
Cream of tartar
Cinnamon
1 tablespoon caster sugar
1 rounded tablespoon treacle
Milk to mix

Method
Preheat the oven to gas mark 8/220°C/450°F and grease a baking tray.

Rub the butter into the flour, and then sift in all the remaining dry ingredients to make a mixture with a fine breadcrumb consistency.

Gently warm the treacle with two tablespoons of milk and then pour onto the dry ingredients, bringing the mixture together to make a soft dough, adding more milk if necessary.

Knead a little and then roll out on a floured board to about three-quarters of an inch thick.

Cut out circles (I like to use a cutter with a fluted edge), making about eight small scones. Reform any leftover dough to make a final one.

Put on the baking tray and bake for ten to fifteen minutes.

Cool on a wire rack.

Old English Jumbolls

Variations of this simple recipe (sometimes called Jumbles or Jumbells), go back to ancient times and were included in the very first British cookbooks, sometimes as a drop biscuit or, as here, a slightly firmer dough that can be shaped.

Ingredients
2½oz/62g caster sugar
2½oz/62g butter
1 egg, well beaten
5oz/150g plain flour
1oz/25g ground almonds.
Grated zest of an unwaxed lemon

Method
Preheat the oven to gas mark 4/180ºC/350ºF and grease a large baking tray.

Beat the butter and sugar till soft and fluffy and then beat in the egg.

Sift in the flour and stir in the ground almonds and lemon zest. Mix well to a soft dough.

Divide the dough into small balls and press flat onto the baking tray with two fingers, which makes a sort of 'wave' pattern. (This recipe also works if you press the dough into small madeleine moulds.)

Bake in the oven for 15–20 minutes, until pale golden brown at the edges.

Cool on a wire rack and then store in an airtight tin.

Sugar Mice

I'm sure the sugar mice for the Rhymers' annual Mouse Hunt were made by Em the traditional way, using uncooked egg white for the fondant, but for this recipe I've simply combined icing sugar and Carnation evaporated milk. Add a little liquid glycerine for a slightly softer fondant. I just form my mice by hand, but plastic and silicone mouse-shaped moulds are available.

Ingredients
6oz/175g icing sugar
A small tin of evaporated milk
Sugar balls for the eyes
Thin string for the tails
Food colouring, if desired
½ teaspoon of glycerine (optional)

Method
Put the icing sugar into a bowl and stir in the evaporated milk a spoonful at a time until you can form a fondant dough. If you overdo the milk, just add more sugar till you get the right consistency.

Divide up the dough and add a tiny drop of food colouring to each batch, kneading in well. I like to leave half my mice white and colour the rest pink.

On a board sprinkled with icing sugar, form the fondant into little pear shapes, pinching one end into a pointy nose and two small rounded ears. Press in little silver sugar balls for eyes.

For a traditional tail, pierce the back of the mouse with a skewer and then push in the end of a short piece of thin string.

Allow to dry and harden, then store in a box or tin lined with greaseproof paper till needed.

Why was her marriage to Mr Right making her long
for Mr Wrong?

Buy *Good Husband Material* now in
all good bookshops!

The perfect gifts aren't always found under the tree . . .

Buy *Wish Upon A Star* now in all good bookshops!